I0684579

Also by JA Sanborn

The Lost Cipher

The Orion Factor

All books above are available in Kindle edition or softcover at Amazon.com

Death
Comes
To
Ely

Copyright © 2015 Dr. Jon A. Sanborn
Cover Copyright © 2015 Dr. Jon A. Sanborn

All rights are reserved. The reproduction or utilization of this work in whole or in part in any form by any electronic, mechanical, or other means is forbidden. This prohibition includes any methods now known or hereafter invented, including xerography, photocopying, and recording, or in any information storage or retrieval system is forbidden without the written permission of the Author.

Swift River Publishing, LLC
P.O. Box 30965
Savannah, GA 31410
swiftriverpublishing.com
swiftriverpublishing@gmail.com

ISBN: 978-0-9968082-4-8

DEATH COMES TO ELY

To
Dave and Phitsamon, lifelong friends.

This book is a work of fiction. All names, characters, organizations, events, and places in this novel are from the imagination of the author or are fictitiously used. Any similarities or resemblance to any persons, living, or dead, business establishments, events, or locales are entirely coincidental.

Death
Comes
To
Ely

A Karen Hunter Mystery

A novel
By
JA Sanborn

Acknowledgements

I am indebted to many friends who have encouraged me to continue this series.

Prologue

Whatever the universal nature assigns to any man at any time is for the good of that man at that time. Marcus Aurelius

In the mid-1700s, land-poor farmers began to move to an area near a tributary of the Oconee River in the central region of the Georgia colony. There they launched toppling trees, removing stumps, and tearing into the virgin soil, thus laying the groundwork for their farms that were to follow. Finding the settlement suitable with rich soil and pleasant terrain, they called the place Ely in remembrance of the village of Ely in Cambridgeshire, England.

They knew by the teachings of their religion that they did not want to be part of the small, but growing, nearby village named Middlefield. By its reputation and behavior, Middlefield residents were less religious and worldlier in manners and morals, which the God fearing Ely farmers shunned.

The steady beat of time would eventually dull the fervor of independence of Ely, but not its spirit. Surviving many years as an unincorporated village, Ely was eventually annexed into Middlefield as many similar villages were unwillingly combined with larger cities and towns whose thirst for expansion matched the zeal of earlier settlers taking land from the indigenous peoples of the area.

Annexation, however, did not mean capitulation. Members of Ely maintained fierce loyalties to each other and to the village by following their own rules and ethics well into the twenty-first century. As the city of Middlefield would find out, ordinances, rules, and laws only work when people are willing. Such stock comprised the citizens of Ely, but over the years, succeeding generations have become less dedicated to the beliefs and religious dogma of their ancestors.

The village of Ely lies totally within the bounds of the prestigious city of Middlefield in central Twiggs County. Situated to the southwest area of the city it is backed by rolling hills where the fertile land produces high-yielding crops of cotton, hay, and corn. Only the weather limits the yields. Farmers in Ely know and appreciate their God who looks upon them with great favor if they just follow His commandments.

Over the years, most of the farms had been sold for development and today the village has become an exclusive community for the rich and very rich. Homes built here boast five car garages attached to seven and nine thousand square foot abodes. The community manages its own roads and schools to the relief of Middlefield and the County.

As idyllic as the Ely lifestyle seemed, events would take place over the next year, which would lead the city of Middlefield and the village of Ely in unexpected directions.

Chapter One

Don't judge any man unless you have walked two moons in his moccasins. American Indian saying.

As part of Karen's physical fitness program, she would run on Wednesday mornings before work and again on Saturdays. It was a ritual not to be broken or changed even during bad weather, and with good reason. Middle age was starting to take a toll on her body; she felt that the best way to keep her trim figure and health was to remain physically active while religiously watching her diet.

To date, she had been successful, managing to maintain her weight at 125 pounds, which for her height of five feet seven inches was not bad for a woman nearing forty-four years. Of course, her hair spoke a different tale and her monthly visits to her hairdresser were imperative to keep back the increasingly noticeable gray strands.

Added to life's normal worries was the daily stress Karen experienced as department head of the Major Crimes Unit for the Middlefield Police Department. It was this pressure that Karen attributed to her graying hair and penchant to overeat at times, not to her loneliness, which at times overwhelmed her.

Early one Saturday morning, Karen went for her usual run in McCrery Park. On this particular morning, the moon had set before she had left her apartment, and the sun had not yet risen enough to peek over the horizon, so only wisps of twilight found their way through the treed canopy dimly lighting the jogging trail. As Karen clomped along the path, she became aware of a feeling; really a chilling sense of her surroundings; an awareness that something was different this morning. Karen slowed her pace to a walk; staring ahead at shadows moving with the slight breezes that briefly cooled her face.

A short distance away, she could barely make out a shape, a form beside the path that moved slightly, but not with the rhythm of the other moving shadows. Karen stopped and unzipped the pack belted around her waist. She had not lost the sense of being a vulnerable woman after the near death she had experienced a few short years ago.

Retrieving her service firearm, she slowly approached the mysterious shadow. With relief, she saw that it was a black leather jacket caught on a low broken branch of a small oak jutting into the path. As the breeze caught the top of the tree, the jacket swayed in an opposite way compared to the foliage beside it.

Oh, what is this doing here? Who wears a leather jacket this time of year? It can't have been here very long. I'm sure I would have noticed it before. Well, this is one of my favorite trails but it is the least used trail, so perhaps no one else has ever noticed it.

Karen put away her firearm; grabbed the jacket and turned to jog back home. She was well aware that several women had been attacked along these trails even in the daylight hours. A proposal had reached City Council to have crews broaden the trail routes by removing vegetation on both sides of the trails. As of this date, the proposal sat in limbo.

Later, back at the office, Karen looked closely at the jacket and realized that the leather was badly scuffed, as if it had been dragged along the ground. Perhaps it was nothing, but she had a nagging feeling about it. People are usually careful with their leather; this coat was obviously not discarded by the owner. The question was; how did it find its way to the tree limb?

I'll have Sarah put it in an evidence bag and store it. The owner may come along, who knows?

Sarah had joined the MCU after completing a degree in Criminal Justice. Sarah had been in a serious automobile accident in high school and was bound to a wheel chair. Her spirit, perseverance, and positive attitude constantly impressed Karen and her fellow MCU members.

* * *

The bones were definitely human. Dr. James Gordon, the Twiggs County Medical Examiner for over twenty-five years, had pronounced them so.

"This humerus is from the body of an adult. Ossification is complete. From the pelvic bones, she was a woman, possibly late twenties to mid-thirties, that's as far as I can tell."

"Can you tell her race from these?"

"With only the pelvic bones, and likely no salvageable DNA from the marrow of the humerus, no. I will send the bones to the GBI lab to see if they can extract anything of value. If anyone in that outfit can find something

5

worthwhile, it will be Sue Miller."

"I agree that she is the best the GBI has. Can you tell how tall this woman may have been, James?" Karen asked.

"Have you found the femur?"

"No. We don't have either femur. These two bones were found well away from the jogging paths down an embankment. A man had to chase his dog after it bolted from the path. When he reached the dog, it had the humerus in its mouth."

"Without the femur, it would only be a guess, but she may have been roughly five foot five to five foot six; that's the average height of women today. Of course, with the femur, I could give a better estimate."

"Too bad, that's not much to go on. This case will be a tough one; I can feel it in my bones."

"Is there any chance of finding anymore bones, especially the skull, Karen?"

"I haven't been to the site myself, but Susan told me it is heavily overgrown in the area, so not much hope of easily spotting anything more. Animals undoubtedly dragged away most of the others. The rest of her bones are likely scattered around other remote sites in McCrery Park, or they have been devoured by nature's creatures.

"We haven't given up though. We have three cadaver dogs as part of the search going on now to locate any more bones or evidence.

"You wouldn't be able to tell how long she has been dead, would you?"

"Not really. The bones have been weathered; the marrow in the humerus is decayed, but I really couldn't say; a guess would be four to six months. One last comment, Karen; the circumstances of how and where she was found, obviously makes her death very suspicious, however, her death may have been natural. There is no way to tell from this scanty evidence."

"James, unless we can find more of her, the only thing left to do is to check missing person's reports. Maybe something will turn up there for her identity."

"Let me know if I can be of any other help, Karen. If any more evidence is found, please contact me."

"Of course, James, I need to get back to the office now. Thank you."

Back at the office, Karen sat down at her desk just as her phone rang.

"Good morning, Major Hunter, this is Denise Lee from the *Patriot*. I heard something about the finding of some bones in the Park. Can you give me an update?"

"Hello, Denise. The only thing I can tell you now is that we have found some bones of a person. At this point, we don't have a name for that person. As soon as we have any further information, we will call a news briefing."

"We had an agreement on our last major case, remember?"

"That depressing serial case was closed, and I did honor our agreement back then. We have no agreement now, but if we do discover something, I can let you know where the

7

briefing will be held."

"Don't ever ask for anymore favors from me."

"Denise, I don't want you as an enemy, but I do have to be fair to all reporters."

"If you change your mind, Major, give me a call. Goodbye."

With that, Denise Lee hung up.

Karen called the MCU together for a planning session. The team consisted of Detectives Susan Ramos, Richard Burnham, Carol Morgan and Sarah Green.

Susan Ramos was Karen's strongest detective and had become her closest confidant after the horrific serial killer had nearly killed Karen.

Richard Burnham had been hired to replace, Robert King, a young MCU detective who had been fired from the force after unbecoming conduct with another officer. Burnham had come from the Chicago police force being tired of the level of crime in that city. Karen had had lapses of judgment because of her loneliness, but she had prevented any personal involvement with Burnham.

Carol Morgan had been hired by Karen from the Boston PD to replace Caroline Sprague, the other detective involved with Robert King. She was young and the newest arrival to the MCU.

"I've sent you all the information from Doctor Gordon. It isn't much to work with, but it is all we have at this time."

"Karen, I have looked at our local 'missing persons' reports. The only thing we found is a report of two teenagers last week, but they have returned home. Out for a fling I guess. Their folks are not happy about it, but they are home safe. I've also checked towns and cities in Georgia, but I haven't found anything that matches yet."

"Thank you, Susan. Our next task is to ask neighboring states for their lists. You are aware how daunting this work will be. The nationwide numbers of people missing or identified as unsolved homicides are staggering. Since our unidentified woman has been dead for perhaps six months or so, we can focus to this year only. It will still be a massive task, but I believe we can find our woman; perhaps not easily, but we'll find her."

"Karen, I suggest that since there are five of us, we could divide up the country with each taking ten states," Richard advocated.

"That sounds like a good suggestion; Richard, you take the Northeast states; Susan can manage the Southeast; Carol, you take the Midwestern; Sarah can focus on the Mountain states; and I will take the Western ones. That divvies it up evenly; please get started immediately; keep all of us informed, if you spot anything."

At the end of the day, the MCU had corralled over fifty possible candidates to investigate further. Of these, Karen selected five for immediate analysis. The most promising lead was a missing woman from Stoneham, Massachusetts.

Richard requested the Stoneham police to send all of the woman's information to him.

Karen reassembled the MCU members to their dismay,

due to the time of day.

"All right, folks, I know it's late but before we break for the day, I think we should hear what Richard has found."

"There have been seven missing persons in the Boston area in the last six months. Two of those are men; both have since returned home. Of the five remaining reports, three women have been located and are safe. That leaves two women who are not accounted for. One, named Jane Swanson, is a nurse who was last seen in Haverhill, New Hampshire, at a gas station convenience store last month."

"Was she seen with anyone?" Karen asked.

"At the store, she was apparently alone. She hasn't been seen since, but her debit card was last used in Swansea, Massachusetts. And, her ATM card was used at a Swansea Bank by a man, but the camera was not able to fully catch his face. A woman was recorded by the camera sitting in the front passenger side of the car. The police have no idea if she is voluntarily accompanying the man. Her husband said that Jane wouldn't leave with someone else. He said that she has been depressed lately, but they were working things out."

"Perhaps the Boston police should put more pressure on the husband," Susan said.

"They have four children and the husband has been with them. The Police say that he's not a suspect," Richard responded.

"So, she could be our person, but we have no way to verify that."

"Yes, it's possible, but I agree; we have no way to say positively that it is Jane Swanson."

"What about the other possibility?"

"Okay, Karen, the other woman's name is Kaye Billington, a nurse from the city of Stoneham, age 46, five foot six, blond hair, dyed that way, blue eyes, medium build, no tattoos or other identifying marks. She was reported missing by her estranged husband three days after she did not return to her home. She has two grown children, both girls…"

"Please, Richard, women. They're women. Continue."

"The younger daughter still lives with her. The other daughter is a flight attendant with American; she had come back from a two-day business trip to California. The last time she had seen her mother was the day she departed for her duty."

"Hmmm, both nurses. Did the daughter say if she noticed anything unusual about her mother that day?"

"No, she called her father who, in turn, called the Stoneham police and reported her missing. The Police followed up with an interview of the daughter and her husband. They both indicated that alcoholism was Kaye's problem. It was that that led to the estrangement with the husband. The husband had an alibi, which they are still trying to vet."

"Do we have any reason to assume that Billington came to Middlefield?"

"All three said that Kaye would sometimes go off with

some guy she picked up at a bar, but she was usually back the next day. She was still working as a nurse, but the hospital was nearly fed up with her lateness and absences."

"Does the Stoneham PD have a list of possible men she would trip off with?"

"There were only two men the family knew of. The police had their names and pictures; they are both well known to the police; they have long rap sheets. Not nice guys for a drunk to hang around with."

"Are they going to interview them?"

"As soon as the Police can locate them, they will."

"Stay with your contact at the PD. Give us the results of any interview that they have with them."

"Okay, Karen, they also sent a picture of Kaye, which we should take to bars and hotels to see if anyone, recognizes her or the two men."

"Why do the Stoneham Police believe she came to Georgia?" Sarah asked.

"By following the money, Sarah. The Stoneham PD had warrants to check her cell phone records and her charge cards. Her credit card was used for gasoline in Connecticut on I 95; then in New Jersey on the Jersey Turnpike; next use was in Maryland for gas and motel in Baltimore; one in North Carolina; and the final use for gas purchase was near the airport in Atlanta."

"What did they find about her cell phone?" Susan asked.

"There was only one call from her phone the entire trip. It was to her home phone, but it only lasted two seconds.

Not enough time for a message."

"What kind of car was she driving?" Karen asked.

"It is a 2009 red Toyota Camry with pin-stripes along the side."

"Was the airport area the last place her credit card was used?"

"No, Karen, it was used at Mueller's Inn on the south side of Middlefield."

"I didn't ask before, but was anyone with her?"

"Yes, I called the motel before the meeting today. A man and woman had checked in with a red Toyota three months ago. They were there for four days; then the man came to the lobby to say his girlfriend had left to visit some friends in the area. He wasn't sure when they would be back. The motel owner last saw him driving away with the car."

"Did they give a description of the man?" Karen asked.

"They said he was about my height, ruddy complexion, and probably in his forties."

"Did they get his name?" Karen asked.

"No, they checked in with the name Mr. & Mrs. John Smith. Good luck tracing that."

"Okay, folks, that's all for today. Please be here early tomorrow. We will spread out with pictures of the men and her; we'll check any places she may have gone to after she left the motel. See you tomorrow."

The following day, all the bars, motels, hotels, and restaurants were shown Kaye Billington's photo. Later in the day, at a bar named Jacks Place, she was identified by the bartender.

"Yes, I do remember her. She was in here alone; drinking heavily; I finally had to shut her off."

"Do you recognize either of these two men?" Richard asked.

"No, I have a good ability to recognize faces, but they aren't familiar."

"What was she wearing, do you remember?" Susan asked.

"I'm not much for women's fashions, but I remember she had on a red dress with way too much cleavage showing. I guess that's why I remembered it. Too much showing for a tipsy woman alone in a bar. It got quite a few looks by my patrons I can tell you that."

"What did she do after you refused to serve her any more drinks?"

"She got angry. That happens a lot around here. A clean-cut looking guy; not a regular, came up and stood beside her. He talked to her for a few minutes and then they left. That's the last time I saw him or her."

"How would you describe the guy?" Richard asked.

"If I remember right; he had light colored hair, no beard, young, probably in his twenties; he was a typical young guy."

"Did you notice any tattoos or other identifying things."

"Nah, he did wear nice clothes, not expensive, but clean. That's sort of unusual for people who come in here."

"Thank you very much. You've been a great help."

Later at the MCU meeting, it was learned that other than the motel's owners and the bartender, no one had seen Kaye Billington or her mysterious escorts.

"Well, this is just great. She was here; she disappeared, but we don't know if our bones belong to Kaye Billington. The possible men she was with are unknowns here. We have nothing more to work on, right now," Karen complained.

"Doctor Gordon said he thought that the marrow was too decayed to be of use, but he said that he may be wrong. I'll check with him and Sue Miller at GBI," Richard said.

"Okay, Richard, please do that. Give us the sad news in the morning. See you all tomorrow."

Karen felt disgusted.

Why do our MCU cases always seem to have knots that take incredible skill to untie? If it's not some cipher, then it's troublesome reporters, mendacious witnesses, or serial killers. Wouldn't it be great to have an old-fashioned murder committed in the heat of passion? You're tired, Lady; go home.

As Karen was putting on her coat, her phone rang. It was an outside call.

Oh no, why a call this time of day?

"Hello, Karen Hunter speaking."

"Hello, Karen, this is Sloan Harrington. I would like to come and see you again."

"What is it this time, Sloan?"

"I need to come to Middlefield; would that be all right?"

"I'm not sure that is a good idea. You know that many people here don't have great faith in what you say."

"I know, but wasn't I correct with my theory of the two murders of the professors?"

"In a way, but it was a matter of interpretation."

"Does that mean no?"

"No, Sloan, when were you planning to be here?"

"Can I come tomorrow around one o'clock in the afternoon?"

"Yes, I will call the group together. Don't be late."

"I will be on time. Thank you."

Karen assembled the MCU late that morning without telling them that Sloan Harrington would be coming to the meeting. But first, Richard had heard news that he wanted to share.

"Good news from Atlanta. Sue Miller says that they think that they have found enough useable marrow to try testing. She will put a priority on it," Richard said.

"That is great! Please tell Sue to let us know as soon as she has anything," Karen pushed.

"That's not all; New Hampshire State Police called to let us know that someone pretending to be Jane Swanson was picked up in Portsmouth. They are investigating that situation, but Swanson remains on their missing person list until it's resolved."

"Thank you, Richard, we'll see how that one turns out."

As Miller's good news was ingested, Karen told them of Sloan Harrington's impending visit.

"Christ, Karen, wasn't once enough with her?" Richard exploded.

"I understand how you feel, Richard, but she did assist us. We can't forget that. With this latest case, we have nothing; no leads; no one to interview; we have nothing but some bones."

"Richard, give her a chance," Susan admonished.

"Let's give some of our time. If it has been a waste, I will not ever allow it again, okay?"

At exactly one in the afternoon, Harrington appeared at the MPD dressed in her prim and proper best suit, which displayed her slim figure and ample bosom. The middle-aged woman had been a God-send when the MCU had faced the death of two college professors, but most of the MCU was not enamored of her intrusion into the group's business.

"Come in, I think you know everyone here."

"I don't think I know the handsome man here."

"Sorry, Sloan, this is Richard Burnham. He came aboard after your last visit. What is it you wanted to share with us?"

"I recently read about the unidentified woman you have in Middlefield. I am here to tell you that she is not the only one you have. There are at least eight more to be found in the city."

"Where are they, or doesn't your crystal ball tell you that?" Richard said with a snarl.

"I understand your disbelief, Mr. Burnham, but you

must understand it is not a crystal ball that informs me."

"What is it then?"

"It is a sense; it is a feeling; it is not something I can explain in a scientific way. I did not ask for this gift, but it is with me. I cannot ignore it. If I do, I am complicit with the murderer. I hope you understand."

"I don't know if I can, Mrs. Harrington, but I will try."

"That is all I can ask, thank you."

"Please continue, Sloan," Karen said.

"I can only tell you that there are bones scattered throughout the city, but there are some that are not scattered. I cannot see which are which, but the sense is very strong that that is true."

"The last time your premonitions were of things not yet done. Is this true of these?" Karen asked.

"Karen, I always have the feeling that what I sense has been already done. This time, though, I see more that will be done unless the aura changes."

"Aura? What do you mean?"

"I see the energy of the killer is waxing. The energy must be slaked for this curse to be stopped."

"How soon, Sloan?" Susan asked.

"I can't tell you that, I don't know."

"One last question, does your sense have an idea where the ones not scattered are located?" Karen asked.

"I see darkness broken by spots of light shining through from somewhere beyond that constantly shift in brightness. In front of the darkness, there is great cross. In front of the cross, I see an expanse of movement. Things sway to and fro."

"Can you see anything else?" Susan asked.

"I see a moonless night. A man is carrying something; it is heavy for him; he goes into a building; he puts down his burden. I see movement and then the man is gone."

"Can you see what he is carrying?"

"Now I see that it is a woman, but I have no feeling who she is. She is frightened."

"Can you see anything else about her?"

"Only that she will be dead in two days from that night."

"When did this happen?"

"The shadows blend. He has done this before. I cannot tell you when."

"Sloan is there anything else that you can tell us?" Karen asked.

"No, I am sorry."

"Well, thank you very much, Sloan. If anything else comes to mind, please phone me. I will listen."

"Wait. There is a place in your city where nature is allowed to develop as she wishes. It is normally peaceful, but now it is a place where I feel the fearful energy."

"I wonder if she means the Park." Richard added with a sneer.

"Is it McCrery Park?" Karen probed.

"I cannot say."

"Well, you have given us enough to ponder."

"Thank you all for hearing me out. It is a great relief

when I can purge these things from my mind."

With that, Sloan left the MCU to mull over what they had heard.

"Well, Folks, what do you think?"

"Karen, my mind wants to say it is just bull, but what she says is intriguing," Susan said.

"It is hard to believe her because what she says is so general. Could be anything, anywhere," Carol added.

"Well, let's leave it at that. Have a relaxing weekend. We'll tackle this more on Monday."

Chapter Two

Certain signs precede certain events. Cicero

On late Friday afternoon, GBI confirmed a DNA match with Kaye Billington's DNA. They had a possible murder, but no leads. They had a seer's vision of another murder but no body. Ever since her discovery of the leather jacket along the trail in McCrery Park, and now Kaye Billington's bones positively identified, Karen's old fears rose up again. She had overcome the trauma of the serial murderer who had wanted to kill her, but at times, the pangs and stress of her responsibilities returned.

Since that time, Karen felt nervous doing her early morning Saturday running ritual. Today, as usual, she belted the fanny pack to her waist feeling safer knowing her department-issued firearm was within easy reach. Tying her running shoes, Karen walked to the Park; stretched her muscles, and began her usual four-mile run.

It's a shame that the Council has taken this long to fix the trails in the Park. What are they waiting for, another rape, or murder?

This day her run was uneventful, but her thoughts about the leather jacket left by the trail were a constant concern. Sloan's visit had not helped, either. If anything, Sloan had added to other problems the MCU would have to consider, if they believed her, that is.

Back at her apartment, Karen showered; dressed casually for the day; then sat down to eat a cold bowl of granola while reading the morning paper. Munching on the cereal, she opened *The Middlefield Patriot* to the third page, intrigued by the headline on the front page: "Wealthy Farmer Missing in Ely." The story was the usual headline that was intended to induce people to read a story part truth and part reporter's personal bias masked as research.

After finishing the article, Karen thought that the news could have potential consequences for the Major Crimes Unit if the story was accurate. The reporter had implied but not openly said that this was a possible kidnapping for ransom.

This was only a few months after she and her team had solved the murders of Doctors Kelly and McPhee, but this disappearance could be just a case of senility and age, not a kidnapping, or something worse. Karen checked the "By line" and found it to be Denise Lee.

As I suspected, Denise, you are at it again. In any case, this story is not promising. If it is a kidnapping, then Denise is very unprofessional to suggest it without the family and police involvement. I hope this story is only that Jeffrey Waters simply wandered away from his home; then the family will find him and this can have a happy conclusion. I hope, he will be found quickly.

But, at his age, if Waters has wandered off somewhere into the woods, it does not bode well for him. He could be anywhere on that property; it's a huge farm with many places to search; at his age, the weather is quite cold at night, it may be dangerous for him.

If Denise has scooped a kidnapping, we'll have to be

22

involved, but Ely folks are not easy to work with. I admire their independence, but the joy of helping them wears off quickly. I need to check with Jim at Missing Persons.

Karen reached for her phone and called Detective Hardy at the Missing Persons Division.

"Good morning, Jim. Do you have a report on a Jeffrey Waters over in Ely?"

"I do; his son called in last evening."

"The paper said that he lives alone."

"He does; his son was visiting for a couple of days. Apparently the old man went for his usual walk with his dog. Two hours later the dog returned, but Mr. Waters didn't. The son and his wife searched the usual trail, but didn't find him. We sent two officers to help look for him, but it was dark by then and nothing turned up."

"Do you think he has just done a walkabout, or does Denise Lee really have some information about a possible kidnapping?"

"Sometimes I think that paper should get rid of her. The son said nothing about a ransom note or such."

"Well, that's a relief."

"Walkabout? That must be your Aussie blood coming to the surface."

"Hardly, I'm so Italian that olive oil runs in my veins. I couldn't think of a better term, that's all."

"As I said, we don't have any better news to report than what appeared in the paper this morning but the kidnapping thing is rubbish. We have a search party out there right now. His daughter is flying in from California."

"Can you send me some information on Waters in case this turns out to be more than his being lost? I would like to get the Unit up to speed."

"Things slow over in Homicide?"

"No, I'd like to be ready if there is anything that would involve us, so can you send some info?"

"I'll send it over by Monday."

"Thanks, Jim. I owe you. Please keep Richard Burnham updated if something changes; he has duty this weekend."

"Will do, Karen."

Karen dialed the station.

"MCU, Burnham here."

"Good morning, Richard. Has Jim Hardy called you?"

"No, he hasn't. I read the paper; is there any more news about the old man in Ely?"

"I've asked Jim to keep you updated. Also, forget about the kidnapping, it's Denise's bunk, but keep an ear out for any change, especially if it involves us."

"Well, I'm happy to hear that we don't have kidnapping to deal with," Richard replied.

"Call me if anything changes with Waters."

"Okay, Karen, will do. Enjoy your evening."

On Sunday morning, Richard called Karen to give her the latest update on Jeffrey Waters.

"Karen, Jim Hardy just called to say that Waters has been found, dead I'm afraid. It looks natural; hypothermia got him; Doctor Gordon will have to certify that."

"Thanks, Richard. In a way, that's a relief. It's terrible that he died, but for selfish reasons I am happy we don't have to get involved."

"Doctor Gordon called to say he will perform an autopsy tomorrow at Waters' son's request. He'd like someone there."

"Let's talk tomorrow and flip a coin to see who attends."

"Don't need to do that, Karen, I'll go."

"Thanks, Richard. See you sometime Monday."

On Monday morning, Jim Hardy sent over all the information he had. The report began with some early family history:

By 1956, Jackson Waters, the latest in the line of great-great-grandsons of Ebenezer Waters, managed to bring all the former pieces of the original Waters' farm in Ely under his control. In the Waters' tradition, he farmed the land over forty years before he took his place among the listing of the Ely dead.

As expected, Jeffrey, his only son, managed the farm in the same tradition as his father had. Jeffrey was a sensible and wise farmer having lived and worked on his farm with his father all his life.

The farm was large and it had the prime advantage of location. The fields were flat and fertile with several natural artesian wells that provided water for his house and furnished irrigation water for his crops during the dry spells of summer.

Recently, neighbors had observed that Jeffrey was

declining in health, both physically and mentally for the past few years.

He had begun to complain that he was having stomach pains and feeling weak. Jeffrey told family and friends that he could not keep the farm going much longer. He would have left the fields to farrow if it hadn't been for the support of his good neighbors.

His niece, Caroline who lives in Middlefield, noticed that lately he seemed to be slipping very quickly. He was forgetting important, personal things, such as brushing his teeth, washing up dishes, and even laundry. She said that was unusual for him because he was always so independent. For years after his wife died, he kept house as well as anyone did.

She pleaded with him to see a doctor, but he refused. In fact, he had not seen a doctor in more than twenty years.

Caroline has been visiting him every other day to make sure he eats and has clean clothes. She last saw him on Wednesday. His son and his wife were visiting, so she felt no need to return on Friday.

A search party of friends, neighbors, and police searched the property and found him Sunday morning in the woods about five hundred feet from the house. The night temperature has been averaging thirty-five degrees for the past week. At his age and frailty, it is not surprising that the elements killed him.

Karen then called Richard.

"Richard, Waters' death seems be entirely natural, but if anything suspicious is found, would you please ask James to get his report to us as fast as possible?"

The autopsy started promptly at ten o'clock on Monday. Since Jeffrey Waters did not have a family physician, the task fell to the Twiggs County Medical Examiner, Dr. James Gordon, to sign the death certificate.

Doctor Gordon did not expect anything unusual with the death of an older man, particularly a man who eschewed the medical world as Mr. Waters had for most of his life. Even with the circumstances of Waters' death, he felt that an autopsy was an unnecessary expense in view of the man's age. Nevertheless, the state proscribed such procedures unless the family objected for religious reasons.

The body showed no outward evidence or signs of violence, as was determined by the Middlefield detectives who had arrived with the ambulance. The preliminary judgment of the police was death due to hypothermia.

The results of the autopsy did not disclose a cause of death directly. Waters' core body temperature was extremely low as would be expected due to the night long exposure to nearly freezing temperatures. Worse, he had not been warmly dressed for his walk.

Waters' heart was enlarged somewhat, and Gordon noted thin, grey-blue lines visible along the margins of the gums at the base of the teeth.

Gordon knew these were well known symptoms of lead poisoning called Burton lines. He also knew that the element bismuth could also give these Burton lines but that seemed unlikely due to the relatively low toxicity of bismuth.

Examination of Waters' stomach revealed he had eaten late in the day. The best estimate of the time of death was early Sunday morning.

* * *

Not surprisingly to Gordon, when toxicology test reports were received, they confirmed the presence of lead with a blood level concentration of 279.6 micrograms per deciliter (μ/dL). The liver and kidneys also had elevated levels of lead. Brain, spleen, kidneys, liver, lungs and other soft tissues had been tested indicating unusually high levels of lead.

Bone samples revealed high levels also. Hair samples were tested. The lead levels from oldest to youngest parts of the hair strands were consistently similar essentially ruling out a sudden overdose ingestion. This fact was a sure sign that lead had been ingested continuously in small doses.

Doctor Gordon knew that these were signs that this poisoning was chronic and occurred over some length of time, but it wasn't clear what was responsible or how it had been administered.

The Medical Examiner's expertise and years of experience in these types of death had given him a basis for understanding lead poisoning. Gordon knew that blood lead concentrations in occupational poisoning victims had rather large ranges.

People working with pottery glazes often had concentrations up to 105 micrograms per deciliter, (105 µg/dL). People eating contaminated herbal medicines or drinking acidic juices from lead glazed earthenware often had levels as high 300 µg/dL.

Gordon's opinion of the cause of death as required by the death certificate was hypothermia. He also noted that the level of lead poisoning in Waters' body would have led to general body organ failure, if Waters lived much longer.

Doctor Gordon first contacted Waters' niece, Caroline Fielding. She revealed that she visited her uncle a couple of days a week for the past number of years after Waters' wife had died. She felt that her uncle was not eating well on his own.

Gordon learned that Caroline often brought meals prepared at her home some fifteen miles away from the Waters' farm. His niece would place the meals in the freezer for his later use. Whenever she visited, Caroline would make up two gallons of lemonade for his use while working the farm.

Gordon probed the family history and found that Caroline and her husband Randolph had lived in Middlefield since their marriage twelve years ago. They had met in their senior year at college and married after graduation. Caroline was an elementary school teacher in Middlefield.

Randolph was a chemist at National Paper in Macon. Whenever asked, Randolph bragged that National was the prime purveyor of fine writing and archival paper. His position at National was manager of quality control and nothing shipped without his approval.

With nothing but his concern and facts of Waters' condition at death, Gordon contacted the Middlefield Police to ask if they could investigate whether someone had intentionally poisoned Waters. The unexplained lead poisoning of Waters' neighboring farm owner, Mr. McKinney, a few years earlier still grated on his nerves.

With that request, Karen assigned the MCU to put together plans to gather information. Initially they would interview people who usually had contact with Waters. The team universally felt that the work was 'busy work,' a waste of time, but dutifully made their plans.

At the same time, Karen decided that the MCU could use some additional help. She felt somewhat concerned, but decided to ask her friend from Middlefield College to help.

Dr. Joshua Robertson was the department head of the Chemistry Department at Middlefield College. Standing 6 feet 2 inches, he had dark brown hair and sported a full but well-trimmed beard. His facial features reminded people of Gregory Peck. In his younger days, people often asked if he was the famous actor.

Joshua had married a local beauty shortly after coming to Middlefield. Many women had tried to bring him to the altar, but only Betty Wells had succeeded.

Robertson had been in the Department for fifteen years, serving the last three as Department Head. His scheduled term as Head would end shortly.

"Good afternoon, Joshua, this is Karen Hunter."

"Hello, Karen. David told me you two are going to have dinner some Saturday when you are both free from work."

"He asked me the other day and I said yes, but it probably won't be for a while, unfortunately."

"It's the first time in quite a while that he babbled on about meeting a nice person. You have him very interested."

"Well, I can say that I did enjoy talking with him at the Mayor's Ball a while back."

"How can I help you, Karen?"

"Have you read the story about Jeffrey Waters' disappearance?"

"I did. It was in Saturday's *Patriot*."

"Yes, he was found dead Sunday morning. Doctor Gordon performed an autopsy earlier today."

"James and I have worked together in the past. He called me after the autopsy to let me know what he found. Has he given you any information about what happened?"

"Not yet; Richard was at the autopsy, but I'm just going over his notes now. I do have sort of a historical report about the family, but otherwise not a lot. Doctor Gordon found that hypothermia was the cause of death, but he also found significant evidence of lead poisoning."

"Yes, Karen, do you remember about the lead problem at the McKinney farm a couple of years ago?"

"I vaguely do, but we had the appalling serial killings at that time and, frankly, I could only provide minimal help. Why do you ask?"

"Well, it lies adjacent to Waters' farm and strange things began to be noticed about old man McKinney's behavior.

"I was involved pretty heavily in the search for the lead source. From conversations with Mr. McKinney's neighbors, Gordon noted that McKinney might have displayed behavioral symptoms of chronic lead poisoning. Friends noted McKinney had increasingly poor physical health and had increasing difficulty with memory over the years but they had attributed that to his age.

"McKinney also had sudden bursts of anger railing at neighbors. He often complained about stomach troubles but again that was discounted as a function of aging. People began to suspect that John McKinney might be a victim of some kind of poisoning.

"McKinney submitted blood samples for testing to verify the suspicion. The results were positive for lead, and he died soon after."

"Was the source ever found?" Karen asked.

"To determine the cause of the poisoning, the Georgia Environmental Protection Division was notified to perform tests at the McKinney farm. Water, soil, cooking, eating utensils, foods, and all other potential sources of lead contamination were tested and cleared.

"After all tests were completed, it appeared that the farm had no sources of lead contamination above the accepted EPA maximum contamination levels. The farm was deemed safe in this regard.

"With this stamp of approval, there were no EPA remediation requirements. No conclusion was forthcoming in the report as to the cause of lead levels in McKinney's system.

"At the time, the large bottle of sweetener solution was a point of interest to me. John Reed of the Georgia EPD asked me to assist in the survey of the McKinney farm lead contamination study. I felt that the sweetener might be a link to the chronic lead poisoning.

"We decided to take samples of the liquid sweetener to his lab and perform simple qualitative tests on the liquid. If lead were in the sweetener, it would have to be in a form that was soluble in water. Reed tested it and dismissed it, as it contained no lead. Therefore, the cause of the chronic ingestion of lead by McKinney was determined not to be from the sweetener. The problem was that no one ever figured out how McKinney ingested so much lead."

"Was that the end of the investigation?"

"No, Cathy Swanson from GBI worked to find a cause, but nothing ever came of it. We still don't know if someone planned to kill him or not. I'm not certain that we will ever know. Nevertheless, it was clear that lead led to his demise. No pun intended!"

"None taken, Joshua."

"Well, is there something you want me to do about this case, Karen?"

"Gordon has asked me to look at the Waters' death in terms of a possible intentional poisoning by someone. Since you worked on the McKinney poisoning, perhaps you could help us on this case."

"I can certainly try, Karen, but unlike the McKinney death, Gordon's preliminary report on Waters indicates that lead poisoning did not directly contribute to Waters' death, but he is very concerned that the poisonings of the two farming neighbors are very unusual, which is why he wants you to look at it."

"Is the State going to try to find the poisoning source?" Karen asked.

"I don't believe they will. They spent a huge amount of money trying to solve the McKinney poisoning with little to show for it. As I said, the McKinney study at last focused on the foods that he habitually used. There were many different canned vegetables furnished by caring neighbors. Those kinds of foodstuffs were all tested and found to be free of lead.

"At the time, we made assumptions that commercially produced foodstuffs could be eliminated because other controls were in place for them. In light of the McKinney autopsy report, the fact that no lead sources were found at his farm has always bothered me."

"Do you have any ideas how we can work this case?" Karen asked.

"I haven't had much time to think about it, but I think that a cursory examination of the farm is in order. My suspicion is that extensive testing of the farm similar to what was done by the State at the McKinney's farm will be a waste of time and money again," Robertson replied.

"My suggestion is that the process should be two-fold. One, my group will focus on the niece and neighbors. Gordon talked to Waters' niece and she told him that she often brought Waters home-prepared meals and sometimes made up lemonade for him. Perhaps, you could focus your energy on items at the farm, which may provide clues to how he was poisoned."

"I'll do it, Karen, but it seems like 'needle in the haystack' kind of work."

"I'm sorry, Joshua, unless you have another idea, that is the best I can do."

"Okay, Karen, let me see what I can find out. Can you keep me informed about your interviews?"

"I will; talk to you soon."

* * *

Three days later, Joshua called Karen.

"Good morning, Karen. I went to the Waters' farm after we talked the other day, and spoke to Waters' son, Jason, who was still at the farm. I asked him if he knew what his father's favorite foods and drinks were. When he said that lemonade was his dad's favorite drink, which he prepared for years in an old family terra cotta pot, my interest was piqued."

"Why was that, Joshua?"

"Because there have been cases of accidental poisonings due to the leaching of lead out of containers."

"What did you do next?"

"I asked for the containers that his father used for the lemonade. Jason told me that his father bought powdered lemonade mix and then prepared the lemonade in a large Tupperware container, which he mixed with the correct amount of water. I decided to test that lemonade solution."

"Joshua, what did you find?"

"I did some simple qualitative tests on the solution. One test was for lead ion and another for the anions of lead that are soluble in water. Most lead compounds are insoluble or only slightly soluble.

"Not to bore you, but I tested for lead acetate in particular because they are quite soluble in water. Sorry to disappoint you, Karen, but there was no lead in the lemonade solution, so I knew that it was back to square one."

"That is disappointing, Joshua; I had hoped we could get this off our plates, no pun intended."

"It upset me also, but I went back to the farm and talked more to Jason. I asked him if he knew where the terra cotta pot was that his dad used for making the lemonade. He said that he didn't know, but called his cousin with the question.

"Caroline said that she had accidentally broken the jar three months ago while washing it out. His father had gotten very upset about it and tossed the broken pieces into the barn. As far as she knew, they were still there.

"I asked Jason why his father would have been so troubled about an old terra cotta jar. He told me that the pot had been in the family for years. It was brought to the country by Jason's forefathers when they immigrated. Caroline told Jason that his father had brought it down from the attic several years ago and decided to put it to use. That piece of history made me think we were on the right trail."

"Why do you suspect the jar is the problem?"

"It will be easier to describe if I put it in writing rather trying to explain it on the phone."

"Okay, were you able to find the pieces?"

"Jason and I went to the barn. Luckily, they had not yet been thrown out. Jason was in the process of cleaning the barn and they would have been tossed the next day. I gathered all the pieces and took them back to the lab where I leached them in a solution of the lemonade powder mix in the way we believe Jeffrey Waters did. His niece provided the preparation steps that she saw him use."

"Okay, Joshua, enough of the chemistry for me. Do you think this will solve the mystery?"

"I do, but I have to do some testing later. It will be a simple qualitative and quantitative approach, but it will be accurate enough to determine if it is the cause."

"Thank you, Joshua. Can you send me a report if it is the culprit?"

"Yes, it has to be unofficial, but it will be accurate. If you want my opinion, I think he accidentally poisoned himself simply because he didn't understand how lethal it could be."

"Thank you, Joshua. That takes a possible mess off my plate."

"You are welcome. I will prepare a brief procedure of the analysis written up, and to you by the end of the week. In the meantime, I will send a brief email about the terra cotta pot with my explanation of why it is suspect."

* * *

The next day, Robertson's email to Karen arrived.

Dear Karen,

Per our discussion yesterday, this is the explanation of the terra cotta pot problem. Pottery is glazed today, as well in the past, many times using lead oxide as a flux. The main ingredient in glazes is silicon dioxide, which forms the glass surface on the pottery. Fusing substances such as lead oxide is added to lower the high fusing temperature of the silicon dioxide. Generally, today aluminum oxide is also added to glaze material to increase the physical and chemical resistance of the glaze, and to decrease the lead solubility. In today's kilns, at about 500 degrees Celsius, the lead fluxing begins and forms lead bisilicate with the silicon dioxide. This pot used by Mr. Waters is over two hundred years old and may have a high lead content in the glaze. Highly acidic fruits can leach this lead out of the pottery glaze if the acidic substance is stored in it.

I believe that this is the case for Mr. Waters. I will begin testing the pottery shards today.

Sincerely,
Joshua

Chapter Three

Loneliness and the feeling of being unwanted is the most terrible poverty. Mother Teresa

As promised, in Friday afternoon's mail, Karen received the report from Dr. Robertson.

Dr. Joshua R. Robertson, Chair
Department of Chemistry
Middlefield College
118 Powdermill Road
Middlefield, Georgia 31044-1180

Dear Major Hunter:

Using the solution, which I described in my letter to you yesterday, we used the same techniques to test the lemonade found in the Tupperware container and the resultant solution from the "leached" pottery pieces.

The supposition that Mr. Waters experienced lead poisoning from the lemonade solution led us to assume that the solution may have contained lead citrate in some concentration. This assumption is based on the fact that many lead compounds are not soluble in water at room temperature, but the storage of citric acid in a glazed clay pot can leach lead out of the glaze.

The following is a brief, general, description of a qualitative procedure that we used to determine the solution's lead content. Although several of us felt that this step was unnecessary because we knew that the lemonade

mix used by Mr. Waters had sodium citrate and citric acid listed as ingredients, for completeness, we still felt compelled to test for citrate.

1) The first test was to identify the anion *(citrate)*. We removed a 25 milliliter (mL) sample by filtration of the lemonade solution by filtering. We then added 10 drops of the sample solution to a previously prepared 3:1 pyridine-acetic anhydride solution. As we added the sample solution drops, a red-brown color developed indicating the presence of a citrate.

2) To identify the cation *(lead)*, we removed another 25 milliliter (mL) sample by filtration of the solution and added 10 mL of a dilute solution of sodium sulfate. The formation of large quantity of a precipitate occurred immediately. This precipitate was only slightly soluble in plain water. We believe that this precipitate is lead sulfate, confirming the presence of lead leached from the pot. We have purposely generalized the anion because more than one anion may be active, but we feel certain that citrate is most likely the major one.

$$Pb^{2+}_{(aq)} + (anion)^{2-}_{(aq)} + Na_2SO_{4\,(aq)} \rightarrow PbSO_{4\,(s)} + 2Na^+_{(aq)} + (anion)^{2-}_{(aq)})$$

3) Since we had prepared a known concentration of sodium sulfate solution for test 2, we were able to calculate the concentration of lead in the solution to be 110 µg/dL.

We, therefore, concluded that the continual use of

lemonade solutions prepared in the old terra cotta pot was most likely the cause of Mr. Waters' chronic lead poisoning over time. This quick analysis was done at your request due to your time constraints.

We will also submit the samples to further analysis using spectroscopic methods, but these wet chemical results should be of some use for your investigation.

Sincerely,
Joshua R. Robertson, Ph.D.

After reading the brief report, Karen called the MCU together to report on the Waters' case.

"Folks, as far as I and Tom Hansen are concerned, the Waters' case is closed. Believe it or not, he accidentally poisoned himself with homemade lemonade."

"I'm sorry, Karen, but we've wasted time working on something that shouldn't have concerned us," Susan said.

"I don't agree, Susan. It was important to find out what caused the poisoning even if it didn't cause his death directly. Gordon had a great concern about this, and Gordon has been such good support for us that I couldn't refuse. It was the right thing to do."

"I think we can all agree that the exercise was worth the time," Chief Tate added.

"Let's break for now. We have some serious cases in front of us. Send your reports to me as soon as possible," Karen said.

As the meeting members dispersed, Richard approached Karen.

"Karen, can I speak to you privately?"

"Yes, Richard, is this a serious discussion about our talk the other day? Let's go to my office for privacy."

Richard and Karen had had words about Richard's insistence on a relationship with Karen. She remembered the painful conversation they had had.

"I am a little miffed that we haven't been out together."

"Richard, you need to find somebody. You know damn well that we cannot become involved. You know how policy works."

"You're right Karen, but it seems so natural for us."

"Richard, I had to fire somebody and transfer another somebody for having an affair. It didn't matter if they were unmarried or not; they had to go."

"I've got the message, Boss."

* * *

As they walked to her office, Karen wondered how to handle the situation.

Richard, I hope you are not going to say anything, which puts us into a confrontation. I've told you, no sex, and no personal relationship. Regardless of what some may think, I do have high standards.

"Take a seat, Richard. What can I do for you?"

"Okay, ever since the scolding the other day, I've been giving this whole situation a great deal of thought. I'm ashamed that I have been forcing myself on you. Frankly,

I was smitten with you. It's due to my loneliness, but that's no excuse. After my divorce, I found it almost impossible to look at other women in the way I did Anne. I found women attractive, but those I dated had more interest in the relationship than in me."

"What does that have to do with me?" Karen pushed.

"I think you can understand that. You were the first woman who made me feel comfortable. You seemed to understand what I've been going through these past years. All the time I spent with the Chicago Police was not satisfying when it came to the topic of women. There have been countless women who could have satisfied my physical needs, but that is not what I want out of my personal life."

"I do understand to a degree, Richard, but it can't be for us. When I was at your home when we were solving the ciphers of the Orion Case, I had thoughts that were inappropriate for us. I weakened and you probably could have tried to make things happen, but you didn't. I respect you for that."

"Karen, I think what I am saying to you now is that I am not sure it is good for me to stay here. Perhaps I should look for another position away from here."

"I would hate to lose you, Richard. You have been vital to our group. You and Susan are my right and left hands. The group would suffer by your leaving."

I wonder if Susan might help us out of this mess. Her sister, Aretha, is a bit younger, but she would make

Richard a solid partner. I'll check with Susan.

"Will you make me a promise, Richard?"

"What's that?"

"Don't make any inquiries or decisions until I sort some things out."

"Does that mean that there is some hope for us?"

There's not a chance that will ever happen. I have that womanly feeling for you in some ways, but not that way.

"Absolutely not; there are no commitments or promises on my part nor will there ever be about that, but I do hope you can grant me that promise."

"I will make it time limited, Karen. In six months, if nothing changes my mind, I will be on my way. I don't see what will be different enough to keep me here. Fair enough?"

"Fair enough. Let me get sorting."

After Richard left her office, Karen called Susan for a chat.

"Susan, I have a personal problem that you may be able to help me to fix."

"I already know what your problem is, Karen. I was wondering when you would talk to me."

"Richard mentioned that he had a conversation with Carlos when they were golfing. He didn't tell me what was said, but I know you can."

"I am guilty for urging Carlos to speak to Richard. At the time, Karen, you were telegraphing your emotions where Richard was concerned. Carlos and I thought you two were intimate, but Richard said you weren't."

"You're right, we weren't and aren't, but the thought crossed my mind. You know that I have to maintain a high moral standard with subordinates, especially after firing Robert."

"Well, Carlos told him to be careful."

"Good. The reason I asked us to chat is that I need to focus Richard in another direction. I don't know if it will work, but I have to try. We can't afford to lose him, but I have to shut him down as far as I'm concerned."

"What can I do?"

"Your sister, Aretha, is unmarried, yes?"

"Yes, she is. Are you thinking of playing matchmaker?"

"You have it. Why hasn't she ever wed? Is she a man-hater or just not found the right guy?"

"From what she has told me, it's finding the right man that's the problem."

"Sounds like she may be hard to please. The times I have talked to her, though she seems reasonable and pleasant."

'Aretha is her own woman. She would make a good wife for someone, but the right someone has so far been MIA."

"What can we do to get her interested in Richard?"

"I'm not certain. She is the youngest of our family, so you know; they're sometimes a bit spoiled by parents. She didn't date much in high school or college."

"But you think that she has healthy interest in men and their appetites?"

"If you're asking whether she is a virgin, I have no idea,

but the times we have talked; she has said she wants a family, so…"

"Unless she is the 'my way or highway' type, being a bit spoiled probably isn't the reason."

"Well, being a nurse, her hours are varied and a bit wacky just as ours tend to be. Here's a thought. Why don't I have Carlos invite him over for dinner on some Saturday evening? I'll invite Aretha and see if they find a spark. When I can get her scheduled, you have to make sure Richard is available. I want to make this very clear, Karen, if she is not interested in him, you will have to step in. I don't want her to feel threatened if she turns him down."

"It's a deal. I hope this works, Susan. I don't want to lose him, but I'm not going to stand for his shenanigans, either. Besides, I've got my own romance to work on."

"I'll keep you posted. It's going to take time, Karen. Love can't be rushed."

I think this may have a chance. Aretha has a pretty face, a good figure. Not so large in the chest department, but I think Richard is a leg man from what I've noticed. Richard is a perfect mate for someone; I hope Aretha feels the same way.

* * *

"Karen, I think we are set for next Saturday evening. Carlos called Richard and invited him for dinner. He accepted, but said he would have to make sure he didn't have duty that night. Has he spoken to you yet?"

"No, but he asked to see me later this morning, so that

may be his reason."

"Well, free him up because I do have Aretha coming."

"Does she know that Richard will be there?"

"Yes, I told her. She said that she thought it would be nice to meet him."

"Great! I hope this works out. I have to get him focused to someone else."

"Karen, I want this to be good for Aretha. I'm not pimping her to Richard."

"Susan, I want them to respect each other. I'm not looking for anything else. If it works; it works; if not, then…"

"I know, Karen. It's just that I have watched over her ever since my mom died, and I don't want her hurt."

"I'm with you, but of course, I can't say anything to him unless Aretha complains. Then it will be unpleasant to say the least."

"Now I'm not sure I was smart in agreeing to this."

"Susan, it is only dinner. You're not setting up a tryst for them, right?"

"Right."

"In any event, Susan, if he doesn't act properly, I will send him packing. I have made it clear to him about me and women in general."

"Thanks, Karen."

* * *

After introductions and greetings were done, Susan, Carlos, Aretha, and Richard moved to the living room for a cocktail before dinner.

"So, Richard, how did you find your way to Georgia, or did Georgia find you?" Aretha teased.

"I think it's a bit of both, but it is a long story so I won't bore you with the details."

"Well, I should tell you Aretha, he is a good golfer. Our round a month ago left me wondering what my skills are," Carlos said.

"Carlos, you exaggerate there. I'm not that consistent. It was a lucky day for me."

"Aretha is quite a golfer herself," Susan added.

"Now who's exaggerating, Susan. I try to get out once a week, when my schedule permits, but I often have to golf alone, since there always seem to be a schedule problem planning a golf day," Aretha said.

"While you talk golf, I'll take up dinner. I hope you like authentic Mexican food," Susan said.

Susan served her delicious bistec with side dishes of lemony rice and refried beans.

"Kudos to the chef, Susan, that meal was delicious," Richard complimented.

"She puts me to shame," Aretha said.

"Nonsense, Aretha, I'll bet you are a fine cook," Richard insisted.

After dishes were done, a final after dinner drink was offered; Aretha and Richard gave their thanks to the hosts and went home their separate ways.

* * *

On Monday, Karen couldn't suppress her curiosity and asked Richard how his weekend fared.

"Do anything exciting this weekend, Richard?"

"Not much really. I did have dinner with Susan and Carlos. Her sister was there. I was surprised you weren't invited."

"Well, I've had dinner with them many times. Susan is a great cook. I always love her food."

"Yeah, the meal was great. Her sister was interesting to talk with, but she seems a bit too focused about her job. All that interested her seemed to be nursing, but she did say that she enjoyed golfing when she could get a tee time."

"She's single. That is her life at this point. I'm sure if she met the right guy she might broaden her views."

"Do you think Susan would be okay with my asking Aretha out? I know she and Aretha are very close. I don't want to start anything that could affect my working with Susan."

Let's see. You want to take me to bed, but you're worried that Susan might not want you to take her sister on a date. For a rich, and I thought, a sophisticated guy, you are just a puppy.

"Of course, she wouldn't mind. The person to worry about is her sister. What does she think?"

"We did have a few minutes alone when I walked her to her car. I almost asked for a date, but something stopped me."

"Seize the day, Richard. Ask her out."

You have never gotten over your divorce have you, Richard? You are tough on the outside, but inside, you are just a kettle of mush. Believe me, Richard, I understand, I understand.

"If you want my advice, you should at least try to change your social world. Rambling around in your beautiful home by yourself is not healthy for you. Just my opinion."

"Well, you haven't remarried yourself, Karen. Your advice seems hollow."

"Richard, the direction of this conversation needs to stop right now. We both have things to do to reorder our personal lives, but not with each other. I have given you my advice as a colleague, not as a boss. You have to make your own decisions and I, mine. Let's just drop it here."

"Okay, Karen. Thank you for your concern."

"Richard, I wish the best for you."

"I'll have to decide where I go from here."

"I understand. Keep me posted on your decision."

After Richard left, Karen called Susan.

"Susan, how did dinner go this weekend?"

"I think it went very well. Aretha called me on Sunday and said she is a bit taken with Richard. She hopes he will ask her out some time."

"Well, that's progress, but I am afraid that Richard is still in love with his ex-wife in some way; it drains any thoughts he has about women."

"I'll put a bug in her ear to call him."

"Thanks, I owe you. I need to get back to work."

Chapter Four

It is hard to free fools from the chains they revere.
Voltaire

Karen's Saturday's run began as usual, but had the added anticipation and excitement of this evening's promise. She felt the delicious feelings experienced so long ago as a schoolgirl and looked forward to an outing with a gentleman for dinner. It had been a long time.

I wonder how dinner with David will go. He seems nice, but I don't really know him. Just met him at the Mayor's party, but people usually put on their best behavior, unless they've drunk too much, then... We'll see how this doctor's charm works.

Several weeks ago, Doctor David Robertson had called Karen for a Saturday evening dinner date, which she had accepted cautiously. She would meet him at the restaurant rather than having him fetch her at her apartment. He had told his brother, Joshua, who was happy that his bachelor brother was finally thinking of something other than medicine.

She had met and spoken to David Robertson briefly at one of the social functions so important to members of political strata of Middlefield elite. Robertson was a medical doctor on staff at Middlefield General Hospital.

At the function, they had not been able to ask each other too many questions of themselves, so the call to ask her out had been unexpected. For lonely Karen, however, the brief meeting with him had stirred some basic emotions. She had hoped he would call her, but several months had passed with no contact.

At the social party, she had learned that he had a brother, Joshua with whom she was acquainted. She and Joshua had worked together recently on the Waters' case requiring a chemist's expertise. Joshua was the current department head of the Chemistry Department at Middlefield College. He was married, in his mid-forties, and very handsome. In fact, both the Robertson brothers were extremely handsome having attractive faces bearing warm smiles. They stood over six feet tall, were slender, obviously took pains to keep in good physical shape.

If this date doesn't work out, then why not accept the invitation from Ben who's been calling you once a week? I like him, but he's my dentist. If we go out to eat, he'll be watching how I chew my food. I can't have that!

He's nice enough, but I want someone a bit taller. He's only five six. I tower over him. Well, your husband, Bill, was tall, but he also cheated on you. I did too, and I am forever sorry about that. Divorce is not pleasant. You're getting fussy in your old age, sister.

Besides, he's not manly enough for me. Seems too much of a milquetoast for me. All he sees in me is a set of teeth. I guess that's better than viewing me as a pair of boobs, but then I think that's where the milquetoast part comes in. That's not what I want or need. Let's see how David works out this evening.

Okay, gal, you need to get ready for tonight's dinner. I

think I'll wear something a bit seductive tonight. Show a bit of leg and some discrete cleavage. Maybe that will interest him. Course, I don't want him panting... On the other hand, do I want him to lose control?

* * *

McCarthy's was the first class restaurant located in the heart of Middlefield on Thayer Street. The owner, Robert McCarthy, had designed the interior with rich wooden paneling tastefully accented with paintings of local talented artists. The dining area, which could seat over two hundred people, was appointed with oaken tables covered with fine linen table cloths while delicate overhead lighting brought out the detail of the interior finery. Soft lights in the center of each table setting added to the aura experienced by diners. The leaded glass windows permitted diffuse light into the rooms creating a sense of imperial dining.

Guests used only the best flatware and china to cut and consume their preferred choices of the finest cuisine served in the area. It was to this fashionable restaurant that David had invited Karen.

When Karen walked in, eyes of the already seated guests were drawn to watch where this well-dressed, stunning woman was headed. David, in gentlemanly fashion, rose to greet her.

"Karen, you look lovely tonight. I'm so glad we could get to have dinner."

"Thank you, David, I do appreciate the compliment. I don't get many these days."

"I can't believe that."

"It's true. When women age, we find ourselves less and less interesting to men of the same age. Some become cougars."

"That's not you. I would say you are an exception."

After ordering dinner and a vintage bottle of wine, they began to talk about their interests.

"How long have you been in Middlefield, Karen?"

"Quite a few years. I took a police position here after college. Haven't thought of moving on."

"That's good for me."

"Why do you say that, David?"

"I have been looking for someone whom I can share my thoughts and feelings."

"I understand that feeling, David; loneliness is a terrible disease."

"Is that your life? I thought you would have many beaus and an active social life. You are beautiful."

"Thank you for the compliment, David, but I've led a not so spectacular life, and beauty is only in the mind."

"I would like to get to know you better."

This low cut dress must be more powerful than I thought. Apparently, boobs play a great part in his fantasies. I hope I haven't gone too far this evening. I only meant to tantalize him not seduce him. What do I do now? I can't go to bed with him even though my juices are flowing. It wouldn't be right.

"Josh told me that you are divorced."

"I am, that was a few years ago."

"Haven't found someone special yet?"

"David, there are a lot of good men out there, but none have interested me. I know Joshua is happily married. How did the ladies let you get away?"

"I just haven't found the right person yet."

"Tell me a bit about you."

"Josh and I grew up in Milledgeville. Mom and Dad owned a small hardware store. They've both retired now and are in their seventies. Health is beginning to fail. We both keep a close eye on them."

"What attracted you to come to Middlefield?"

"Josh and I are only one year apart in age. After college, he went to graduate school at Yale, and I went to Harvard and then on to med school.

"He took a position here at the College and I followed four years later after my medical internship was done. I was offered a position here at Middlefield General; it is a great place to work. I guess it would take something special to make me decide to leave the town."

"I feel that Middlefield isn't perfect, but except for a few nut cases that pop up now and then, it's a great place to raise a family," Karen agreed.

"Josh told me you don't have any children."

"That's true. I was pregnant, but miscarried. It broke my heart."

"I'm sorry, Karen, that was unkind of me to ask."

"The pain is still there, but each year it gets better."

Karen and David continued their general exploration of each other's beliefs, politics, and life goals over dinner. When the wine and meals were done, Karen decided she had been too prissy with her insistence on meeting at the restaurant.

I think I'll invite him to my place for a nightcap. Oh Karen, are you thinking right? Yes, it's my turn to enjoy life again. However, what will he think of me? Oh, God, no, I couldn't stand for him to think bad of me.

"David, would you like to come to my place for a drink to top off the evening?"

"I would, Karen. I'd like to get to know you even more. I feel a certain bond forming with you. I know it's too soon to talk this way, but I've been lonely. I have wanted to meet someone like you for a long time."

"Well, let's go to my apartment for that nightcap."

Karen had always left a light on in her apartment when she was out for the evening.

As they entered her apartment, Karen took his jacket intending to hang it in the coat closet. When her hand touched his, she could feel the tingle of electricity pass from him to her.

He makes me feel like a giddy girl. Why does that have such a control over me?

"Humidity is low tonight. Static electricity," Karen remarked.

"I'm not so sure of that, Karen. What I felt was a lovely

hand of a lovely lady."

"You must say that to every woman, especially your patients."

"No, Karen, many of my patients are well beyond what one would call lovely. I'm not saying they're not nice people, but time has passed them by. You know what I mean."

"I do, but it awaits us all. Someday you would be saying that about me."

"I can never imagine that would ever be you. I can see you gliding into old age as lovely as you are now."

David, you have a bedside manner most women could not resist.

Looking around, David appreciated the warmth and good taste Karen had used in furnishing her apartment.

"I must admit, Karen, that you have excellent taste. Your apartment reflects you with its warmth," David said while Karen was in the kitchen.

Karen returned to the living room with the drinks.

"Here we are. I have some brandy for the nightcap."

Karen sat down on the couch close to David and poured two small glasses of Cognac, handing one to David. As they sipped their drinks, conversation turned more direct and intimate.

Why did I sit so close to him? Am I daring him to kiss me? What are you doing, Karen?

"Have you anyone special in your life these days, David?"

"As I said before, no one, I haven't found the right woman yet. You said at dinner no one occupies your time."

"That's true. No one is part of my life."

"Tonight I am feeling as though I have met that someone."

"Well, David, it's hard to tell after only one dinner date."

"I'm not sure of that, Karen. You are doing something to me that I can't explain, or control."

Karen put her hand on his leg as if to say that he was just overwhelmed by the evening and drink. He turned to her and slowly brought his lips to hers. She felt herself weakening and eagerly returned a long, slow kiss.

Karen's resolve melted by his kisses and the pleasant feeling of his closeness. She knew she did not want to stop him or herself.

"Karen, I have to tell you that I love you. I would like us to continue together."

"David, this night has been something special for both of us. We have each been alone for a long time, perhaps not by choice, but without that comfort of a willing and loving mate. I think we should move ahead slowly. I have given my heart too quickly in the past, and it didn't turn out well. If you can be patient, let us find out more about each other. Can you live with that?"

"I can manage that. I want you to love me as I feel I love you."

"Thank you, David. Let's see how things work out."

Chapter Five

The tolling bell reports a death, but tells us not who, how, or why. Anonymous

Monday morning, Karen called the MCU together for a meeting. Before the rest of the staff entered the room, Richard approached Karen.

"How was your dinner Saturday evening?"

How does he know about my date with David Robertson? Word gets around fast.

"It was fine, Richard, it was fine."

Give it up, Richard. Please ask Aretha out. You may find what you have been looking for, but you must stop bothering me before I have to reassign you to somewhere that you will consider not nice.

"Speaking of dinner dates, have you asked Aretha out yet?"

"I have, Karen, we have a date for next Saturday. Was McCarthy's worth the prices he charges?"

"It was great, Richard. I highly recommend it."

At this point, Susan, Carol, and Sarah ambled into the conference room. Karen started the meeting.

"Richard, what information do we have from the Stoneham PD's interviews of the two possible escorts of Kaye?"

"They did manage to locate them and brought them to the station. Both denied going to Georgia with Billington. Neither had good alibis; they are pretty much homeless. No one would vouch for them, so we have nothing in that direction. Even so, the police are confident that neither one went with her. We know that she didn't come to Georgia alone, but who came with her and who met her in the bar that night is a mystery."

"That's too bad, Richard, I was holding out some hope that one of them might be able to help us."

"I have some news. The bartender at Jack's Place called me this morning. He saw the same man who left with Kaye reappear in the bar last night. He said he tried to call me, but I only got a missed call notice. He didn't leave a message," Susan said.

"Did you get in touch with him?"

"I did. He said the man told him that his name was Sherman Smith, a computer sales rep. He only comes to town every four weeks; he doesn't necessarily stay at the same hotel, eat at the same restaurants, or drink at the same bars. That is why the bartender hadn't seen him for a while."

"Susan, did the bartender find out where he is staying?"

"No, sorry."

"Let's break from here. Call every hotel in town and locate him," Karen ordered.

Two hours later, Carol called Karen. Smith was staying at the Marriott Hotel. Karen and Richard rushed to the hotel to interview Smith.

"Mr. Smith, I am Major Hunter of the Middlefield MCU. We have a few questions to ask you. Are you willing to talk to us?"

"What is it you want to know?"

"Several months ago, you were seen with a woman who has subsequently gone missing. Take a look at her picture. Do you recognize her?"

"Who said I was with her? Am I a suspect? Do I need a lawyer?"

"The bar tender at Jacks' Place said that he remembered you with her. Mr. Smith, you are not a suspect at this point, but since you are the last known person to have been seen with her; it would be a great help if you could tell us what happened that night."

"Let me check my calendar."

Slowly thumbing through his record, he finally said.

"I was here in Middlefield that night and for the next two nights. I had met her at Jack's Place. I bought her a drink, but the bartender said that was the last he would serve her."

"What happened when he said that?"

"Well, she got angry and started bad mouthing him. I calmed her down a bit, and told her we should finish up our drinks and leave."

"Was she really drunk?"

"She'd had a little too much, but she wasn't falling down drunk if that's what you mean."

"Where did you two go after the bar?"

"She said she wanted to make love, so we went to my hotel room."

"Are you married?"

"Divorced."

"Did you give her any money for the favor? You realize that if she was drunk, she couldn't give consent for sex."

"She wasn't that drunk and besides she asked for it."

"What happened after that?"

"I took her back to the bar and dropped her off. She said her car was there."

"So you let a woman whom you just had sex with and was drunk drive a car?"

"Come on, officer. You're making me sound like a hard-hearted person."

"Maybe you are not hard-hearted, but you are certainly callous when it comes to treating people."

"Is this all you want to know?"

"I have a couple more questions."

"Shoot."

"Can you describe what this woman was wearing?"

"If I recall correctly, she had a short red dress with a low cut neckline. That's what caught my eye."

Boob man, huh. Probably anything in a skirt would make your little heart go aflutter.

"It was cool that evening, was she wearing a sweater or jacket?"

"Yes, in fact, after we left the bar, I had to go back to get her leather jacket that had slipped to the floor from her barstool. The bartender had already picked it up by then and set it on the bar."

"Do you remember the condition of the jacket?"

"Not really, but I can say it looked expensive, like it was from Italy–you know, soft and supple."

"So it wasn't scuffed at all?"

"I didn't really notice that."

"Was there anything else you noticed about the jacket?"

"When I held it to help her put it on, I did notice that the left sleeve cuff was torn, so it couldn't be buttoned."

Damn, I missed that. I'll check it out later.

"All right, Mr. Smith, here is my card. If you think of anything else, please give me a call. I have your card from your company, so if we need to reach you, I will call there."

"Did something bad happen to her?"

"Yes, something bad happened. Thank you for your time."

Karen and Richard returned to the station.

"What do you think of him, Richard?"

"I think he took advantage of a drunk, but I don't feel he is our killer."

"I agree. He was calm through most of the questions. I don't feel he is hiding anything."

"What could have happened to her that evening?" Richard thought aloud.

"Your guess is as good as mine, but perhaps nothing happened that night."

"What do you mean, Karen?"

"Did the Stoneham PD say anything about her hobbies, habits, etc.?"

"Do you mean was she a jogger or something like that?"

"Yes, but I'm thinking that she didn't have a run in the Park that night. Perhaps she did the next day, that may be where she met her murderer. It would make sense because he could have dragged her off the trail and left her where her bones were later found. She certainly couldn't have been seen from the trail. That could explain the scuffing of the leather jacket, but who hung it up on the tree, and more importantly when?"

"You know, Karen, we don't even know if she was killed. She may have had a heart attack or something else. The trail at the point we found her bones drops off steeply. She could have fallen to the bottom of the gully. That alone could have killed her, perhaps."

"What you say could be true. The prevailing winds would drive any putrefaction odors away from the trail. However, there is the jacket; I still can't let go of that. Smith said it had damage to one cuff."

"We are assuming that the jacket that you found was hers. Maybe it isn't. Maybe someone just found it along the trail and hung it up expecting that the owner would return for it," Richard said.

"I know, Richard, that is a huge assumption, but we can prove it."

"Do we still have it?"

"I had Sarah put it in storage. It's time to take another look at it."

After Sarah had retrieved the package, they put on gloves and examined the jacket. The torn left cuff was obvious.

"Sure enough, Richard, Smith was right. This jacket is the one worn by Kaye that night."

"The scuffing of the leather means she was dragged while wearing it; we know that she was killed in the Park."

"Not necessarily, Richard, she could have been killed somewhere else, and dumped off the trail where we found her bones."

"What now, Karen?"

"We can tell Tom Hansen that we feel certain Kaye was murdered. Who, what, how, and why remains unknown."

"He's going to love that case."

"Well, at this point, that is all we have, too bad."

"I've been meaning to ask you about Ely village. I don't know much about it, but with old man Waters' death, it has gotten me thinking."

"It's now a very exclusive place. It was mostly a farming community until about twenty years ago. Then money rolled in. There are a couple of farms left, but most have been sold off; Waters' farm is one of the last. As I was saying, rich people have moved in; building their fancy houses and driving their fancy cars."

"We don't seem to have much crime reported in that area, do we?"

"No, we don't have many calls out that way. Their Owners Association begrudgingly works with us, but to their credit, they police themselves quite well. They can afford neighborhood patrols; that is a big crime stopper.

They have an interesting gate keeping system; visitors must pass by a gate guard for admittance, but residents have a special entrance, which is gated, but unguarded. Their entrance is not in sight of the gate guard."

"That is interesting; I suppose it keeps the gossip down for errant husbands and wives," Richard said.

"You could be right."

"Karen, I read somewhere that a big shot lawyer moved to Ely a few years ago."

"Yeah, it was the talk of the town; a family named Reynolds. I think the old man came down from Boston where he made oodles of money representing underworld figures in New York and Rhode Island. He still runs a practice in Atlanta. The *Patriot* did a major puff piece for the family. I kept a copy of it, Richard. Let me see if I can find it. Yes, here it is; I'm not sure why I saved it, but take a look."

Details of the following story have been taken from the Reynolds family diaries and other memorabilia saved by the family. Quotations have been faithfully reproduced from other written family records. Eds.

In June of 2009, noted barrister Lincoln Reynolds relocated from Boston to the prestigious enclave of Ely, Georgia with his wife, Mary, daughter Lizbeth, and son Flynn aged seventeen and eighteen respectively. He is a well-known lawyer who has had many famous clients. He has now decided that a slower life, which will help him ease into retirement in a few years suits him better than the bustle of Boston. He has nothing to prove. His plan is to re-establish a law firm in nearby Atlanta, the business center of the southeast.

Lincoln Reynolds is a large man standing over six feet tall with pleasant facial features and the overall brawn that has come down through the years from his ancestors. Balding slightly at age fifty-five, Lincoln has managed his weight impressively over the years, such that his present dress suits are the same size that he wore in his thirties.

Mary, his wife of twenty-five years, on the other hand, barely stands five foot three with graying hair that, by her own admission, she is reluctant to color. She has allowed this reporter to say that Mary has managed her weight over the years, but not quite as effectively as her husband. The family has high praise for Mary's preparation of balanced, delicious family meals, which they insist have been responsible for the health that the entire family now enjoys.

As for family hobbies, Mary and Lincoln are well known in the world of rose gardeners. At their home in Boston, they have grown roses of every color and size; some being types that she has perfected. The Boston elite and friends were dismayed when Lincoln decided to move to Georgia.

Mary is proud that she encouraged Lincoln's interest in roses in the early years of their marriage. He became as enthusiastic about roses as she, often breaking new ground in their backyard garden to plant the latest variety he found.

Also in the family unit, is their son, Flynn, who was disappointed to leave Boston, where he has certain unnamed interests. However, the timing has been perfect for Flynn (named in honor of his immigrant ancestor). He has just graduated from Boston Latin where he excelled in academics. He also had a formidable career as quarterback in football and center in basketball for the Wolfpack teams. Now, his academic goal is to attend a small liberal arts college and follow his father into law. He has just heard of his acceptance to our own Middlefield College, an outstanding liberal arts school. This has made the family move to Georgia much sweeter.

Flynn resembles Lincoln in many ways. Taller than his father, he carries the muscular build from generations past. His dark brown eyes and brown, wavy hair complement a pleasant face with its perennial warm smile.

When the fall of 2009 arrives, Flynn will move from the plush house in Ely into the dorms at Middlefield College to begin his journey of study. As a freshman, he has been encouraged to try out for the football team. Coach Johnson feels that Flynn will have to earn his quarterback position for the Tigers, but expects he will be a first stringer in his second year.

The basketball coach is also interested, but Flynn believes that his time will be better served focusing on academics when the basketball season rolls around. For the summers, Flynn would return to Ely to get ready for the next football season and to shadow his father to see how he will like the legal world.

The couple is also very proud of their daughter Lisbeth who has no interest in roses, but has an academic interest matching her father, and wants to be a doctor.

Lizbeth had been named in honor of her long past grandmother, Caleb Reynolds' wife. Lizbeth is tall and towers over her mother. She is shorter than her father and brother. She is beautiful, intelligent, and has been gifted with a common sense that she says seems to be missing from most of her friends in Boston.

Lizbeth is also very interested in sports and will play basketball and soccer at Middlefield High. Both the basketball and soccer coaches are optimistic that Lizbeth *will add greatly to their squads. After her graduation from Middlefield, her career goals are to attend Harvard and then on to medical school, if all goes well.*

One last thing to report for this illustrious family. Lincoln graciously shared a family secret with this reporter. It involved his many great-grandfather, Caleb Reynolds, who wrote a letter to his wife.

The letter was sent by Caleb from California in 1857, and its contents have been a family mystery for many years after Lincoln's father discovered it. It was put in a safe deposit box, which Lincoln recently brought out to show this reporter. He has allowed us to reproduce it here for you.

The cipher has never been decoded. The editors are pleased to welcome such distinguished new neighbors into our City. Eds.

August 1, 1857

My Dearest Lizbeth,

I am sending this letter to you by overland mail. It is so important that I don't want to carry it with me. I leave from San Francisco tomorrow to Columbia. I am returning to Boston on the fast route through the Isthmus. I leave early September and should be home sometime later that month.

I have written down the directions to a fabulous gold mine, which will make us rich beyond our wildest dreams. When you receive this letter; put it in a safe place; I have put the directions in a code so that no one can read them. The directions come from a Dr. Wolfgang Schröder. He nursed a sick old man who gave him the directions to a lost gold mine. I met Schröder last fall when he was very ill himself, not sure if he would live or not. One night he told me these directions and I wrote them down. He wanted to make certain that someone could benefit from the mine. He survived the night and told me that if anything happened to him, I was to have his claim to the mine. I heard a month later that he had been shot by someone in a bar after an argument during a poker game. He died later that night.

I will write down some more information and send it to you in another letter when I reach New York. I am in a hurry to catch the ship home. Here is the code:

L	D	N	S		R	T	H	T		L	A	N	D		E	D	A	E
M	O	E	E		U	O	I	C		E	H	U	A		I	O	N	H
F	C	E	F		R	O	L	D		R	R	T	S		E	H	H	D
L	T	L	W		T	W	R	N		R	N	C	L		D	O	L	E
A	U	R	W		P	U	V	E		E	T	S	R		G	U	T	E
B	A	D	O		I	N	D	I		U	O	A	U		N	T	E	L
F	L	S	E		E	N	E	S		D	W	A	E		B	L	R	R
A	E	E	T		S	A	U	O		E	L	D	B		H	E	N	C
O	B	V	C		S	M	F	A		N	G	O	O		D	B	E	T
R	K	A	A		D	N	K	P		S	I	H	T		R	E	E	E
T	R	E	T		T	I	N	M		T	K	P	O		I	R	C	A
A	W	E	A		I	A	E	E		N	E	E	D		T	T	O	B

Do not show anyone this letter and place it in the back of our family Bible. Tell the children I love them. I will see you soon.

I am your ever-faithful husband,
Caleb

Lincoln says that he has searched for the second letter from New York, but has never been able to locate it. He says that Caleb's Lizbeth wrote a short family history in 1858, but he has refused to show it to this reporter.

We wish the Reynolds all the best for the future.

"That is quite a story. Am I expected to bow down when I speak to these people?"

"Hardly, but you can see what to expect when we have to do business in Ely. They've been trying for years to have their own police force. They don't feel we give them enough service."

"What will happen to the Waters' farm now that he is gone?"

"My suspicion is that developers will stumble over each other trying to outbid for the property. The farm is over six hundred acres. You can build many houses, even if lot sizes are ten to twenty acres. It's a gold mine."

"And I thought my family had some bucks."

"Tough to compete with old money."

* * *

Over the next couple of weeks, Richard could not let go of the intriguing letter by Caleb Reynolds. Always up for a challenge, he spent considerable personal time thinking up a solution to the code. Finally, one day he approached Karen with a request.

"Karen, are you willing to let me work on the cipher in my spare time? It would help to use equipment we've used for the last ciphers we solved."

"I don't know if that's a good idea. What happens if you solve it? Do you turn in your badge; go off in search of this elusive mine?"

"Of course not, Karen, it's just the challenge. Like you."

"You don't give up, do you?"

"No, I'm teasing you."

"You should realize, Richard, this is becoming very serious. You need to stop it."

"I apologize, Karen."

"Okay, let it go. As far as the cipher, you can work on it, but don't let it interfere with this murder investigation."

"Thank you."

"Do you have a plan for attacking it?"

"Not yet, but I'll come up with something."

"Richard, I have to confess. Ever since the *Patriot* did that piece on the Reynolds, I have considered trying that cipher for some time. I haven't had time to explore it more, but I'm thinking that old Caleb wasn't a master at this sort of thing, but he was no fool either."

"What are your thoughts about it?"

"I suspect that, at first, he probably used a substitution cipher plan, which most people do. Given the way he presented it in his letter, I'm betting that he used a transposition cipher. His saying that he would have more information about the cipher when he got home leads me to make that assumption. Of course, I could be wrong."

"A transposition cipher makes it tougher since I, we, have to find the key."

"I'm happy that this has nothing to do with Billington's murder; perhaps just a puzzle to keep our crypto skills honed."

"I enjoy puzzles like this, Karen. Sometimes I feel that I should join a cipher club. Fill in my spare time."

"Do you wonder what gold mine he had in mind?"

"A thought came to me when I was reading his letter of his trip to the Arizona territory. With all the rumors of lost mines around what is Phoenix today, the Lost Dutchman's Mine is an easy guess."

"Richard, those are just spooky old tales. I doubt if the mine ever existed, Superstition Mountain and all of that."

"I know, but what if he had glommed onto something real."

"I'll leave it to you, Richard. I have my hands full."

"I wish my hands were full…."

Forget it, Buster. You are never going to be with me anywhere. Take Aretha, she is more than willing, according to Susan. Be man enough to treat her right.

Chapter Six

There is one who kisses, and the other who offers a cheek. French proverb

A week later Karen stopped by Richard's office.

"Any luck with the cipher? Are we going to be rich?"

"Very funny, Karen. Much of my money is tied up in the market. You probably haven't noticed how it's tanking these days. I can't get out now though. I don't want to turn a paper loss into a real loss. I just have to wait it out."

"I'm sorry; just trying to be glib. It was unfair."

"That's okay. I have cracked it. I was going to surprise you later. We'll have to book our trip to Phoenix; spend time in the desert; sleeping with you under the stars; finding the mine."

"Okay, that's enough. What have you found?"

"Here is the cipher again.

L	D	N	S		R	T	H	T		L	A	N	D		E	D	A	E
M	O	E	E		U	O	I	C		E	H	U	A		I	O	N	H
F	C	E	F		R	O	L	D		R	R	T	S		E	H	H	D
L	T	L	W		T	W	R	N		R	N	C	L		D	O	L	E
A	U	R	W		P	U	V	E		E	T	S	R		G	U	T	E
B	A	D	O		I	N	D	I		U	O	A	U		N	T	E	L
F	L	S	E		E	N	E	S		D	W	A	E		B	L	R	R
A	E	E	T		S	A	U	O		E	L	D	B		H	E	N	C
O	B	V	C		S	M	F	A		N	G	O	O		D	B	E	T
R	K	A	A		D	N	K	P		S	I	H	T		R	E	E	E
T	R	E	T		T	I	N	M		T	K	P	O		I	R	C	A
A	W	E	A		I	A	E	E		N	E	E	D		T	T	O	B

"Counting the rows; we get twelve, so that means the

key has to have twelve letters."

"Right and the key shouldn't have repeating letters for clarity."

"Since he knew what the plaintext was, he could have violated that rule, but I suspect he didn't. That way he could leave it to his wife or son to decipher if something happened to him."

"The problem was, Richard, that he never got the additional letter written and, of course, he was killed in a hurricane."

"I tried quite a number of keywords, but none worked. Finally, it dawned on me that he may have believed it was the lost Dutchman mine. Why wouldn't he use that as part of the key?"

"Sound logic there, Richard."

"I finally used this for a key: Dutchman view. Please don't ask me how I settled on that because I don't know."

"That's bizarre. I just added up the total number of cipher characters. There are one hundred ninety-two, so each column under each key letter is sixteen characters long. The spaces are just to fool someone."

"If I remember the rules correctly, Karen, the sequence order for the rows he gave us would start with the 'A' of the keyword and proceed all the way to the letter 'W' in the alphabetical sequence of the key letters."

"That's right, Richard, so the first row is turned vertical and lies under the letter 'A'."

"Here is what I got:

D	U	T	C	H	M	A	N	V	I	E	W
4	21	20	3	8	13	1	14	22	9	5	23
F	R	O	M	A	F	L	A	T	B	L	A
C	K	B	O	U	L	D	E	R	A	T	W
E	A	V	E	R	S	N	E	E	D	L	E
F	A	C	E	W	E	S	T	T	O	W	A
R	D	S	U	P	E	R	S	T	I	T	I
O	N	M	O	U	N	T	A	I	N	W	A
L	K	F	I	V	E	H	U	N	D	R	E
D	P	A	C	E	S	T	O	M	I	N	E
R	S	N	E	E	D	L	E	T	U	R	N
R	I	G	H	T	W	A	L	K	O	N	E
T	H	O	U	S	A	N	D	P	A	C	E
S	T	O	A	R	E	D	B	O	U	L	D
E	R	D	I	G	B	E	H	I	N	D	T
H	E	B	O	U	L	D	E	R	T	O	T
H	E	E	N	T	R	A	N	C	E	L	O
D	E	T	H	E	R	E	C	A	L	E	B

Richard then read the message:

"From a flat black boulder at Weaver's Needle, face west toward Superstition Mountain. Walk five hundred paces to Miner's Needle. Turn right; walk one thousand paces to a red boulder. Right behind the boulder to the entrance lode there. Caleb."

"Those directions are useless, Richard. I believe that old Caleb was scammed big time."

"Well, you never know. When do we make our reservations?"

"Very funny. We don't, Richard. Neither of us is going anywhere except to work Billington's murder case, but I

78

suggest that you contact the Reynolds; I'm sure they would love to know that somebody actually solved the family secret."

"Do you suppose someone from the family will be trying to find the mine?"

"As I think I said before; 'X' doesn't mark the spot on that useless 'map'; all it will do is lead someone to a pile of sand."

"I will send them the deciphered message. With their money, I bet they will launch a safari to Arizona."

* * *

Two months after Jeffrey Waters' death, his farm was sold to investors. Surveyors were dispatched by the new owners to plat out sixty building sites.

As the surveyors continued their work, they began to notice unusual depressions in various places in a field on the outskirts of the farm. These depressions were found in the areas reserved for haying where timothy, red clover and alfalfa grasses were allowed to grow to three or four feet before cutting, tedding, drying, and baling by neighboring farmers. Even though plats were being surveyed, the new owners had agreed to honor existing haying leases for the next two years.

One day, one of the surveying teams stumbled across a depression site where several human bones lay scattered. The police were called, who in turn notified the county ME who immediately stopped all activity in the field.

Since the grass was ready for cutting, the reason for

concern was that heavy reaping equipment would destroy the site; thus obliterating any possible forensic evidence. The fact that more than one depression had been found by the surveyors, signaled that an investigation needed to be underway. Susan and Karen immediately went to the Waters' farm.

"Well, Karen, it looks like there is another killer at work here."

"I have a crew on hand to identify all the depressions and dig for any more remains. Once that is complete, I want the grass in this field cut and the debris removed," Karen said.

"I asked the surveyors if this field was leased to anyone. The foreman said that the neighboring Jenkins' farm leases this field for haying," Susan said.

"Good job, Susan. Okay, get in touch with them."

"Karen, I've been looking at the stand of loblolly pine trees next to this field."

"Yeah, what do you see?"

"Do you remember what Sloan said?"

"Some of it, I do. She said that she saw a huge cross with some sort of movement of things in front of it."

"Look across the field. What do you see?"

"I see a stand of huge pines."

"Don't you see what looks like a huge cross?"

"Susan, you're right. It appears that one of the tall pines snapped off half way up. It's being held up by something, so that it is held horizontally across the front of another huge pine. You can see a cross from this view! I'll be damned."

"She may have meant that the grass in this field is what she saw moving to and fro."

"If she was right, there are more bodies in this field."

"Work with an officer; have each depression staked. We need to have GPS readings recorded for every depression."

"Actually, I have already put that in place."

"Susan, we need to get the Jenkins to clear this field. If they can't do it soon, I will have it done for them. They will not be allowed the option of using their heavy equipment. Cutting the hay will have to be done by hand and no grass will be cut within five feet of a depression."

"I'm sure they aren't going to like that. I'll check with them now."

"That's just too bad for them."

District Attorney Tom Hansen had been notified and came to the farm. As he walked around the site, it was obvious that the depressions in the field were unnatural.

"Tom, I believe those depressions are shallow graves. They have to be opened," Karen said.

"How are you going to clear the field?" Tom asked.

"The Jenkins' family is coming over to hand cut the hay. We can't let them in with heavy equipment."

"Karen, this is incredible! I cannot believe that this has been going on."

"I can't believe it either, Tom. I thought Ely only had the upper crust living here," Karen lamented.

"I know. I hope that you are wrong about more bodies," Tom agreed.

"I will have all the other sites dug up," Karen said.

"I know you know your stuff, Karen, but take special care in handling all the evidence. James Gordon will take charge of the bodies, uh, bones, so you might want to wait for him. I know this sound macabre, but I hope some sites have actual bodies we can DNA test," Tom instructed.

"All right, Tom, we will. I contacted the Archaeology Department at the College and they are sending out a crew with state-of-the-art ground radar equipment. It will make the search easier and we will know if there are more bodies, so we will not be wasting time digging empty sites.

"The first site may be old, say a few years. We'll see what the others look like. I am not that hopeful, though; the land here is low; it's often very wet in the spring. It dries out well by June but by then damage to flesh and bones is already done."

"Let's hope for the best. Who will be your contact for this?"

"I will ask Richard and Susan to oversee our part of this investigation."

"Good. You have two fine support people, but I guess I'm not telling you anything you don't already know."

"Yes, I couldn't agree more."

* * *

Because of possible damage to the graves, Karen had insisted that the Jenkins field workers hand scythe the grass; then carry and load the cut green hay onto trailers. She also ordered them to take it to another field to be dried.

"You know, Major, I can't bale hay without equipment, and I can't bale green hay because it can result in spontaneous combustion. I have to let it dry in the field. I have seen several farm barns go up in smoke for that reason," Edgar Jenkins said.

"I'm not a farmer, but I appreciate what you are saying. I am also grateful that you responded so quickly. We had to declare this whole field as a murder site. So, thank you," Karen replied.

"I hope you realize how much this is costing me."

"I gave you a choice. You do it, or I would have someone else do it. Stop your complaining. How soon will it be done?"

"Probably several more hours."

"Good, please get it done as soon as possible."

After the Jenkins' work was done, Karen's digging crews began theirs.

Nineteen depressions were found and the ground radar confirmed that the soil had been disturbed. Subsequent digging yielded bodies in various states of decay. Gordon felt certain that DNA profiles could be obtained from some of the bodies.

"Whoever killed these people had the time to dig graves nearly four feet deep," Karen said.

"The first grave, which the surveyors discovered, was only two feet or so deep. That's why animals had been attracted to it," Susan added.

"We need to have Doctor Gordon help us identify the sex of each body, so it will be a few days until we have that information."

"James has been looking at each body as it is dug up, Karen. He is mystified by the fact that there are no heads in the graves."

"I know, that will make the identification process harder without dental profiles. Now I wonder if the woman found in the Park was decapitated. We never found her skull. It could be that animals did not carry it off, as we first thought. Was that also the work of this killer?"

"The isolation of this area of the farm means the killer had the time to do what he did."

"Susan, we have to get back to the station and lay out a plan to interrogate all the residents in Ely."

"That's not going to be easy. You know how these rich folks circle the wagons."

"Yeah, I know, but we have to find the way to break their defending each other. Something else comes to mind. Whoever this killer is, he, and I'll assume it's a male, must be invisible, Susan."

"By that, you mean that he is able to come and go without people noticing."

"That's exactly what I mean. Young or old, whoever it is, no one questions his movements, or if they do, folks close to him protect him."

"Karen, I can't believe that someone would protect a

killer. Of course, there have been rumors of poaching for years in this area, so that may be what people thought was happening."

"I agree, but they may not understand what they have been protecting. If they thought it was poaching, I can appreciate that."

"Karen, since we've only just discovered these graves, the word hasn't reached everyone in Ely."

"There is a crowd already at the road leading to the farm. The uniforms blocked it off," Karen answered.

"How silly of me. Of course, news like this spreads like wildfire."

"Okay, Susan, let's gather up Richard and head to the station."

* * *

At the station conference room, Karen spoke to Richard before the rest of the MCU arrived for a meeting.

"Richard, how are you and Aretha doing?"

"Well, it is personal. I thought that you didn't want anything personal dealt within the office."

"Sorry, Richard, I was just asking. I didn't mean to upset you."

However, Richard, you need to direct your intentions in another direction. You just don't stop with the innuendoes. I hope Aretha can divert or better yet, fully capture your attention.

"I'm not upset, Karen. I just wish things could have worked out for us. Aretha is nice, but…"

Maybe I should ask him to leave. I've already talked to the Chief, but I don't want to lose him from the group. It's a mess no matter how I handle this.

"Give Aretha a chance, Richard. Things like this take time. She is attractive, smart, has a great job, and is falling for you. Don't be a cad."

"I know what you say is good advice, but…"

"For all the reasons I've given you, I cannot be your paramour. Why do men insist on knocking at a door when no one is home? We have work to do. Let's stop this…"

Karen heard Susan's high heels tapping along the tile floor to the Conference Room, and abruptly ended the conversation with Richard. As Susan and Carol came into the room, Karen put up a proposal on the screen.

"Folks, let's get started. I'm showing the basic plan I have for us to cover the Ely interviews in light of the discoveries there. There are eighty homes in Ely; not counting the two remaining farms. Nevertheless, they cover nearly half of the acreage of the Village.

"Susan, I want you, Carol, and me to work as an interview team. We will split up and go to each home with a form I've prepared. I want them to answer several key questions. This is a big job, because I want each member of a household to give their answers separately. Sarah will collate our questionnaires and have them typed up, so they'll be ready for a wrap-up meeting."

"Whew, you aren't kidding, Karen. Separately? What if they refuse?"

"These folks are very cliquish, I don't know if they will hear, see, or speak no evil, but if that happens, we will have to put pressure on them here."

"You mean drag them to the station?" Richard asked.

"You've got it. Uniformed officers will do the heavy lifting for us, but I hope it doesn't come to that."

"I don't either, these folks are armed," Susan said.

"Look, Georgians are good citizens and know how to behave themselves when it comes to guns. It's the thugs, drugs, and gangs that are the problems."

"True, Karen, but we are talking about a serial killer here. We don't know if one of the Ely folks is the one we're after."

"That's true, Carol, but my questionnaire doesn't accuse anyone. It seeks to identify anyone or thing unusual that someone may have seen or heard. I'm sure no one is going to come out guns-a-blazing over that."

"I hope you're right."

"Georgians, including Elyites are basically good people. If I thought we were putting ourselves in danger, I would say so. Plus, a uniformed officer will accompany each of us."

"What's my task, Karen?" Richard asked.

"I've arranged for another officer to go with you to the two farms. I have gotten a search warrant for any outbuildings on the Jenkins property. It's my feeling, and it's only my feeling, that the Jenkins clan is not involved, but our killer may have used one of their buildings for his carnage."

"What about the Waters' farm; since it's been sold, do we need another warrant?"

"No, the buyers have given us written permission to inspect anywhere we feel we need to. They don't want things torn up in the farm house or the old farm house."

"There's an old farmhouse?"

"Yes, it was the original building used as a home for years. In 1956, Jeffrey Waters built the current farmhouse. The old one is rented out, so that has to be checked out also. Okay, let's get moving."

Chapter Seven

It is not upon thee to finish the work; neither art thou free to abstain from it. The Talmud

Two weeks after the interrogation assignments were completed; Karen assembled the MCU to discuss the results and latest news.

"Before we get started with your interview reports, I have some information from Gordon. He has finished the nineteen autopsies, if you can call them that, with support from the GBI. The consensus of thinking is that these women's bodies were buried in the field over a five-year span; that means this killer may have started sometime around 2010; the last body was probably buried just a couple of months ago. He is still active."

"Karen, that means these killings were happening around the time we were cleaning up the prostitute murder cases. Did we have another serial killer operating that we didn't know about?" Susan asked incredulously.

"We must have had one. We had already stopped the other murders by early 2012. Remember, at the time, we weren't certain if we had a copycat murderer. You, Grace, and I discounted it, but it appears that we might have been wrong; if there was another killer operating; we just didn't know it."

"Do you think that Billington's murder is related to these cases in the field?" Richard asked.

"I don't have a good feeling about that yet. The Kaye Billington murder is recent; it could be involved with those cases, however, the MO seems different; she was just dumped, not buried. Scraps of her clothing were found with her bones. Moreover, don't forget her leather jacket hanging on a tree, which was found before her discovery. That jacket still ruffles me when I think about it. It just doesn't make sense."

"Perhaps the jacket isn't important except that it gives us solid reason to think she was murdered because of the scuffing showing that she was dragged along the ground," Susan said.

"It could be that her murder was the latest one he did; the field became too hot for him to use anymore; or perhaps Billington's murder was one committed in a pique of passion unrelated to the field bodies. Unless we find a suspect, we may never know."

"Was there anything else that Doctor Gordon found unusual about the bodies?" Susan asked.

"Yes, two things stand out. The first is that there were no heads, skulls, found with them. The killer decapitated them and took the heads with him; or buried them someplace else; or had some other nefarious purpose for doing that."

"This dude is sick. We had one case in Chicago, which was similar, but only one murder. We never did find the killer, though," Richard said.

"What was the second thing?" Sarah asked.

"Not a stitch nor a scrap of clothing was found with the bodies. He must have undressed them and taken the clothing also."

"Karen, I think that the reason for doing that was to prevent us from identifying the victims. To me, that takes him out of the insane killer class; it puts him definitely in the 'cold-blooded killer' category," Richard said.

"Well, I think we're all in agreement about that. The DA and Gordon feel that way also. Because of the bodies' conditions, we don't how they were killed."

"Has anyone at GBI come up with a profile we could use?"

"Yes, I was going to show you that. Marcus Strong at GBI conferred with the FBI's lead profiler. They believe that in general, he fits this:

- **The killer is most likely a white male, but that may be wrong**
- **He is probably a loner without friends**
- **He has the ability to blend into the Ely area**
- **He has flexible work hours, or doesn't have a job**
- **He may live with a wife or his parents**
- **He may have been abused as a child: sexual/physical**
- **He may have a hatred of his mother or wife**
- **He is physically strong**

"It's not really much to work with, but that's all we have at the moment."

"Is there anything else about the site that we should

know?" Susan asked.

"Yes, the oldest body is the one that was discovered by the surveyors. It may have been his first; he may have panicked, which is why he only dug a shallow grave for her at the edge of the field, which is adjacent to Sloan's Cross."

"We're calling it 'Sloan's Cross' now?"

"Come on, Richard, stay focused. He then moved farther into the field; fashioning the graves in the form of an 'X' pattern, which you know already. Whoever did this must have a creepy sense of humor; 'X' marks the spot? Are there any more questions? If not, Richard, would you take the lead? What did you find at the Jenkins farm?"

"Okay. The Jenkins farm's primary business income these days is providing hay for other farmers across Georgia and the country. They grow soybeans, corn, a few acres of tobacco, and have a large apple orchard. The farm is over three hundred acres, of which, twenty-five acres, is the homestead area; the rest is for farm use, but they also rent out some hundred additional acres from the adjacent Waters' farm for haying.

"At one time, they had dairy cows, but today, they only have a few hogs, chickens, and beef cattle for use by the family and for sale as animals on the hoof.

"They ran an abattoir for years to slaughter and sell their hogs and cattle, but the USDA gave them such a hard time requiring that they provide a shower for the USDA inspectors; they gave it up."

"That is interesting, where is the abattoir?" Karen asked.

"The Jenkins farm has four outbuildings. Two of them are very large barns. One is used for storing tractors, trucks, plows, harrows, along with haying equipment, and general tools. It is huge. The other is used for storing the hay that they harvest. One of the two smaller barns is used as a workshop, and the last one is a garage for the family vehicles.

"I'll ask again, where is the abattoir?"

"Sorry, Karen, it was torn down late last year. It was located adjacent to their property line; you know to keep it as far away as possible from their farmhouse."

"Does the property line abut Waters' field?" Karen pushed.

"It does, but…"

"Does that raise any concerns?"

"It could, but there is nothing there for us to evaluate, in any case."

"Okay, Richard, move on."

"I should mention that the Jenkins have three sons, Larry, James, and Edgar, Jr., and two daughters, Alicia and Anne. All live on the farm. Mary and Edgar Jenkins gave each kid an acre to build their houses. The sons work on the farm, but the two daughters and their spouses work in town. Unbelievably, they are all nurses. One last thing, there is a small house that they rent out to a worker. He lives alone; he has no spouse or kids."

"Sounds like as if they're a typical Georgia farm family. Make sure that the renter is on the interview list. Was there anything suspicious that you noted, other than the abattoir?" Karen asked.

"Over the past week, I finally interviewed each member of the family. Each one said that they had not seen or heard anything unusual. What…"

"That doesn't surprise me. Gordon said that he feels the oldest murder in the field was over five years ago judging by the extent of deterioration. The latest body was buried there only a couple of months ago. Please continue, Richard," Karen interrupted.

"I went to the farm late one night, unannounced to them. I drove past several of the houses on the farm. A few dogs barked in the distance, but no lights came on, and more importantly, no one came out to investigate a strange car. When I drove by the old folk's home, the same thing happened, no one stirred. I found that strange."

"I can't imagine them not waking up; I wake up at the slightest sound out of the ordinary," Susan said.

"It certainly makes them unreliable as witnesses. What time did you go there?"

"I arrived there at the farm about ten thirty. I didn't leave until midnight."

"I'm still surprised that no one woke up. Not sure what that means," Susan said.

"Did you get the feeling that anyone was not being honest with your questions?" Sarah asked.

"All of them were open, but guarded with their answers. I don't understand that, but rooting it out the reasons may never happen. The two sons-in-law unnerved me for other reasons that I can't explain."

"Who are they?" Susan asked.

"Greg Moran is married to Alicia Jenkins; Jack Mullen is married to Anne Jenkins."

"What bothers you about them?" Karen asked.

"Again, I can't put my finger on it, but they seemed shifty when I talked to them. Plenty of snide remarks about the father-in-law."

"By any chance, do they work night shifts?" Karen asked.

"They are both male nurses at Middlefield General. Their shifts vary, but many times they work the three o'clock shifts, so they do come home around midnight. Something that is strange to me though, is that they always work the same shifts."

"Did they tell you that?"

"They did, in fact, they made a point of it."

"Well, Richard, what do you make of them working the shifts together?" Karen pushed.

"I can't really explain it, but doesn't it seem odd for two brothers-in-law to be so close that they don't want to work separately? Too much togetherness for me."

If you want to know what I really believe, Karen, it's this: they don't trust their wives, so they work the same shifts to be home together. Both wives separately said how much they enjoy being with the other sister's husband. Seems strange to me. By my thinking, either one or both are having a bit of fun.

"Well that's interesting, but it doesn't help us; does it?" Susan asked rhetorically.

"Richard, the discussion about light versus sleeping patterns is interesting because it could help explain why the killer can operate without someone noticing," Sarah said.

"I think Sarah might be right about this 'not hearing things' in the night. The logic seems valid; people do become accustomed to sounds and smells such that they are filtered out of the consciousness," Karen said.

"As far as night noises are concerned in Ely, there are rather loud natural sounds from animals," Richard replied.

"That may partially explain why no one notices things. They won't hear cars, which they are used to hearing, and normal animal noises because they all get filtered out," Susan said.

"Animal sounds are one thing, but cars make different, louder sounds; the closing of car doors, or muffler differences, for instance. More to my argument, it would be a miracle if my police car made identical noises as their cars do. It would be the unusual 'sound' that was mentioned earlier; I believe people would not filter them out and wake up. Spending time in the middle of the night in Ely is different than in a city. Unusual noises would be detected," Richard countered.

"If you're correct, Richard, why didn't Jenkins' folks notice you?"

"I wish that I could answer that, Karen, maybe they did."

"Since you were there at midnight, did you see Mullen and Moran come home?" Karen asked.

"No, I didn't, and that is another strange thing about this family.

"Let's table this discussion for a while. I need to bring up another issue. The worker, John Jackson, is someone we need to keep an eye on."

"Why is that, Richard?" Karen asked.

"He told me that he is a direct descendent of Brigadier General John Jackson, CSA, not Stonewall Jackson. He has the General's saber on his wall.

"When I went to see him, he invited me in, but he insisted that I remove my shoes before I entered. He has a fetish about cleanliness."

"That is not that unusual," Susan interrupted.

"As I was saying, the house is small; well furnished, but Spartan with furniture finishes that can be easily wiped down. There is probably not a fingerprint in the joint to be lifted."

"I agree that is a bit over the top, but is that all?"

"He says that most nights he doesn't get to bed until one in the morning. I asked him if he ever hears people coming and going in the night. He replied that he does, but he doesn't bother to get up."

"Well, for all our sleep sleuthing discussion, perhaps the answer is as simple as that. Please continue, Richard," Karen said.

"I asked him what he does with his evenings; he said

that he works on his computer. He says he seldom watches television. He showed me what he calls 'puzzles' on his computer; they're ciphers!"

"Did you probe that more?"

"I did. I asked him what types he uses; said he likes the Polybius ciphers."

"Did he impress you as a competent cryptographer?" Karen asked.

"Not really, but he did say he makes up his own ciphers, whatever that means. He had a number of examples that he let me see. Nothing special in my opinion."

"Why should we keep an eye on him, then?"

"Because he said he often goes out at night. He likes to go to bars and meet women. Sometimes he brings them to his house, and they spend the night. When one of his lovers does stay, early the next day he drives them back to town. He is a bachelor, so I can understand it, but…"

"Well, we can't really keep an eye on him at the farm; it would be too obvious. We can check the bars, though. Did he say he favored any particular bar?"

"Yeah, he favors Jack's Place."

"Spend some time there and get any information from the bartenders about Jackson. Also do some background checks on the two Jenkins' brothers-in-law."

"Will do."

"What about the Waters' farm?" Karen asked.

"Nothing outwardly suspicious, although, did you know that the old farmhouse, which is located below a rise from the 'new' farmhouse is occupied by a renter?"

"Yes, did you interview him?"

"No, apparently he is on vacation someplace. I did call Caroline Fielding, Jeffrey Waters' niece, about it. She said his name is Michael Pitts. He comes from the New York area; rents this place to get away from the hubbub there. She said he has a home in Spain. She will try to find out where. She said he is a freelancer for a big software company, but she can't remember the name."

"Does anyone live with him?"

"No, Fielding said that he is single."

"Did she know anything about his schedule?"

"Not really. She said that he pays his rent on time every month, but he told her that he travels very often. She did say that he is a ladies' man."

"I suppose I can guess what she meant, but did she explain it?" Karen asked.

"She told me that he hit on her a couple of times, but she is married. She said single women might not be able to resist his charms."

"Anything else about him?"

"If he were our killer, he could come into town; pick up a woman; do his deed; leave for New York, or wherever with none the wiser, especially with the remoteness of Ely."

"Your scenario is not a stretch, but we need to find out for certain," Karen said.

"Okay, Karen, I'll follow up on that. The first of the

month will probably be the best time to get to him."

"Well, Susan, your turn."

"My twenty-seven houses were 'A through J.' As we all know, there isn't one family living in Ely that isn't rich or super rich; well, that probably excludes the Jenkins.

"I interviewed forty adults and twenty-one children aged fourteen through twenty. There were six children under seven; I didn't talk to them. I thought that all of the adults were open with their answers, but similar to Richard's experience, most adults were cautious how they answered the questions. It wasn't that I suspected them lying to me, but they didn't volunteer anything, either.

"There is one exception to my previous remark. When I interviewed Jason Arnold, he wouldn't make eye contact; he told me later that if I had any further questions to contact his lawyer. Something bothered me, so I did a background check on him.

"In 2013, his wife ran off with someone that she had met on a tour. She has never been heard from since. Arnold and his wife had no kids. He reported her missing a month after she had run off. We only have his word then or now about the reason his wife went missing."

"I do remember the incident, but no one ever accused him of anything, as I recall. Did his wife, Ruth, if I remember correctly, have any siblings?"

"No, she was an only child. Her parents are dead. As far as anyone could discover, the family is extinct. The parents died mysteriously on an Alaskan cruise with Ruth and Jason. Their bodies were never recovered from the frigid water."

"Whew, that is a strange tale, Susan."

"I know. What he does in that seven thousand square foot house is anyone's guess. He did tell me that he has a housekeeper, not a live-in, who cooks his meals and does light housework. He also has a cleaning lady who comes in twice a week'."

"If you haven't already, I think you should interview them."

"Okay, Karen, I will follow up. I believe the other people that I've interviewed are clean. All the kids below the age of seventeen were respectful, but had that spoiled attitude, well, I guess most are spoiled rotten by the money. The older ones were actually fun to talk to. They told me of their ambitions and life goals. I don't have any qualms about the lot of them."

"Thank you, Susan. Okay, Carol, shoot."

"I had only ten houses to work. Compared to Richard and Susan's experiences, I had it easy. All of my adults and kids were welcoming; they answered all my questions without any hesitation. One woman, Laurie Melville, told me that she and her husband, Gene, had gone for a walk one evening around two years ago. Their home is close to the Waters' farm.

"During that walk, she and her husband had taken a hiking trail that led near the Waters' field where we've found the bodies. On that night, they heard a scream, but couldn't place where it came from. They saw some sort of light flashing in the field. They got scared and went back home. They had left their two children in bed asleep.

"They said they called the police when they reached home. Her husband said they did not use their cell phones when they were on the trail because they were afraid whoever it was in the field would hear them.

"To their surprise, no one ever followed up with them from the police or ever visited the area as far as they knew. I checked the blotter. They were right. No one ever responded to their call."

"I'll check with the Chief. It's a hole in our system, but maybe it's been fixed. Carol, I would like you to re-visit the Melvilles; ask them to take you out along the trail they took that night; look for anything that we can use to identify this killer. Please continue."

"Everyone else I spoke with seems fine. Did anyone get the feeling that there is a level of jealously between the families in Ely? I have that thought because whenever I asked for information about their neighbors, they always made snide comments about the family or their kids, or some other odd statement."

"I did notice some of that. Things like "she's been sleeping with the gardener," or some little gem that they couldn't help but pass along to me," Susan added.

"We've all seen people under interview pressure; it's a way for them to divert our attention, but I think we have to remember who these Ely people are. They are idle rich with family connections that hark back to famous people. Actors, politicians, adventurers, you name it; but of course, that doesn't mean they are connected with any of this mess."

"Well, Karen, I'm not sure this two-week enterprise was worth the time," Richard said.

"Perhaps not; we do have some leads we need to check out. I hope this work drives us in the right direction, but you know from experience that most leads don't turn out well."

"How did your interviews work out, Karen?" Carol asked.

"Similar to yours, but I suspect that I intimidated them somewhat. The Reynolds family was on my list; those interviews went very well. A cheerful and open family who doesn't seem to have been jaded by money. That may be due to that fact that the money they have is old, not nouveau riche.

"You're all familiar with the Reynolds' saga. There is something good about that family that I respect, notwithstanding Lincoln's clientele. Their home sits on twelve acres. Their land bounds the Waters' burial meadow. The stand of loblolly pines where 'Sloan's Cross' is observed is the northern boundary of their plat; or, if you prefer, forms the southern boundary line of the Waters' property.

"I was curious how the Waters' farm is shaped, so I obtained a tax map from the City. The six hundred acres of the Waters' farm is contiguous with the 'new' farmhouse facing toward the southern property line. The driveway to the farmhouse runs from Carson Hollow Road, which is a dead end road that terminates around two hundred yards beyond the Reynolds' driveway. That is also the road, which cuts through the Jenkins' farm providing access to their fields.

"What's also interesting is that the Carson Hollow Road is the access to the Waters' burial meadow; field if you wish. Jenkins' farm abuts the Waters' farm on the west and north sides; Melville's plat abuts to the northeast; finally, the Craig Richardson's plat extends along a five-hundred-foot boundary to the southeast nearly completing the Waters' boundaries. I say nearly, because the Arnold plat also abuts Waters' property for approximately fifty feet on that southeast side.

"What I am trying to say, is that the Jenkins, the Melvilles, the Reynolds, Arnold, and the Richardsons all have access to the burial field."

"Karen, what you're saying is that anyone driving on Carson Hollow Road can access the 'field' unnoticed. The Richardsons, the Melvilles, and the Reynolds only have access directly to the field using walking trails leading from their properties. Only the Jenkins can directly reach the meadow by car," Richard challenged.

"Richard, are you saying that the killer must be someone from the Jenkins' clan?"

"I had the feeling when I interviewed the three sons that

they could not be involved with these killings, but the two male nurses I don't trust, so perhaps."

"Folks, I didn't want to bias our meeting today, but I have to let you know what Doctor Gordon also said about the bodies we found. Whoever did these murders is an expert at cutting. The bodies were all decapitated; they were also cut through the spine; limbs were severed neatly. Whoever is doing this has medical or butchering skills. I'm not saying that nurses necessarily have that skill, but…"

"Richard, we don't have anything to charge them with much less even to bring them in for questioning," Susan pushed.

"She's right, Richard. At this point, we have nothing; again, run detailed background checks on them. I want to know want kind of early lives they had; what their early friends think of them; have they ever had a sex related charges against them, even if they were dropped," Karen said.

"Perhaps I should go pay them another visit, Karen," Richard tested.

"That is a good idea, but you should first check their backgrounds. In fact, I'll have Sarah tasked to get the court records, if there are any, on all of the Jenkins. Let's break for now. We'll get back together when we have more to discuss."

* * *

"Susan, were you able to interview the domestics for Jason Arnold?' Karen asked.

"Yes, the cook is Mrs. Jane Babson; she is a native of Middlefield. Her home is close to Ely, which is why she took the position with Arnold. She's a widow; her husband died on his second Iraq tour; she is forty-eight years old, not very attractive, childless, with no formal education beyond high school. She is the original 'plain Jane.' "

"What's her opinion of Jason Arnold?"

"Not great. She says he is always complaining about the meals she fixes. They are what he wants, but too cold, too hot, too salty, not spicy enough; you get the picture.

"He threatens to fire her, but she knows no one else will put up with him; she's looking for another job."

"Other than that, did she say anything about his habits, strange or not?"

"She is only at his house from four to seven in the evening, so she has no idea what he does after she leaves. Jane did say that Rose Estes, the housekeeper, told her that Arnold makes suggestive comments to her, which unnerves her."

"Did you speak with Rose Estes?"

"I did. Rose is about thirty years old; she is married with two small children, and is quite attractive. She has told her husband that Arnold makes unacceptable comments. Her husband is furious saying that he will beat Arnold to a pulp. She doesn't think he means what he says, but they can't afford for her to quit without another job lined up."

"That is such a classic story, Susan. I feel sorry for her. Was there anything else she had to say?"

"Only that he told her his wife left him and he knew that she would never be back."

"That's interesting. How would he know that?"

"He wouldn't unless he is the one who made her disappear."

"I agree, Susan. We need to do some more work on the guy. He has the opportunity; he has a strange lifestyle; he lives close to the burial field. We need to find out if one of the bodies out there is his wife."

"Gordon says it's likely impossible. Arnold said his wife went several years ago, so that means if she is there, she is just a few bones."

"Well, if he did away with her, time and circumstances have been kind to him. We'll probably never know if he killed her."

Chapter Eight

Reputation is an idle and most false imposition; oft got without merit, and lost without deserving. Shakespeare, 'Othello'.

"Sarah, were you able to complete a background check on Arnold?"

"I have a partial one done. His family was somehow connected with the food servicing industry. His lineage goes back to the Benedict Arnold timeframe when his ancestor Wolfgang Arnold emigrated from the Austrian area to Boston in 1734. From there, old Wolfgang started making baking equipment becoming a success in the large cities. That financial empire grew and finally making its way down to the present day Jason. Apparently…"

Carol strode excitedly into Karen's office interrupting the conversation.

"Have you two seen the *Patriot's* front page today?"

"What does it say?" Karen asked not a little disturbed at the interruption.

"I'll read it to you," Carol said.

"I hope this is important, Carol. We need to get this investigation moving. We haven't shown any progress. We are at a standstill."

"I think you'll agree that this is important. It directly relates to us. A letter was sent to the *Patriot* and they printed it."

"If it involves us, I wonder why the editor didn't contact us before it was printed? Okay, let's hear it."

"Let me read it to you."

Mysterious letter received by the Patriot Editor

Late last evening, a letter was hand delivered to the Editorial staff of this newspaper by a man unknown to any of the staff. The messenger had been instructed by telephone, whose name and number were blocked, to go to a bar, Jack's Place. He was to sit at the last booth on the west side of the bar. In the booth seat facing the street, he would find an envelope tucked down beside the seat cushion. Inside that envelope, he would find a fifty-dollar bill and a sealed packet. He was told that there would be instructions to deliver the packet to the Editor of this newspaper.

The man said that he did not know why he had been selected to make this delivery. The caller told him that if he carried out this as instructed, he would have another letter for him to deliver. The messenger would not identify himself and left after handing over the envelope.

A copy of the letter will be delivered to the police, but the Editor decided to publish the contents without the consent of the police. The letter ...

Karen interrupted Carol's reading.

"Do you know who received the letter here, Carol?"

"The desk called Sarah and said the letter was being delivered to you."

"Great. That means the letter has been handled by a slew of people; any forensic value has been compromised," Karen said with exasperation.

"I know. Shall I continue?

The letter is published as it has been received. It contains information about the nineteen graves found at the Waters' farm meadow. No editing has been made to its content, spelling, or style.

September 2015
Greetings to the Sleuths of Middlefield. I see that you have finally stumbled upon my handiwork in the field. Here is something for you in your spare time. I will send you a sprinkler to help you along with your work.
Baphomet

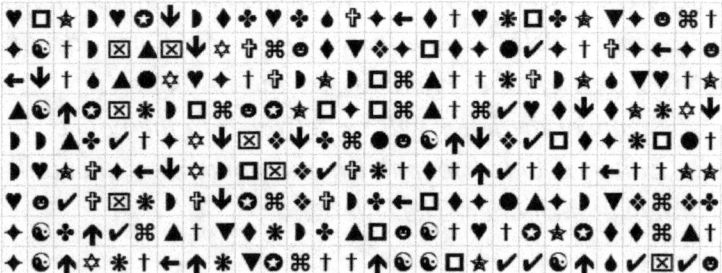

"Where do these people come from? Baphomet? He thinks he's the Devil, wonderful! Another vicious moron in the world," Karen said, exasperated.

"I hope this isn't some jerk expecting to have his twenty minutes in the limelight," Carol said.

"Let's get the rest of the gang to the conference room and discuss where we go from here."

After the MCU assembled and while drinking their morning coffee, Karen opened the meeting.

"As you are all aware from the *Patriot*, we think we have heard from the killer of these women. His letter is pathetic; his cipher may take us some time to break; and there is no indication that breaking it will put us any closer to catching him. Still, we have to do it.

"I suggest that Susan and Carol complete the re-interviews we discussed the other day. Carol, you will need to cover Richard's interviews; he and I will start working this crazy cipher; you need to get with him for his instructions after the meeting."

"Okay, Karen. I will finish my interviews. I can help Carol with Richard's."

"Karen, I still have a couple of interviews to complete. Can we defer Richard's until I finish those?" Carol asked.

"Yes, do yours first."

After the meeting broke up, Richard suggested to Karen a method to divide the cipher work they faced. His idea split the cipher lines between them unevenly, since the code contained nine lines.

"Karen, I could take the first five lines and see what I can do with them. You could start on the last four. My first step would be to try a letter frequency check."

"That's a good idea for splitting the load, Richard, but I don't believe it's the best way to work this. My reasoning is that for frequency analysis to work, all the cipher characters need to be considered together. This cipher looks like a Vigenère analogue."

"On the other hand, suppose he used a nihilist approach; then converted the numerical results to alpha characters; then God forbid, further converted those characters to these iconic characters. That could be next to impossible for anyone to break. I suppose if he wanted to make it unbreakable; that would be a way to do it, but to what end?" Richard rebutted.

"My initial thought is that for all his sophistication of killing methods, he may be a novice with ciphers; he may be acting out 'a la Zodiac.' If this cipher is his statement to tell us why he is doing the killing; then he must assume that we can break it, or it has no value to communicate his thoughts," Karen said.

"Karen, I think you're on to something here, but 'Zodiac' didn't necessarily want his codes broken. The Zodiac's first letter was broken. I have thought that that was part of his demented plan; many of his other letters were not and have not been broken; again I think that was part of his plan."

"I agree; it certainly seems that way. Perhaps, the ciphers he did not want decoded included his name or other information the police could have used to nail him. Just a way to show his brilliance, maybe?"

"I don't mean to sound hopeless here, Karen; but really, we may be out of our depth with this thing."

"Let's give it a try for a few days. If nothing comes of it, or all we get is nonsense plaintext, we'll turn it over to bigger brains in the world. Okay, let's get started. We'll meet daily to share results, if any. I will call on Don at GBI, if necessary, but I have faith we may be able to handle this ourselves," Karen said.

The following day, Wednesday morning, Karen called the MCU members together for a strategy meeting.

"Here's an update on the deciphering work Richard and I are working on; so far, we have nothing solid to report; that doesn't mean that there is no progress, necessarily, but it isn't anything to crow about yet. I wanted to have this brief meeting to see where Susan and Carol are currently with their tasks. Carol can you update us?"

"I'm going out to speak with the Melvilles this afternoon. That is the earliest they can meet. Then I will visit the two Jenkin's nurses, Greg Moran and Jack Mullin that Richard was going to see. He gave me some follow-up questions that he wants them to answer. I will plan to meet them at the hospital at the end of their shifts. I have to admit that I am concerned about meeting these guys."

"Okay, Carol, follow-up with the Melvilles; when you see the nurses, have a uniformed officer with you."

"I will."

"Good, Carol. Keep us posted. Susan, your plan?"

"I'm going back to see Arnold. After what the cook and

housekeeper said, I have a few more questions for him."

"What sort of questions?"

"The housekeeper said that he has made some strange comments besides trying to get her into bed. He referred to the discovery of the bodies as somebody's fun that had gone bad. I want to see what he meant. There is something bothering me, but I can't put my finger on it. Besides being a rich jerk, he's sinister, I can't explain it."

"Take a uniformed officer with you."

"I will. I have nothing else to add here."

"I am wondering if we shouldn't pull him in here for some old-fashioned grilling," Karen suggested.

"I'd love that, but he has a bank of lawyers who will make it tough for us to do. A waste of time, I think."

"Do you have anything substantial to connect him with the bodies in the meadow?" Richard asked.

"No, Richard, but I believe that he is one we must keep our eye on."

"Okay, Susan, let's take it one day at a time. Therefore, it looks as though we have three possible candidates for connection to the murders. Greg Moran and Jack Mullin have strange ways and have the opportunity; Jason Arnold has an arrogance along with this missing wife story that has pieces, which don't add up in my mind. Is there anyone else to consider?" Karen asked.

"Has anyone talked to Craig Richardson?" Carol asked.

"From the response, apparently not. Carol, would you make it point to stop by his place and ask a few questions?"

"Yes, Karen, I'll get to him after I see the Melvilles."

Later that afternoon, Karen and Richard met to discuss the cipher.

"Richard, I have the original cipher the killer sent us for our discussion today, which I show here. I pulled the characters out and put them in a chart; I sorted them from largest number to smallest; I then applied the normal distribution frequency of letters in the English language.

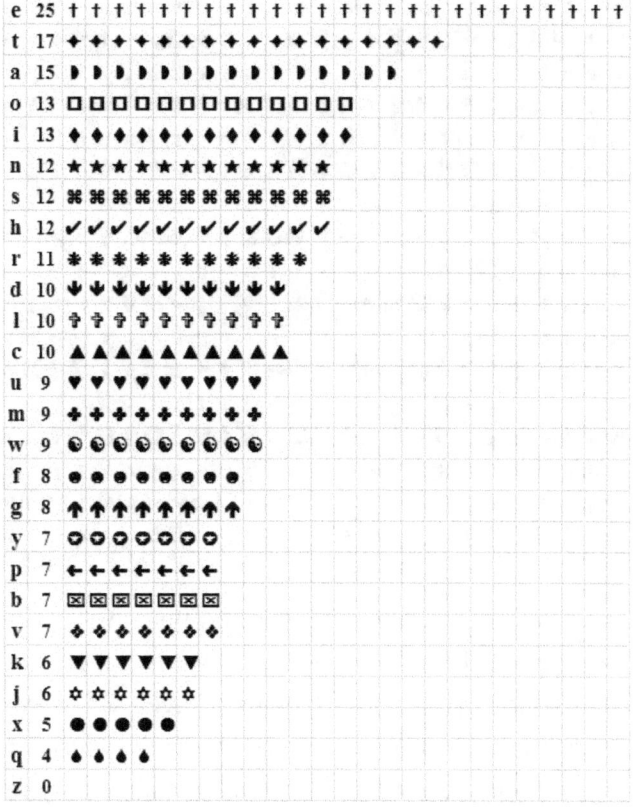

e	25	† †
t	17	✚ ✚ ✚ ✚ ✚ ✚ ✚ ✚ ✚ ✚ ✚ ✚ ✚ ✚ ✚ ✚ ✚
a	15	▶ ▶ ▶ ▶ ▶ ▶ ▶ ▶ ▶ ▶ ▶ ▶ ▶ ▶ ▶
o	13	☐ ☐ ☐ ☐ ☐ ☐ ☐ ☐ ☐ ☐ ☐ ☐ ☐
i	13	◆ ◆ ◆ ◆ ◆ ◆ ◆ ◆ ◆ ◆ ◆ ◆ ◆
n	12	★ ★ ★ ★ ★ ★ ★ ★ ★ ★ ★ ★
s	12	⌘ ⌘ ⌘ ⌘ ⌘ ⌘ ⌘ ⌘ ⌘ ⌘ ⌘ ⌘
h	12	✔ ✔ ✔ ✔ ✔ ✔ ✔ ✔ ✔ ✔ ✔ ✔
r	11	✱ ✱ ✱ ✱ ✱ ✱ ✱ ✱ ✱ ✱ ✱
d	10	✛ ✛ ✛ ✛ ✛ ✛ ✛ ✛ ✛ ✛
l	10	⚕ ⚕ ⚕ ⚕ ⚕ ⚕ ⚕ ⚕ ⚕ ⚕
c	10	▲ ▲ ▲ ▲ ▲ ▲ ▲ ▲ ▲ ▲
u	9	♥ ♥ ♥ ♥ ♥ ♥ ♥ ♥ ♥
m	9	✦ ✦ ✦ ✦ ✦ ✦ ✦ ✦ ✦
w	9	☻ ☻ ☻ ☻ ☻ ☻ ☻ ☻ ☻
f	8	● ● ● ● ● ● ● ●
g	8	↑ ↑ ↑ ↑ ↑ ↑ ↑ ↑
y	7	✺ ✺ ✺ ✺ ✺ ✺ ✺
p	7	← ← ← ← ← ← ←
b	7	⊠ ⊠ ⊠ ⊠ ⊠ ⊠ ⊠
v	7	❖ ❖ ❖ ❖ ❖ ❖ ❖
k	6	▼ ▼ ▼ ▼ ▼
j	6	✿ ✿ ✿ ✿ ✿ ✿
x	5	● ● ● ● ●
q	4	◆ ◆ ◆ ◆
z	0	

"The shape of this frequency curve seems to reflect the statistical frequency charts; however, nothing of value is readily apparent. I tried to place the letters against the cipher lines. However, by just employing the frequency distribution of letters against the cipher without a keyword, as you know, may not work. By doing that, here is what I got. You can see for yourself. Nothing.

u	o	i	t	u	y	d	t	o	m	u	m	q	l	n	p	i	e	u	r	o	m	n	k	t	f	s	e
t	w	e	a	b	c	b	d	j	l	s	f	i	k	v	t	o	i	t	x	h	t	e	l	t	p	t	f
p	d	e	q	c	x	j	u	t	e	l	a	n	a	o	s	c	e	e	r	l	a	n	q	k	u	e	n
c	w	g	y	b	r	a	o	s	f	y	n	o	t	o	s	c	e	s	h	u	i	d	i	n	r	j	d
a	a	c	m	h	e	t	j	d	b	v	d	m	s	x	f	w	g	d	v	h	o	i	t	r	o	x	e
a	u	n	l	t	p	d	j	a	o	b	v	h	l	r	e	i	e	g	h	e	i	e	p	e	e	n	n
u	f	h	l	b	r	a	l	d	y	s	v	l	a	m	p	o	i	t	x	c	t	a	k	v	x	v	m
r	w	m	g	h	s	c	e	k	i	r	a	m	c	o	f	w	e	u	e	y	n	y	i	i	s	c	e
t	w	g	j	r	e	p	g	r	k	y	s	e	e	g	w	w	o	n	h	h	w	g	q	h	b	h	f

"We don't know how sophisticated this guy is with his use of ciphers. If this is really a Vigenère cipher; he may have used a long password; or he may have used more than one password. If it is my worst fear, that it is not a Vigenère; then we have a long road ahead of us. He has given us not a clue about the password, so I am not certain this is worth much more of our time."

"I don't think it's hopeless, Karen, but…"

"I haven't lost the feeling that we can make some progress. Richard, would you experiment running a password generator? I left a copy of the matrix I believe he may have used on my desk. Try substituting passwords working backwards using a Vigenère matrix of the characters. See what you get. In the meantime, I have to check with Susan and Carol. Keep me posted."

"I will, but sometimes I wish the extent of my job in law enforcement was simply to draw the chalk line around the victim."

"Hah, that's a good one, Richard. When I get a chance, I'll try some other letter substitutions. Catch you later."

* * *

Later in the day, Karen received an IM from Susan.

***

Went back to Arnold's house. He is a belligerent guy. He threatened to throw me off his property if I bothered him again. You need to talk to Joe Green at Traffic. I couldn't get a uniformed officer to accompany me; they are too busy. I'm coming back to the station.

***

What do you mean? I will get this fixed. Come back and get your report done. I want ammo to talk to Mr. Green. Have you heard from Carol?

***

She sent an IM earlier. She is going to see the Melvilles later today.

***

Come see me when you get to the station. Thanks.

***

Karen sent an IM to Carol.

***

Where are you?

***

I'm at the Melvilles. We are going to do the trail walk in a half hour. I thought it would be better if we could go after sunset.

***

When are you going to the hospital to talk with the nurses?

***

As we planned earlier, it will be at the end of their shift, about eleven o'clock.

***

Will you have a uniformed with you?

***

Yes. Joe promised one at ten tonight.

***

Good. Keep me posted.

***

Will do.

***

We will meet at nine in the morning on Friday.

***

I'll be there.

Karen had expected at least another IM from Carol by five-thirty.

***

Carol, how is it going?

***

Hi Karen. I'm sorry for not getting back sooner. I just finished the walk-through with Laurie and Gene. Because the field has been cleared, I don't have the same view they had that night, but they could have seen someone even though the grass was high. I'm going to do some more nosing around on the Waters' property. After I leave here, I'm heading home until I go to the hospital. I plan to see Craig Richardson on Thursday. I called him today, but he can't meet until after four o'clock tomorrow afternoon. He is at an art auction in Atlanta.

***

OK Thanks. Be careful. Update us on Friday morning.

***

I will.

***

Karen went back to the cipher work, but thoughts of David and their evolving relationship kept her slightly unfocused from the task.

David, you have stolen my heart! It's Wednesday and we are going to dinner as usual. The old-timers always said it is serious when dates are on Wednesdays. I think they knew what they were talking about. You keep proposing and I keep saying 'maybe.'

What happens if he doesn't agree with my ideas for marriage? Don't be silly, this is what you have craved. He loves you. He carries the ring with him all the time. You're stupid if you don't go for it!

* * *

Over dinner, the conversation between David and Karen turned serious as it usually did on their dates lately.

"Karen, I have been carrying this ring with me ever since we started dating. For the hundredth time, will you marry me?"

"I have thought about this for a long time. I don't want to be hurt again. I will, David, on a couple of conditions."

"And those are?"

"I am too old to have children, so no talk about that. My beautiful baby died before she had a chance to be born. I can never go through that again."

"I understand, Karen. I'm cranking up in years myself."

"Second, under no circumstances will I give up the work I love."

"Agreed. I wouldn't give up mine for you, either."

"This marriage sounds like a business deal, David."

"No, I love you, Karen, don't ever forget that. What we do in the hours we aren't together is critical to our general health."

"After getting to know you in many ways, David, you must know that I am in love with you, but is it wrong for us to set pre-marital conditions?"

"No, it is good to set expectations before marrying. I respect what you need."

"Do you have any conditions?"

"I have seen enough in this world, as you have, to appreciate the value of the person across the table from me tonight."

"That's a sappy comment, David. I am saying that if I marry you, I will give you my heart forever; I love you. What are you saying?"

"I'm sorry, Karen. You must know that I love you without reservations. Yes, I do love you, Karen."

"Keep telling me that. Do you have any conditions for marriage?"

"I have no pre-conditions."

"Then let's set the date."

"Not to rush it, but how does next June sound?"

"June is ten months away; I would say that you're not rushing it."

"Would you rather make it March or something like that?"

"David, June is fine. It gives me time to plan the details. I'll find out what's available for venues."

"Where will we live?"

"Down boy, one step at a time."

"It doesn't hurt to plan things out."

"Let's keep talking."

Chapter Nine

I have known a vast quantity of nonsense talked about bad men not looking you in the face. Don't trust that conventional idea. Dishonesty will stare dishonesty out of countenance, any day of the week, if there is anything to be got by it. Charles Dickens

"Susan, have you seen Carol this morning?"

"Sorry, I haven't."

"She was supposed to be here for our meeting today. Where is she?"

Karen called Carol's police issued cell phone.

"That's odd. It goes immediately to voice mail. I'm going to text her."

"Maybe her phone's being charged."

"Maybe, I'll text her, but this is not like her."

***

Morning, Carol. Where are you? Please answer this message immediately.

***

Carol did not answer. Karen called Carol's apartment and got no answer.

"Susan, swing by Carol's apartment and check on her."

"On my way."

***

Karen, she is not here.

***

Where can she be? Get back here.

***

Fifteen minutes later, Susan returned to the station.

"She's not there, Karen. I asked the Super to let me into the apartment. Her bed is still made up. It doesn't look like she was there last night or..."

"What do you mean?"

"Her apartment complex is small, so the Super is generally aware of who is at home by the parking places. He said that her space has been empty since Wednesday morning."

"Jesus, where can she be?"

"She's a solid cop, Karen., but I don't like what I'm seeing."

"I don't either. You had trouble getting an escort the other day. I hope that didn't happen to Carol."

Karen dialed Traffic.

"Good morning, Joe Green."

"Morning, Joe. This is Karen in MCU. I may have a bone to pick with you."

"What's that, Karen?"

"On Wednesday, Susan Ramos needed an escort from your group; it was denied because you all were too busy."

"I'm sorry, Karen. We had a terrific pile up on I 16 that morning. A tractor-trailer plowed into a car; there were several fatalities. All young people."

"I'm sorry. I read that in the morning paper. Carol Morgan needed an escort last Wednesday. Did you provide one for her?"

"Just a moment, let me check the log...Yes, we did. She asked for an escort for Wednesday in the evening. Officer

Jones met her at the hospital at ten o'clock Wednesday night. He was with her while she interviewed two male nurses until eleven-thirty according to his log entry. He noted that Carol had said she no longer needed him at that time. He returned to the station around twelve-thirty and made his log entry."

"Do you know what he did between eleven-thirty and twelve-thirty?"

"The officers on that shift usually take a break around midnight."

"If I understand you correctly, Carol did not ask for an escort for Thursday afternoon."

"Actually, she did, but the note here says that she later cancelled it."

"That is strange, Joe. We don't like to pull your chain unnecessarily. I apologize for that."

"No need to apologize, Karen."

"Thank you, Joe. Sorry for the misunderstanding."

"I understand. Should I have Jones see you when he comes in?"

"No, thank you, Joe. If I need to talk with him, I'll give you a call."

"Susan, where the hell can she be? I know she was at the Melvilles Wednesday afternoon. She planned to see Craig Richardson on Thursday. I had a text from her around five-thirty on Wednesday after meeting with the Melvilles.

"She said she was headed home; everything went well. I didn't hear from her on Thursday, but that seemed okay, but you said the Super noted that her car was not in her parking space Wednesday night. She never made it home."

"What do we do now, Karen?"

"I have to tell Tate; then I want those two nurse assholes brought in for questioning, <u>now</u>. Put out an APB for her car including Ely."

"On my way."

Karen called Richard.

"Richard, I want you to go to Ely with two uniformed officers; talk to Moran and Mullen about their whereabouts Wednesday night after Carol's interview; if you don't like their answers, bring them in for questioning. Carol is missing. Get to it."

"Carol is missing?"

"She is. Please move it, Richard. I'll explain things later."

"Okay, got it."

Karen looked up Craig Richardson's home phone number and called.

"Mr. Richardson, this is Karen Hunter from the MPD. I need to ask you if a detective, Carol Morgan, came to see you on Thursday afternoon."

"Oh yes, she had called me earlier in the week. I told her that couldn't see her on Wednesday because I would be in Atlanta that day. She said she would come out here on Thursday at three-thirty, but she never came. Is there anything else?"

"Thank you, Mr. Richardson. If we need something else,

we'll contact you. Thank you, again."

Karen then called Sarah.

"Sarah, I need a background check run on a Craig Richardson."

"Karen, I just heard that Carol is missing. Susan sent an APB for her car."

"Yes, it's true. Please get the check done as soon as possible."

"I will start right away."

Moments later, Susan came to Karen's office.

"Karen, Carol's car has been found in the McCrery parking lot. The keys are in it; it's unlocked; there is no sign of her. If you're going to ask, they checked the trunk; she's not there."

"Susan, this is terrible; I am worried for her. You know that she is quite independent, but not foolish. This is not like her at all. Start a search of the Park. I need to talk to Joe again."

"Joe, this is Karen again. You did say that Carol Morgan asked for an escort on Thursday? I'm trying to trace her movements."

"Yes, but she later cancelled, as I said."

"Thanks, Joe. I appreciate your help."

"Okay, Susan, let's go to the hospital. We need to question those who were on duty in that ward Wednesday night. I know they won't be on duty now, but we can get their names."

* * *

"Mrs. James, you were the Head Duty Nurse Wednesday evening in the Recovery Ward?"

"Wednesday night? I was; how can I help you?"

"We had a detective who came to the ward to talk to two of your nurses, Greg Moran and Jack Mullen."

"Yes, I remember. She came in around 10:45 and asked for them. I let her use a room for her discussion. A police officer was with her."

"What time did they leave?"

"I believe they were finished by 11:30. Your detective and the officer left together."

"How are you certain of the time? Doesn't your shift end at eleven?"

"No, the Duty Nurse's shift is staggered from the nursing shifts for continuity."

"Did you happen to overhear any conversation between the officer and the detective?"

"Yes, they stopped at the desk before leaving; I heard the officer ask if she would like to get a bite to eat."

"When did Mr. Moran and Mr. Mullen leave?"

"If I recall right, they signed out at 11:45."

"Is that their usual time to leave?"

"Because of your officer's visit, it was a little later than usual. They are generally out the door by 11:35."

"Thank you, Mrs. James. You have been very helpful. I appreciate your willingness to talk to us."

After they left, Karen and Susan reviewed the information Mrs. James had given.

"Susan, I think we need to have a little talk with Officer Jones."

* * *

Later that day, Karen met with Officer Walter Jones.

"Walter, I need to know where you and Carol Morgan went on Wednesday evening after her interview at the hospital."

"I asked her if she would like to get a bite to eat, so we went to the local burger place, Sandy's Giant Burgers. We each ordered a meal and talked. She and I have been on dates before."

"How long have you two been dating?"

"On and off for probably a year. It's not exclusive, if that's what you mean. She dates other guys."

"So, it's not a serious relationship?"

"I guess if I had my way it would be. She says she is too unsettled at this point in her life to make any serious commitments."

"What did you two discuss that night?"

"Nothing special. Just how we are each doing in our professional lives."

"Nothing about personal lives?"

"Well, she did bring up that we should get together more often."

"What did she mean about 'getting together' more often?"

"Well, you know…"

"Actually, I don't know. I'm from the other generation.

Tell me."

"Today's single woman is not what you remember."

"Really? What is different about yesterday's single woman?"

"You know. Today's woman feels it's okay to hook up."

"What does 'hook up' mean?"

"You can't be serious, Major."

"I am, enlighten me."

"Hook up means what you probably called 'one-night stands' or something."

"So today's young woman goes to bed with a man whenever the urge hits her?"

"It's something like that."

"And yesterday's woman never did that?"

"That's something you would have to answer for me, Major, but from what I've heard…"

Buster, you think your generation invented sex. I have a long, personal story to relate around sex, but I will tell you my generation is the reason that your generation exists!

"So, Carol goes out with other guys; 'hooks up' and that is okay with you. And yet, you say you want a serious relationship with her?"

"You're making me sound stupid, Major."

"Sorry, no. I'm just trying to understand what drives your feeling to want a 'special relationship' with her."

"I'm sorry. Are you her mother or something?"

"I suggest you get rid of that mouth, Walter. Carol has

gone missing; you are the last person known to have been with her."

"She's gone missing?"

"Stop it, Walter. The news is all around the station. You came in today. Don't play dumb with me."

"Honestly, Major, I hadn't heard."

"What time did you leave the restaurant?"

"I left at twelve-fifteen, she was going to finish her meal and catch the last round at Kelly's Bar before going home. I went directly to the station from there."

"Did she often go to bars?"

"She did. She wasn't a bar fly or anything like that, but she did go to them."

"Okay, Walter, thank you. I may need to talk with you again."

"Fine, you know where to reach me."

Karen went to her office and called Susan.

"How did Officer Jones interview go?" Susan asked.

"Iffy. Very iffy. Go over to Sandy's Giant Burger joint. He and Carol supposedly went there for a bite after the hospital. Check on that. He told me that Carol said she was going to Kelly's Bar from Sandy's."

"Kelly's Bar? I heard that place is a dump, Karen."

"It could be. I don't know anything about it. What do you know?"

"Carlos told me that before we were together, he went there often. It was a real meat market back then, probably still is."

"Carlos? I don't believe it."

"Well, he is driven by hormones like the rest of us sometimes. Back in his earlier days, they probably ruled."

"Since Jones said Carol was going there after he left, I should go there and check it out. Let's get back together at two o'clock. I'm going to Kelly's Bar."

Karen's cell phone beeped with an IM from Richard.

***

Karen. Talked to Moran and Mullen. Moran said that he went directly home after his shift, so Moran got home at twelve-fifteen, but Mullen didn't come home until after two. He went to a bar. He doesn't want his wife to know about some things he likes to do. I'll fill you in.

***

Okay. Come on back. We'll deal with them later. You, Susan, and I will meet at two.

* * *

Karen drove over to Kelly's Bar and surveyed the atmosphere. A couple of bar stools were occupied by workers taking a morning break from the setup for the opening at three o'clock. The main bar room itself had a smelly drabness. Booths lining the sidewalls hadn't had a facelift in years. The oak-topped booth tables with their red vinyl benches carried scars from careless overuse and downright vandalism.

Yellowed detritus laden foam rubber made its appearance peeking out from the many rips in the seats proving that many of Kelly's clientele were not particular where they plunked their drunken butts.

The room exuded the smell of stale beer driven by six ceiling fans that slowly rotated giving the place an air of occupation while ensuring that any reeking odor would not find its place along the floor, but would be gently wafted into the nostrils of anyone with nasal sensitivities.

Kelly's is a poor excuse for anyone to consider as an evening out. This place is a real dive. Why the hell would Carol come to this place? We don't know you, Carol. Is there a dark side? We need to have the building inspector and the health inspectors in here; this place needs to be shut down.

Karen walked up to the bar, which ran the entire length of the room. Behind it was the usual display of hard liquors, mixers, and the myriad of paraphernalia needed to serve Kelly's discriminating clientele, and behind that array of necessaries, hung the proverbial huge, dingy mirror reflecting the smattering of framed photos of famous visitors who had supposedly graced the place with their patronage at one time or another.

Taking out her ID, Karen approached the burly man standing at the beer draft taps.

"James Kelly?"

"Yeah, what's up?"

"I'm Detective Hunter from the MPD, Major Crimes Unit. Were you bartending on Wednesday night?"

I was. I had another guy working with me that night also."

"I need to know if a young, blond-haired woman came

132

in around midnight or so. Here is a picture of her."

Kelly took the photo in his fingernail-chewed, infrequently washed hands and immediately tossed it back to Karen.

"A lot of young stuff comes in here. Regulars call it 'fresh meat.' If she did come in, I didn't notice her. It was busy that night. I was busy talking to a couple of the regulars, so I wasn't keeping an eye on girls looking to make a hit."

I think you can keep Carol's picture; I don't dare to handle it after your tender touch. The more I talk to you, the better I like my dog. We need to keep a closer eye on you, Buddy.

"Would you be willing to show this to your 'regulars' to see if they can remember seeing her?"

"Sure, but most couldn't recognize their own wives after a while in here."

"Well, I'd appreciate it if you could do that for me. Is the other barkeep here? I'd like to talk to him."

"He doesn't come in until five."

"Here's my card. Please have him call me."

"What's she wanted for, hustling?"

"No, she's a police officer in my group. Just have him call me."

"Yes, ma'am," Kelly replied with a smirk that sent Karen's blood pressure soaring.

* * *

At two o'clock, Karen, Richard, and Susan met to

determine the facts and set a strategy for finding Carol.

"Okay, Susan, what's your report?"

"We may have a problem with Jones' story. For some reason on Wednesday night, Sandy's was very busy. A couple of the College frats were having parties there. The owner said he did not notice a cop there, but he was so busy and it was noisy, so he just may not have noticed."

"Couple that with the fact that Jones made no mention of the place being very busy or noisy, just saying."

"Karen, they may have been there, but it can't be corroborated."

"Richard, I know you sent me an IM of your visit to Ely, but for Susan's benefit, what did you find out?"

"According to Mullen, Jack that is, he and Moran took separate vehicles to work that evening because Greg had to pick up something at Home Depot that afternoon before their shifts."

"Is that unusual for them?"

"Yes, normally they car-pool to work. Here's the interesting part, though. Jack was going to a bar for a quick one before he left for home. I hadn't told him why I was questioning him; he said that whenever he and Greg don't ride together, he often stops to mingle with some woman who frequents a place called Kelly's Bar. I've never been there."

"And you don't really want to, in my opinion, Richard."

"Karen, what did you find out about Carol at Kelly's?" Susan asked.

"I talked to the owner. He's a disgusting man. He said he didn't notice Carol that night. However, his bartender called me before this meeting to say that he knows Carol; she did not come in that night."

"The strange thing is that Carol's car was found in the McCrery Public Parking lot, which is right next door to Kelly's," Susan added.

"That would make some sense, but of course, she didn't go to Kelly's, so where did she go?" Richard mused.

"It would, except you all know better than to drink and then drive a department car. So, I don't know what Carol was thinking by telling Jones that she was going for a drink.

"I'll tell you what is worse; Carol seems to be a regular there. Were either of you aware of that?"

"She did mention one time that she often goes to a bar in town; she never said where and I never asked," Richard answered.

"Carol told me that she had met a guy at Kelly's bar whom she thought was very nice. They apparently hit it off and date often," Susan offered.

"You both knew that she goes to bars, and you never said a word to me? I'm disappointed."

"I'm sorry, Karen, I don't like to pry into people's lives," Richard apologized.

"Never mind. Do you know who this guy is, Susan?"

"No, she did not tell me. I never met him."

"She did tell me that he was going to law school in Atlanta and lived in the Middlefield area, but she didn't identify him. I did get the feeling they were getting serious," Richard said.

"So you both knew about a beau? Richard, after our meeting, would you go to Kelly's and talk to the bartenders? Find out if they know who this guy is that Carol met."

"I will. Why don't I go now before the place gets busy?"

"Go. I think we're done here anyway. I need to meet with the Chief and Gene from Missing Persons to coordinate resources. Give me a call if you hear anything."

Chapter Ten

There is so much good in the worst of us and so much bad in the best of us, that it's rather hard to tell which of us ought to reform the rest of us. Sign in Springdale, Connecticut.

"Chief Tate, this is Karen. Have you heard any more news around Carol?"

"No, except that, Dave Brown, night editor of the *Patriot* called to say that they have received another letter from the jerk calling himself 'Baphomet.' He promised not to print it until we have reviewed it."

"Do you have a copy? I'll gather up my team."

"I'll walk it over."

When Tate reached Karen's office, Karen said, "Before we discuss this newest letter, Chief, can we plan how we can coordinate the resources to find Carol?"

"Karen, my suggestion is that you and Gene get together to make a plan. Obviously, it has to be done quickly."

"I have to admit that I've recently learned some things about Carol's personal life that I wasn't aware of before."

"What do you mean?"

"I learned she had told Susan and Richard that she has a special man in her life. He is a law student at Georgia State. When Richard gets back from Kelly's Bar, I'll have him follow up on that. Sarah can assist him."

"What's this about Kelly's Bar?"

"Apparently, Carol frequents the place. The owner claims he doesn't know her, but his other bartender does.

He is the one who told me that as far as he knew, she didn't come in on Wednesday night."

"Was she on duty?"

"No, she had finished an interview with two male nurses at the hospital around 11:30 that night. She had one of Joe's uniformed officers, Walter Jones, with her. She released him after that, and they were overheard by the Head Nurse planning to go for a bite to eat."

'Karen, what about Kelly's Bar?"

"Sorry Chief, Jones told me when I interviewed him that Carol was going to have a drink after they split that night, but she never showed up. May I take a look at the letter?"

September 2015
Greetings to you again. I hear that you have a missing detective. So, so sorry about that. She was so pretty with her blond hair top and bottom.

Have you found her yet? Since you have not been able to make heads or tails from my last note, I offer you another try. Put your solution in the paper. Baphomet

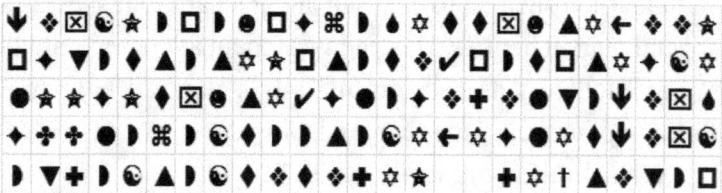

"Chief, this letter doesn't try to disguise his sickness.

He is flaunting his supposed cipher skill even though it might make it easier for us to identify him. There is an arrogance that stands out, as well as his terrible message. Why this letter doesn't demand a ransom baffles me right now, unless he's just faking this. The *Patriot* had a short blurb about an officer missing; he could have read that."

"That may be true; Karen, but the article in the paper didn't mention her name or anything physical, especially her hair color. I'll tell you something else I've noticed, he used the past tense for her. I'm worried if he is not bluffing, he has killed her already."

"Oh God, I hope you're wrong, Chief."

"So do I, but we have to face facts. We are dealing with a smart psychopath. He may outwit us, as sad as it is to admit."

"Just so you know, Chief, Carol's description was in the later edition of the paper."

"That's too bad. We should have held that back. I'll talk with Brown to prevent this kind of problem."

"Richard and I have begun to work on the first cipher with no hint of a solution so far. We will start on this one shortly. If we have no success very soon, we will ask for help."

"Let me know where I can help. Keep me informed on any developments with Carol or the ciphers. By the way, I hope this isn't normal behavior for your people."

"Excuse me?"

"I mean going to bars after duty and then driving their

issued cars after drinking."

"If it has been happening, I will stop it immediately."

"See that you do. I have enough trouble with the Mayor right now. He is disappointed that we have not found the serial killer in Ely. All we need is to have a drunk officer driving a city vehicle and killing someone. As it is, the GBI and FBI feel they should be involved. I've told them that we can handle it."

"It will be stopped. I am worried also about her service weapon. Not only is Carol missing, but also her firearm is gone. If it's in the killer's hands, we have trouble."

"We've got to find her, Karen."

"Obviously that's my wish, Chief."

* * *

Later that evening, Karen met with the MCU to plan their next steps.

"Richard, did the bartender know who Carol's beau is?

"No, he never saw or even met him. All he knows about the person is what Carol told him. He did say she described him, though. He is six feet tall; has short brown hair; has brown eyes and has a nice body."

"That's a bit silly. Do you think that is how a woman supposedly in love describes her hunk?" Karen asked.

"I think he's having you on, Richard," Susan chipped in.

"Maybe so, but it's a good starting point. I assume you want me to head to Atlanta and find this guy."

"Nope, in the morning, I want Susan to visit State. Richard, you and I will work on the latest cipher."

"Sarah, I need to ask you to assist Susan with the search for this lover boy. I think that is all we can do for tonight. See you in the morning."

After Susan and Sarah left, Richard said, "Karen, I thought you and I would be working cheek by jowl tonight."

"You never give up do you? I have told you a number of times that you do not get to sleep with the boss. Have you noticed the rock on my finger? David and I are going to be married in the spring. That is the last time I will talk with you about this fetish you have."

"My apologies, Karen. I did not know. You have not announced anything, so I kept trying."

"Well, now you know. See you in the morning."

"Maybe I should leave the department."

"Maybe you should. I'm tired of this."

* * *

Nevertheless, at eight o'clock the next day, Richard and Karen met in the conference room to start the task.

"Before we start, Karen, I want to apologize again about yesterday. I do enjoy working here for you and with the group. I think things with Aretha may be progressing."

"That is great, Richard. I am very happy for you. Is there a wedding date in the future?"

"It's a bit too early for that, but we have talked."

"Good, Richard. Let's get started. Last night I looked at the cipher and decided to count the characters and to assign the normal letter frequency distribution. It is labeled 'N.'

"However, as I reviewed the chart, I realized that this simple approach may be wrong."

"Why do you say that?"

"Well, he may be trying to waste our time.

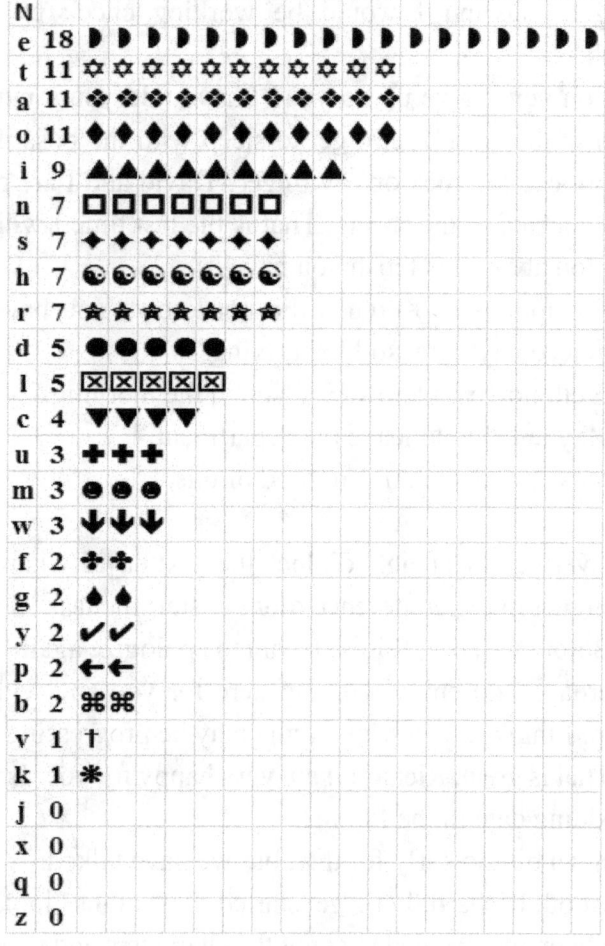

"It is just a feeling, but I think he understands the

distribution problem and played with the cipher, but he gave us a clue with his name. It is not clear to me why, but…"

"So your assumption is that the inclusion of the last eight characters appearing in the second cipher separated from the message is his name."

"Right on, Richard. He calls himself 'Baphomet,' which is an archaic name for the devil. I believe that the last eight characters in the cipher spell 'Baphomet.' If that's true, you can see that I didn't assign the letters in the first chart properly.

"You would think that the normal frequency distribution of the letters in the message reflects the standard charts. However, it doesn't, but he may have given us considerable information, if my assumption is correct.

"As I spent more time last night, I realize that my distribution is wrong. The clue to solving this is his name. He has given us eight letter and symbol combinations. That fact allows us to assign eight plaintext letters to the message. Once I realized that, I revised the distribution and labeled the column 'R.'

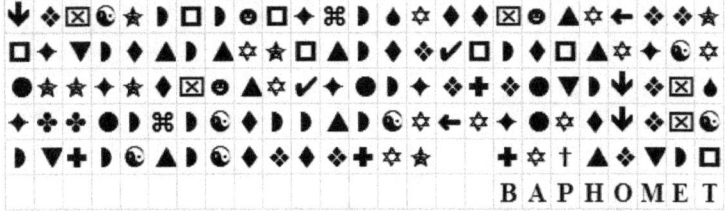

"Take a look at this new distribution chart, which makes much more sense."

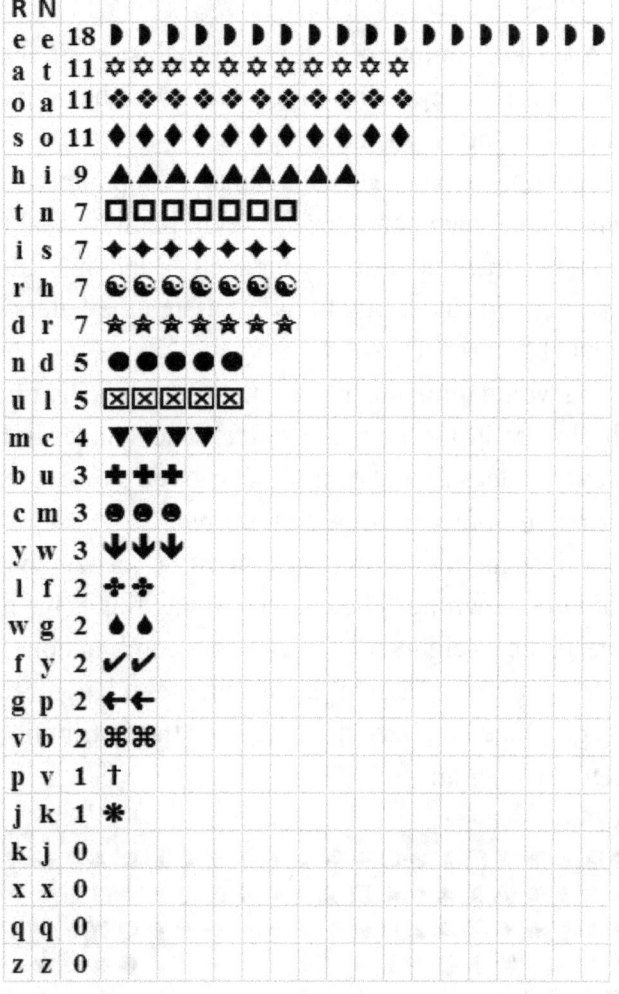

R	N		
e	e	18	▶▶▶▶▶▶▶▶▶▶ ▶▶▶▶▶▶▶
a	t	11	✿✿✿✿✿✿✿✿✿✿✿
o	a	11	❖❖❖❖❖❖❖❖❖❖❖
s	o	11	◆◆◆◆◆◆◆◆◆◆◆
h	i	9	▲▲▲▲▲▲▲▲▲
t	n	7	▢▢▢▢▢▢▢
i	s	7	✦✦✦✦✦✦✦
r	h	7	☻☻☻☻☻☻☻
d	r	7	✩✩✩✩✩✩✩
n	d	5	●●●●●
u	l	5	⊠⊠⊠⊠⊠
m	c	4	▼▼▼▼
b	u	3	✚✚✚
c	m	3	☺☺☺
y	w	3	⬇⬇⬇
l	f	2	✙✙
w	g	2	◆◆
f	y	2	✔✔
g	p	2	⬅⬅
v	b	2	⌘⌘
p	v	1	†
j	k	1	✳
k	j	0	
x	x	0	
q	q	0	
z	z	0	

"Now I'll show you the method I used to populate the rest of the message with letters."

"Yes, Karen, I can see the changes from the chart, but this distribution shows no frequency usage of k, x, q, and z."

"I know; the first chart also exhibited no usage of j, x, q, and z, but that's possible. His message may not have those letters in it. My greater concern is whether the sequence of letters I have chosen is, in fact, correct."

"Karen, by assigning the letters guided by 'Baphomet,' I think you've hit on it."

"Thank you, Richard."

"Now I'm convinced that your '**R**' list at the left, the first column of the frequency chart, has the right assignments. You're pretty good at this, Karen."

"You're giving me too much credit here, Richard. This guy made it easy for us this time. Since he gave many of the plaintext letters from his name, I took the cipher and put in the plaintext letters we know. You can see some words beginning to display themselves.

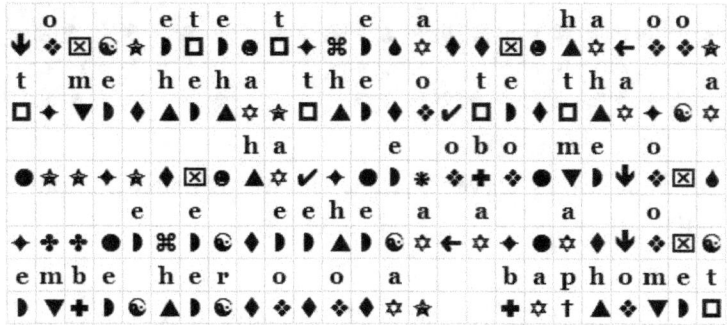

"Then using the revised frequency chart, I placed the

letters **r, u,** and **s** into the cipher as I show next.

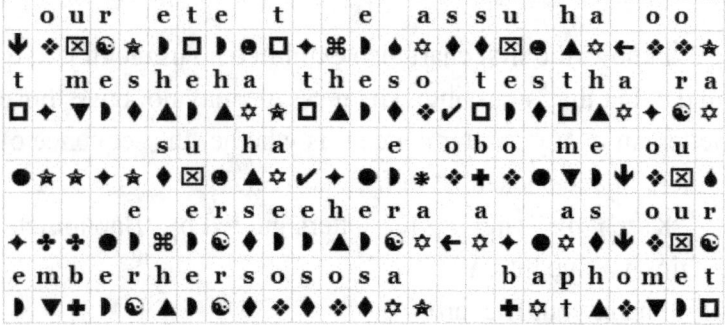

"Afterward, I placed **d** and **i** into the cipher since they are the next two most used letters to get:

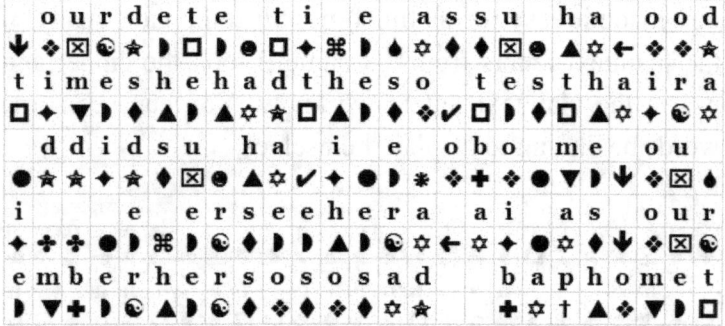

"That is very clever, Karen. The words really pop out. I believe that I could place the next letters into the cipher to complete it."

"Be my guest. I was so tired last night that I didn't finish it even though the adrenalin was flowing. Have a crack at it, Richard."

Karen returned to her office.

* * *

Richard phoned Karen, "Can you come to the conference room?"

When Karen arrived, Richard began his explanation, "I placed the remaining letters into the cipher by intuition. At the start of the message, I placed a **y** for the **down arrow;** a **g** for the **left arrow;** an **n** for the **large dot**. The rest I have filled in, as they are obvious. Now I see you were right reassigning the letter **j** in place of **k** in the frequency chart."

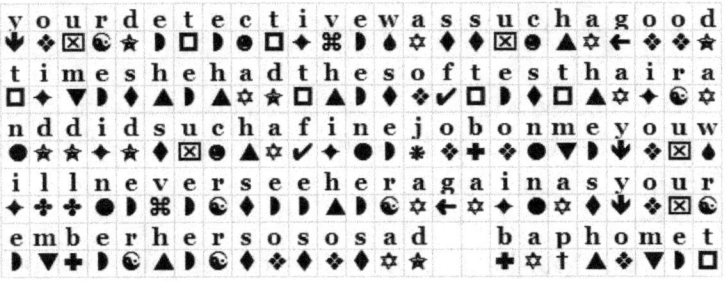

"Reading it, Richard, we get this horrible message."

"Your detective was such a good time. She had the softest hair and did such a fine job on me. You will never see her again as you remember her. So, so sad. Baphomet"

"As I told the Chief; the description of Carol is in the *Patriot*, but he may be playing a terrible mind game with us," Karen said.

"It's possible, but I believe that we should take him at his word."

"After we show this to the group, I need some quiet time to see if I can think as our killer does. We still don't have the first cipher solved, but perhaps…"

"If I haven't said it before, Karen, I have a hunch that the first cipher gives us information about him and the burial ground on Waters' farm."

"You may be right, but I'll bet he doesn't give us much info. He doesn't want us to catch him. He wants his little game and to show just how intelligent he is."

Later that afternoon, Susan sent an IM to Karen.

***

I've checked with State Law School. I have the names of their students. Several are from Middlefield. Most are Georgians or out of state.

***

I guess that's helpful. Come on back. See you tomorrow. We have cracked the last cipher.

* * *

The next morning Karen and her staff met to sort out the information from the local law schools.

"Sarah, what have you found about the Atlanta law schools?"

"I can't believe the number of people going to law school. Between Atlanta and Athens, there are over eight hundred students in full time status and nearly two hundred part-time."

"What the hell do we need that many lawyers pumped

out year after year?" Richard exclaimed.

"I guess we could ask that about science also," Karen answered.

"That's cruel, Karen," Richard replied.

"Do you realize that over the last fifty years, six million plus students have been through law schools? Sarah said, breaking the tension.

"I guess in this country, we can't live without them," Susan said.

"Okay, back to business. How many of those are local to Middlefield, Sarah?"

"Are we only concerned with law students; are we only concerned with local law students?" Susan asked.

"I believe we have momentarily lost the reason we are doing this. Carol has told people that she was in love with a law student in Atlanta. We need to find him."

"Karen, of the one thousand students, we can discount the four hundred who are women. Of the remaining males registered in schools other than State, all have listed their domiciles as Middlefield, but another forty-five live in abutting counties," Sarah added.

"This task is getting out of hand. We are going to need many hands to interview," Karen said.

"I can make the task a tiny bit easier, only three males of the five students at State are from Middlefield," Susan added.

"Our assumption is that whoever Carol's boyfriend is must live in Middlefield. Do we all agree?

"Secondly, we can assume that Carol really meant that her beau was a student in Atlanta, not Athens, so that helps us to narrow down the search," Karen said.

"So, what's our plan to interview these people?" Susan asked.

"Who are the three from Middlefield?" Karen asked.

Susan pulled out her notes and said, "The third year students are Aaron Richardson, Flynn Reynolds, and Eugene Spencer. State has a three-year program, so they will graduate in June."

"Didn't we read an article in the *Patriot* about the Reynolds family moving to Middlefield?" Richard asked.

"We did, but they were moving to Ely."

"Isn't that Middlefield?" Sarah asked.

"I'll answer that, Sarah. Ely is to Middlefield as heaven is to hell. That's a bit of an exaggeration but…"

"Isn't Lincoln Reynolds a big-shot lawyer in Atlanta?" Susan asked.

"Yeah, they came from Boston where he was even bigger, I guess."

"Since you found those three, Susan, why don't you plan on interviewing them?"

"What about Flynn? Since his father is a lawyer, should we give him a heads up that we need to talk to his son?"

"That's a good point, Susan. I'll give him a call. In the meantime, see if you can talk to Aaron Richardson."

"Okay, I will start with him."

"Richard and I will take five each of the fifteen others

who reside in Middlefield. Sarah, I will you ask to take five also, but they will be asked to come to the station. How does that sound?"

"I can't wait to get started," said Sarah.

"Folks, one last thing about these interviews. Yes, we are interested in their whereabouts and such, but you need to really observe their physical attributes."

"The bartender told me that she described him as six feet tall with short brown hair, brown eyes and has a nice body," Richard added.

"Is that it? That could be anybody," Susan exclaimed.

"That's all she said, sorry."

"There is something I need to say about Carol, which breaks my heart to say, but we don't know much. Since she's been with us, she generally has an excuse to avoid attending rare social events of the department. Her familiarity with Kelly's concerns me. It's not that any of us never stop for a drink occasionally, but that place is seedy. I had the feeling when I went there that the clientele is rough, not the place for a young, unattached woman, or I might add, a place for any one of us."

"Are you saying that there are places we can't spend our off time? I don't like that," Richard said.

"Don't get your knickers in a twist. All I'm saying is that we have an obligation to maintain a higher standard in this community. Places like Kelly's are not where we should frequent, but if you do, do not use your Police vehicle. If you do and anything happens, you are out the door, as well as facing charges."

"I think we have the message," Richard said with a smirk.

"I think we all agree with your premise, Karen, but sometimes it smacks of 'big brother,' " Susan added.

"As you know, the City Council has suspended Kelly's Bar's license twice now. Moreover, don't forget that Carol was headed there the night she disappeared. We all need to be concerned."

"Maybe they should just shut it down, Karen."

"Well, be that as it may, Folks, that's what we have to work with. Sarah, please get the names and addresses to Richard and me. Let's get started. I need to have a meeting at six tonight. Get done as much as you can." Karen pushed.

* * *

Later that day, a 911 cell phone call came in from a deer hunter working a stand on the east side of McCrery Park.

"Middlefield Police. What is your emergency?"

"I don't know if this has anything to do with the missing officer, but I'm on Old Macon Road, you know the dirt road that runs along the McCrery border fence. Well, I spotted some clothes in a pile, which looks like trousers, shirt, shoes, socks, and women's underwear."

"What is your name?"

"Aaron Richardson."

"Where along the fence is it?" asked the dispatcher.

"The pile is around twenty feet from an old shed set back

into the woods."

"Stay on the line, Aaron. I want you to remain there. Don't touch anything. A police cruiser will be on the scene shortly."

When the police car reached the site, Aaron showed the officers the clothing pile.

"Have you touched anything?" Officer Brian Tillson asked Richardson.

"I'm sorry, I did. I didn't realize what I was seeing, so I picked up several of the pieces."

"Charley, go check out the shed over there."

Officer Charles Bascomb strode into the woods nearly fifteen feet to where the dilapidated shed sat. The door hung askew where the top hinge had failed sometime over the years. He noticed that the pine needle bed in front of the door had recently been disturbed.

"Did the hunter touch anything at the shed, Brian?" Bascomb shouted to Tillson.

"I didn't. I stayed on the road. I was calling it quits for today; walking to my truck, which is parked two hundred feet further from here, approximately."

"Charley, he says he didn't. Can you see anything in the shed?"

Bascomb clicked on his flashlight; stepping into a place until only recently, untrodden by humans. Peering into the dank, darkness of the building, an odor nearly caused him to gag. In the far corner, his light had startled a rat feasting on a maggot-infested body.

Bascomb hastily backed out of the shed, and called to Tillson, "There's a body here; it's terrible."

Chapter Eleven

And I looked, and behold, a pale horse: and his name that sat on him was Death. Revelation 6:8

* * *

The Medical Examiner, Doctor James Gordon, was called to the scene and was joined by Karen.

"Karen, as you can obviously see, it's a woman. I would say she has been dead for at least two days. Her head is missing, so there is no way to know who she is until we can find a DNA match. I will send samples to the GBI lab. I hope we can get a response within a week," Gordon said.

"The killer is getting brazen; it's the same MO as the other murders."

"It appears that way, Karen."

"Thank you, James. If it is Carol, we will know from the DNA results. Five years ago, Chief Tate required all members of the force to submit samples, which were profiled; I hope we have no match."

"That was a wise decision by Tate. I hope it fails also. If this is not her, are there any leads as to where she went?"

"None at this point, James. We have sent the clothing to GBI also. If it's not Carol, we still have to try to ID her. It is too bad that the hunter who found the clothes touched them. Coincidentally though, he was on our list to interview about Carol."

"Why was that?"

"Carol had told someone that she was dating a law

student; we wanted to schedule him for an interview. Susan was going to see him today, but of course, she probably didn't because he was out hunting."

"What's his name?"

"Aaron Richardson, from Ely."

"Richardson? His father, Craig, is a close friend. We both dabble in art. Well he dabbles quite a bit more than I do; he's loaded as you probably know."

"What can you tell me about the kid?"

"He seems to be a son any man would want. He is very, very smart; a high achiever, scholastically; close to his dad. His mother died in a car wreck ten years ago. It affected both Craig and Aaron deeply as you can imagine."

"Thank you, James. Let me know as soon as you have any results."

* * *

"Okay, Folks, let's get started. I have to bring you up to date on the body found earlier today. It is not known if it is Carol. I won't go into details, but we are not able to ID her yet.

"Susan, the guy that found this woman's clothing is none other than Aaron Richardson from Ely whom you are scheduled to interview."

"Right, I went to his home. His father said he was out for the day."

"I've made it easy for you. He's gone out for a bite to eat. He agreed to return and will talk to you. The desk will call when he arrives."

"That's great, thank you. Saves me a trip out to Ely."

"Susan, have you been able to interview Flynn Reynolds yet? I spoke to his father the other day and he was agreeable for us to interview him."

"Yes, he was at home when I went there. He answered all my questions openly. He said he was at his college that Wednesday night since he had an exam the following day. However, he does not match the description, which the bartender gave. Flynn has a strong physique, not a body builder type, but a big, strong person; he said he works out at the State fitness center. I asked him how tall he is: six foot two."

"Doesn't that match the height description Carol gave to the bartender?"

"It does, Karen, but not the eyes or the hair. Flynn has blond hair sort of the old Beatles style length and blue eyes, which reminded me of Betty Davis blue. I have to tell you that he is personable.

"He and his mother gave me a tour of their rose gardens; Lincoln and Mary each have one. They have a gentle rivalry to see who can produce award-winning blooms. They also develop new types. They have a greenhouse where they hybridize roses by cross-pollination to get new varieties. Mother, Father, and son enter the Boston show each year.

"Many of the bushes were not in bloom this time of year, but they showed me pictures of the gardens taken in June. I have a word for them, gorgeous flowers."

"That's two words, Susan," Richard stroked.

"Yes, Richard. Oh by the way, Flynn asked me to thank you for the solution to old Caleb's cipher. He said his father was excited about it also. He's thinking of going to Arizona to see if he can find the mine."

"Good luck is all I have to say. The directions are so general that they're useless, in my opinion," Richard replied.

"Mary Reynolds agrees with you. She thinks the instructions are useless, and the mine, if it ever existed, is already mined out.

"While I was there, Flynn, who holds himself as a bit of a historian, told me a bit more about his personal life and interests. When he entered Middlefield College, the Fall after the family moved to Ely, he met a student who was also from Boston. It was love at first sight as they say. They have been going together since that fateful day in 2010.

"Flynn explained that Amy Wright was from an old Boston family line, which had been part of Boston's landscape stretching back to the Mayflower days. In fact, her direct lineage reached back to John and Humility Leaver who had a daughter, Patience, born to the couple shortly after their arrival in 1620.

"Through the hard times of the early settlement, the family prospered eventually becoming known as Wrights, since John and Humility Leaver line produced no surviving sons to carry on the Leaver surname.

"Amy's father, Grayson, is a well-known physician

practicing at Boston General. Her mother, Anabel, is also a well-known physician practicing at Boston Women's Hospital. Amy is their only child and Anabel was concerned about allowing her to attend Middlefield College, so far from home. She also had this snobbish idea that southern colleges were not as good as northern colleges, according to Flynn's story.

"Anyway, the couple was inseparable during their undergraduate days, so both Lincoln and Mary expected that they would wed after graduation.

"Grayson and Anabel Wright had met Flynn when he and Amy traveled to their home for a visit during the winter break of their senior year. At that time, Amy's parents had accepted an invitation by Lincoln and Mary to visit Middlefield and stay with them during the intersession. Although the two families had lived in the same city, their paths had not crossed, so the idea was to bring the two families together.

"Apparently, according to Flynn, the visit did not go well. Flynn did not say why, but shortly after graduation, the two broke off their engagement and Amy moved back to Boston. Flynn said he was heartbroken, but has gotten over Amy.

"I think that is why Flynn is talking about setting up a search for the Lost Dutchman mine. It's a foolish idea; I agree with his mother. He is scheduled to take the bar exam a few months after graduation, so I'm not sure this expedition will happen."

"That is quite a love story. Sad, sad Flynn," Richard mocked.

"So he is off our list, Susan?" Karen asked, ignoring Richard's comment.

"As far as I'm concerned, he is. After I interview his neighbor, Aaron Richardson, when he gets back to the station today, I can help with the remaining students on our lists."

"Let me know when he comes in. I want to sit in on his interview. Thank you, Susan. Richard how did your day go?"

"I talked to two of my five here in Middlefield. Nothing there. They don't match the descriptions; they both have alibis, which I need to check out, I guess. I need to travel to Atlanta to interview the last three."

"Thank you. Sarah, how was your day?"

"Three were able to come in today. None matched the physical description. They also have alibis that have to be checked out. The other two are due in tomorrow morning."

"Thank you, Sarah. If you are thinking about the reason why we are checking alibis of people who don't match physically, it is because we cannot afford a mistake here. We have to be certain that anyone we interview is in the clear or not. Remember, the bartender's description is second hand from Carol, so it is sketchy at best.

"As for my five, I was able to talk to three. Only one matches the physical description very closely. Brown eyes, brown hair, large physique, and frankly, an attitude I don't appreciate," Karen said.

"What do you mean by attitude?" Sarah asked.

"Who is this person?" Richard asked.

"Gene Spencer. He is a native of Middlefield. The family lives over in the poorer part of town. He is the first of his family to go to college; he will be the first professional; all his siblings work at menial jobs."

"What do you mean by attitude?" Sarah asked again.

"I asked him if he knew Carol Morgan. He said he did; that they went on a few dates; apparently, they did what couples do today. He said she wasn't that good in bed and they stopped seeing each other.

"When I told him she was missing, he said that she probably hooked up with the wrong guy. He comes across as a callous bastard. 'She didn't satisfy him in bed, so...' He wasn't concerned at all about her. That's what I mean by attitude."

"What about his whereabouts on Wednesday?"

"He needs to be checked out. His alibi is that he was out drinking that night. He was at Kelly's until nearly midnight and then he went home. He says that he may have met up with Carol, but he doesn't remember for sure.

"I am going to check with his parents and siblings. I'm also going back to that slime infested bar and see if anyone can verify when he left."

"Shall I go with you?" Richard volunteered.

"I'm perfectly capable of handling this myself, Richard, but thank you for the offer," Karen said.

I need to slow down. I'm starting to insult my staff and that isn't helping anything.

"On second thought, Richard, why don't you and I check out his alibi? I welcome that."

"Let me know what time you want to start."

"I'll call you in the morning. I know tomorrow's Saturday and I'm asking you all to work; we have to find Carol."

"You don't have to say that, Karen. Carol is one of ours. We will do whatever it takes to find her, God willing," Susan said with a strain in her voice.

"We all agree, Karen. It's something we want to do," both Sarah and Richard said in unison.

"Thank you, all. I'm drained over this whole thing. Let's call it a night; we'll meet again at eight o'clock in the morning."

* * *

In the morning, Karen went to interview the Spencer family before she and Richard were scheduled to go to back to Kelly's Bar.

"Mrs. Spencer, we are investigating the disappearance of a person on our Police Force who your son, Gene, knows. We need to ask you a few questions about him, if you agree."

"What is it you want?"

"We are just checking a few things he said to us yesterday. What time did he come home on Wednesday night?"

"I don't know for sure. I go to bed around eleven and don't usually hear when the boys come in."

"How many sons are living here?"

"Just two. Gene and Harold. My other two sons are married."

"Would your husband know when Gene came home?"

"My husband died three years ago."

"My apology, Mrs. Spencer. Do you know what time Gene generally comes home?"

"He comes home from Atlanta around 5:30; has supper; showers and then sometimes goes out. Many nights he studies until midnight. He's a college student, you know. We are very proud of him. He's the first in the family to go to college."

"Does he have any girl-friends?"

"He was going with a girl from town, but I think they broke up. I know he was upset about it."

"Do you know what her name is?"

"He brought her home once to meet me. I'm not sure. Karri, Carol, something with a 'kay' sound. He's had so many girlfriends, I lose count."

"I have a picture of a young woman. Please take a look and tell me if she is the woman that Gene brought home."

"She looks somewhat familiar, but I couldn't swear to it."

"Thank you. If you can remember her name, please give me a call. Here is my card."

Riding back to the station, Karen said, "Well, Richard,

that was not helpful. Let's head over to Kelly's."

As they drove into Kelly's parking lot, they noticed the door was braced open.

"Maybe Kelly has the door open to air out the place," Richard said.

"I hope so. I don't see how anyone can stand to sit and drink there. The place disgusts me. The health board has its sights on this place."

"Closing it down wouldn't be a bad idea."

"You said it, Richard."

Karen and Richard parked and walked in.

"Oh, you guys again? Can't you leave a poor bar owner alone? I'm sick of answering your stupid questions."

"We can do this here, Mr. Kelly, or we can do this at the station; which one do you prefer?" Karen said.

"What do you want now?"

"We need to know if Gene Spencer was here on Wednesday night."

"I've already told you. I was busy with some regulars that night. I didn't see that tramp or him."

"Careful who you call a tramp, Mr. Kelly. We will get to the bottom of our officer's disappearance, whether you are helpful or not. I suggest you lose that attitude fast."

"I'm sorry that I don't know. Check with my other bartender; he doesn't come in until 5:00."

"Call him. Get him out of bed if necessary. I want to talk to him now."

Kelly reached behind him for a phone and dialed.

"Jim, sorry to call you. The pain-in-the-asses are here again. They want to know if you saw Gene Spencer in here…"

"Give me the phone, Kelly. Jim, this is Major Hunter from the Middlefield PD, did you see Gene Spencer in here on Wednesday night?"

"He was in the bar for a while drinking. He usually only has a couple of beers. He's a student, you know?"

"Did you happen to notice what time he left the bar?"

"That's the funny thing about it."

"What do you mean a funny thing?"

"Well, he came in late, which was unusual for him. Generally, he's in here by nine or so; he orders his drinks, and then leaves. However, Wednesday night was different."

"In what way was it different?"

"He came in roughly at one; you know last call is at two; he seemed very upset. It was as if he had something on his mind. He ordered shots, not beer. I asked him what was wrong; he just shrugged his shoulders and then left. He didn't even finish his last shot."

"Okay, thank you, Jim."

Back in the car, Karen said, "Bring in Spencer for a tough interrogation. He's not getting away with this."

Later that afternoon, Tom Carey, assistant editor of the *Patriot* called Karen.

"We have another letter."

"Oh, great! Did he include any more of his ridiculous

ciphers?"

"I'm afraid not in this letter. Whoever he is, he's got incredible arrogance. Denise Lee, I think you know her, is coming to see you. We want to help wherever we can."

"Denise and I have had a solid relationship over the past few years. She is a good journalist and, I might add, a friend I can trust."

"Please give her any information you can about Carol Morgan's disappearance with any publishing restrictions. We will respect that."

"Thank you, Tom. Can we prevent people from handling the letter?"

"As soon as I saw the envelope, I knew what it was, so I put it in a plastic bag. I'll have someone bring it over."

"Thank you. We'll be waiting for it."

Karen sent an IM to Chief Tate and to each of her staff.
***

Flash. Another letter received by newspaper. Being sent over to us now. No cipher is with it, just ranting.
***

Karen, come see me. Tate
***

I'll bring the letter when I get it.
***

"Chief, here is the letter. I don't think it has any evidentiary value except he is admitting his guilt. More important is that he is staying in contact with us. The more that happens, the better the chance he will slip up. I handled the envelope and note with gloves. I doubt there is any useable forensic value, but just in case."

Tate read the note through the plastic sealed bag.

October 2015

I see you have found my latest gift. Aren't you surprised by my boldness? Have you found out who she is? I know, but I'm not telling. I gave you some easy clues, but you can't seem to see them. In the near future, I will send you another cipher. I will even let you have more clues about me. See if you can solve them. The next one will come in due time; it will not be easy, but it will give you answers to all your questions. Unfortunately, having the Middlefield Police solve my ciphers is like sending a sprinkler to a 3-alarm fire. **Baphomet**

"Have we any news about the identity of the woman found yesterday?"

"Not yet, the DNA profile won't be back for at least a few more days."

"Karen, we need to notify Carol's parents in Boston to let them know that she is missing."

"I know you are right. I have been holding off for another day, but they have to be told right away. I will get to it."

Karen's call to Carol's mother was received at first with stunned silence.

"But Karen, how can this be? She is a detective. How could this happen?"

"I don't have many answers at this point. We love Carol

167

and are doing everything humanly possible to find her."

"James and I will catch the next flight out."

"Jane, wait for my call, if you can. I will give you updates as we find out things. I earnestly urge you not to fly down yet."

"Karen, are you hiding something from us?"

"Jane, it is too early to say anything."

"Tell me!"

"We found the body of a young woman yesterday."

"Oh God. But it's not Carol, right?"

"Jane, we don't know. We have to wait for DNA testing."

"Let us come down. We can identify her."

"Jane, please let me speak with James?"

"Why? Anything you have to say to him you can say to me."

Jane burst out crying; handing the phone to James.

"What's going on, Karen?"

"We found a body. We can't identify her yet because, I can't put this gently, James, the woman's killer mutilated her."

"Oh my God, Karen," James said sobbing.

"I hope it isn't Carol, but until we know for sure; I don't have any further information. I will call every day."

Karen heard the click as the call was ended. Sitting in her chair, Karen broke down, putting her hands over her face and sobbed until her muscles ached.

Chapter Twelve

When I lie down, I say, when shall I arise and the night be gone? And I am full of tossing to and from unto the dawning of the day. Job 7:4

Saturday evening Gene Spencer came to the station.

"Mr. Spencer, thank you for coming in this evening to talk with us. Do you have any concerns about speaking with us without an attorney?" Susan asked.

"I'm not sure what this concerns, but I don't have anything to hide."

"That's good. We are taping this interview; it is standard practice; that way we all can recall what we've said. I will be asking you again some questions that we previously asked in your first interview."

"You're beginning to scare me."

"This interview concerns Carol Morgan. You had previously admitted that you knew her and dated her."

"Where did you first meet?"

"I believe I met her at a party or something."

"Again for the record, did you ever date her?"

"I go out with a lot of girls."

"You have already admitted that you used to date her and stopped seeing her because she wasn't your cup of tea."

"Well, yes, I went out on several dates, sometimes double dating and sometimes just the two of us."

"You do know her. We heard that you two were an item."

"Well, yes, for a while."

169

"Why did you lie to us?"

"I'm afraid that you will blame me for her disappearance."

"Why do you think we would blame you?"

"We had a date on Tuesday night. It didn't go very well. She said that I had gotten her pregnant. I couldn't believe it. I was always careful; we only did it a couple of times."

"Tell us what happened that night."

"I told her I couldn't marry her now. I had no money and I have to complete this year of school before I get my law degree. She said that I had to marry her, or she would make sure I would never be a lawyer."

"What did you do, Gene? Did you hit her too hard? Did she die? Did you panic and dump her someplace?"

"No, no, no it wasn't like that. She calmed down after I told her I would try to help fix it."

"What did you mean by 'fix it'?"

"I told her I would find a way to pay for an abortion."

"What did she say to that?"

"She screamed that she would never get an abortion."

"So that's when you killed her?"

"I'm telling you that I didn't kill her! I told her I would find a way to make things right. She just needed to give me some time to think. She said to meet her late Wednesday night; we would decide what to do then."

"Where were you going to meet?"

"She said she would be at the McCrery parking lot by 12:30, no later than 1:00. I got there by 12:15; her car was not there. I went into the bar; had a few drinks, and left. I looked for her car, but it was not there. She never showed up. I never saw her again. God's honest truth."

"Gene, by your own admission; you were upset that night. There was a major problem between you two. We have only your word that she did not meet with you that evening. No one can verify your story, so why should we believe you?"

"You have to believe that I had nothing to do with Carol's death."

"Why did you just say 'Carol's death'?"

"I meant to say her disappearance."

"Your story is coming apart at the seams, my friend. What did you do with her body?"

"I did not kill her! You have to believe me!"

"Here is what I believe, Gene. She met you on Wednesday night as you planned. When she got there, you two sat in the car, her issued car, to talk. You got into a violent argument. She wanted to have her baby, and you were going to marry her, or support her with awful child maintenance money. Each and every week, you would have to send her a check for taking care of a baby you helped her make."

"You're lying. I did not do any of that."

"You got out of the car and she followed. That thought of her reaching into your wallet drove you mad. When she turned her back to walk away, you strangled her. What did you do with her body?"

Sensing that more interrogation was hopeless, Karen and Susan huddled outside the room.

"Susan, he has been open enough to talk to us without demanding a lawyer, but I think we have to tell him we need to have his fingerprints. I'm afraid that will make him clam up."

"You're right, Karen. However, we do need his prints and a bio sample. You know what was found in her car. I was waiting for him to admit that he had been in the police vehicle after we pushed him."

"Right. We know he has been in her car. Fingerprints were found on the back and front door panels, which all have been identified except for one set, front, and back. I believe they belong to him, and we need to prove it."

"Of course, our problem is semen found on the back seat that obviously doesn't belong in a police vehicle."

"I have say, Susan; Carol has disappointed me with that discovery. She has been the only officer assigned to that car. I cannot believe that she used it for a tryst. If we find her, it could be an end to her career in Middlefield."

"I hope that is the worst problem that she faces."

"We have to find her."

Back in the interrogation room, Karen said to Spencer, "We have some evidence that can possible clear you, but we need three things from you. First, you need to tell us the unvarnished truth. Second, we need your fingerprints. Are you willing to give us those?"

"Yes, but I'm wondering if I should talk to a lawyer."

"That is your right. Are you asking for that?"

"Not yet. What is the third thing?"

"Third, you need to give us a cheek swab."

"Would my lawyer approve that?"

"Gene, you're in your last year of law school. What would you do for a client?"

"I would probably tell him not to do it."

"Would that advice benefit your client?"

"It might, especially if I knew he was guilty."

"Are you guilty?"

"I've told you over and over. I did not hurt Carol in any way."

"Then is your answer 'yes' for the swab and prints?"

"Why do you need them?"

"As I said before, it may clear you. In any event, we can get a court order to take these whether you agree or not. So which is it, yes or no?"

"Yes."

"Thank you, Gene. Sarah will take you over to have the cheek swab done and then get your prints. After that, you will be free to leave. Thank you for coming in. We will be back in touch with you. Would you be willing to take a polygraph test?"

"I will do anything to clear my name."

* * *

"When can we get the polygraph done?"

"I will schedule it for Monday morning. We should have the results of the polygraph by the afternoon. It will give us a better idea, but of course it's not admissible in court."

"Does his story hold water, Karen?"

"It seems plausible, but in any event, we really have no case against him. He admits he saw her on Tuesday. Carol was with us on Wednesday morning. No one saw them together on Tuesday or Wednesday that we know of.

"His nervousness, which the bartender noticed in the bar on Wednesday night, could have been due to the threat, if there was one, by Carol and her not showing up," Karen added.

"So we wait. I'm going home. I have missed another dinner with Carlos and my children. I have to tell you, Karen, that I'm tired; I'm really tired of these murders. Maybe I should find another department."

"Susan, you need a rest. If you need to take some time off, let me know. I don't want to lose you."

"What has gone wrong with the world?"

"It's been going on forever, Susan; we seem to get some of the worst. I'm tired too; let's get out of here. See you Monday."

* * *

On Monday morning, Karen received a call from James Gordon.

"Karen, I have good and bad news for you. Which do you want first?"

"Give me the good news. I'm sick of bad news."

"Okay, the DNA results are back. The comparison to Carol's profile is negative. The body is not Carol. In addition, we made a temperature study of the shed corner where the body was found. Since the shed is shaded most of the day, we found that the average temperature is low enough so that helped to preserve the body somewhat."

"What does that mean?"

"It means that the woman in the shed was killed a few days earlier than Wednesday night; possibly as much as five days earlier."

"What's the bad news?"

"The bad news is that you still don't know where Carol is, and worse, we don't know who this woman is."

"Of course, James, thank you. The good news is actually great news. I've got to call Carol's parents. Thank you again."

Karen called the MCU together and gave them the news.

"So what do we do next about Carol?" Sarah asked.

"I don't know. We have Gene Spencer coming in for a polygraph at 10:00. That may lead us to decide what we have to do," Karen answered.

"If what Carol said to Spencer about her being pregnant is true, maybe she went somewhere to get an abortion," Susan ventured.

"It's too farfetched for me. That's not Carol. I'm sure that she would have let someone here know," Karen answered.

"Carol is proud. If she were shamed enough, she may have decided to just go and take the consequences later," Sarah said.

"Possibly, she may have left the car knowing that she couldn't take a city vehicle. It is one thing to run off; it is another to steal a vehicle," Richard said.

"I've gotten to know Carol a little," said Susan, "It just doesn't sound like her."

"I agree, Susan. I cannot believe that she would leave without telling someone. It's not her way," Karen said.

"If Sarah is correct, she may have taken a bus out of town. The bus station is only a block from the McCrery Parking lot," Richard offered.

"Does anybody have a bus schedule? Okay, Richard head over there and get one. While you are there, get a list of any passengers who left that night or in the morning. Ask the employees if they saw anyone matching Carol's description," Karen ordered.

"On my way."

"I'm going to call her cell phone again," Susan said.

"Okay, but I've called her phone every day since she has been gone. It goes immediately to voicemail, so it's shut off or possibly destroyed," Karen speculated.

"Has Doctor Gordon given us the profile so we can put it up on the national database, yet?"

"He'll send it today. Okay, let's break; do what you can; we'll wait for Richard's report."

* * *

I've got to return Sloan's call. I can't tell the group about it yet. They still can't accept what she says. I may be a fool around it myself, but she has given us good information in the past.

* * *

"Hello, Sloan. This is Karen returning your call."

"Thank you, Karen. The reason I called is that I've had another vision. It came to me late Wednesday evening. I was sleeping; but the dream was so pervasive and terrifying that it woke me up."

"Can you tell me exactly what you saw?"

"It was dark; a young woman was locking her car; a man came up behind her and grabbed her around her neck. He shoved her into a car and drove off. When he got to his destination, he dragged her out of the car and put her in a small building, a shed maybe, I couldn't tell for sure.

"He violated her, Karen. Then he brought out a long knife; he pulled her head back by her hair; he started to slice… It was then I woke up. I screamed. It stopped. I can't remember much else. Many details have evaporated."

"This is probably a hopeless question, but can you see his face or her face?"

"No, I am sorry. The face of the woman and man are blurred. I believe it is because I sense that my vision of the attacks is a collage of images smeared together. He has done this many times."

"Is there anything else that you can recollect?"

"Nothing, except that I had the feeling that the man was well acquainted with the building, as though he has used it for many reasons. I can feel his presence there many times. He uses it when darkness hides his hideous acts. Karen, it

177

is his slaughter house, his abattoir."

"Can you see any details of structure she is in?"

"Not well, but I can see that it sits alone. It has no windows. It is old. I can't perceive the doorway clearly, but it has something different about it; it seems that it takes effort to shut the door. Close by the shed is a road or path; Karen, I am not able to grasp much more. My mind is full of fleeting visions."

"Is it a toolshed or small building?"

"I'm sorry, Karen, I can't really tell."

"Have you been keeping up with the news down here Sloan?"

"No, Karen, I haven't. It is too demanding with the local news here. We have a crime wave in my city. Gangs and drugs, but the city council won't talk about it. They are afraid it will affect precious tourism."

"It's the same here, Sloan. Public safety is at risk because the media colludes with the city leaders to downplay crime. It is sickening to me. I'm sorry for my diatribe. Do you have anything else?"

"No. What is happening in Middlefield?"

"We have another serial killer operating. What you saw may be another of his murders. I told you how valuable your insight was about the burying field. Without you, we probably would not have realized there were many bodies there."

"I was not going to tell you, Karen, but I had had another vision around a week earlier than the one I described. I saw him decapitate someone in the shed."

"No, Sloan, I am so disheartened. Your first vision, I am afraid, is one of my officers. She went missing Wednesday evening. We haven't a clue where she is."

"I am so sorry, Karen. That is all the information I have."

"Thank you. It still amazes me that you seem to tune into Middlefield; do you have visions about crimes in your city?"

"Not my city, but surrounding areas, I do. It is strange to me also. I sometimes ask God in my prayers why he gave me this 'gift.' It isn't something I wanted."

"I'm glad you have it. You have been invaluable to us. Thank you again, Sloan."

* * *

"Okay, Richard, what have you found out?"

"Georgia Trailways has buses leaving Middlefield to Atlanta six times a day, three in the mornings: 4:15, 8:00, 11:30, and three in the afternoons/evening: 2:00, 6:00, and 9:00.

"I spoke with the agent who works the twelve to seven shift. He said that two women answering my description were on board the 4:15 bus. They bought tickets for Chicago and New York.

"Atlanta is the hub for Georgia Trailways. There, passengers transfer to buses going to their destinations, so he wouldn't know if they actually made the connections or not."

"Georgia Trailways would know, right?"

"Yes. He said I had to call the central office for that information, which I did; the two women made it to their destinations."

"You have their names, right?"

"Yes, a Sarah Thomas went to Chicago and a Carol Moore went to New York. The bus agent thought they looked like college students, so I called around to Atlanta colleges. They promised to get back to me."

"Good. Let me know what you find out."

* * *

"Sarah Thomas is a student at State, and Carol Moore is registered at Mercer."

"That rules out Carol, Richard. Our Carol is taking courses at State. She is working on another degree. I just signed her paperwork."

"Well, that's what I have."

"Whether we like it or not, this is a lead we need to check. If one of them is our Carol, she may have just chosen a name from the Middlefield phonebook. Sarah, get busy on the net. Check out families in Chicago and New York. Was it New York City, Richard?"

"Yes."

"Damn, if it's her, that is probably just a stop on her way to a final destination. Sarah, cancel that; instead call Carol's parents and find out if they have any relatives in New York, Chicago, or the New England area. With all the commotion about Carol's having vanished, I never had the chance to ask her parents that question. I did ask her mother if she knew of any place Carol might have gone. She was too hysterical to think. Carol's father offered no answer either. Call me if you have any leads."

* * *

"Okay, Karen, I talked to Carol's mother. Her sister lives in Jersey City. She said that Carol's brother lives in Stamford, Connecticut. She felt that if Carol had gone to either one; they would have called her."

"Sometimes, I feel that we really don't know Carol. She hadn't ever told me that she had a brother or an aunt."

"She is very private about her family. Since Carol and I are both unattached, I tried to get to know her better, but she was not forthcoming with those kinds of details. I finally gave up. Should I call them?" Sarah asked.

"Right now, I would like you to give Susan a hand. I will call them myself."

"I have their phone numbers."

"Thank you, Sarah."

Chapter Thirteen

If a man can remember what he worried about last week, he has a very good memory. Anonymous

"Good afternoon, Mrs. Lindsey, this is Major Hunter from the Middlefield Georgia Police. I'm your niece's supervisor."

"Hello. Which niece is it? My brother has a daughter also."

"Where does he live?"

"Fresno, California."

"I was unaware of that. The niece I'm asking about is Carol Morgan. Have you seen or heard from her?"

"No, my sister called me after the call from your office; it was you, I guess. She had been terribly upset until your second call."

"So you've not seen or heard from Carol?"

"I'm sorry, I haven't."

"Do you have knowledge of any problems she may possibly be having?"

"I am not that close to her, but I haven't heard of anything through the family. I do know that she has said she loves her job."

"If you do, let me know. Here's my direct number."

* * *

"Good afternoon, Mr. Morgan, this is Major Hunter from the police department in Middlefield, Georgia. I'm your sister's supervisor."

"Good afternoon. How can I help you? My parents called me about her disappearance. Please call me John."

"Have you seen or heard from her?"

"Not really. On the night you say she disappeared, I was in bed when my cell phone rang. I usually have it on my night stand, so I answered it."

"What time was that?"

"I still have it on my phone. It was 12:47 am. The strange thing about it was that she started to say something, and then the phone disconnected. I called right back, but it went directly to voicemail."

"I see. Are you close as siblings?"

"We are. We have always shared many things about our personal lives with each other."

"This is a very personal question. I would like you not to share this thought with your parents; would she tell you if she were pregnant?"

"Oh, that is a biggie. I think she would trust me enough to tell me, but I couldn't say for sure."

"Did she ever tell you about any dating problems she's had recently?"

"She has told me of a few issues that she has had with boyfriends in the past. I don't recall anything vital."

"When was the last time you two actually spoke?"

"It was the Tuesday evening before she disappeared, last week. I called her as I usually do. We talk nearly twice a month, generally. She did tell me that she had a current boyfriend who was hassling her for sex. It isn't unusual for dating couples these days, but she wasn't ready for him. She wasn't sure that he loved her and her feelings about him were not certain. However, she said he was so persistent that she finally gave in at the end."

You don't consider dating relationships, which require a woman to have sex as a condition of the connection a vital issue?

"I have a slightly different viewpoint, John, but intimidating a woman to have sex is usually called rape."

"I love my sister, Major. She told me after the fact, not before. I would have advised her to break it off with this guy."

I am surprised that she was not comfortable enough with the group to talk to one of us. She knows better; we would all go to bat for her.

"Did she tell you his name?"

"If she did, I can't recall it. It wasn't a familiar name; so unfortunately, his name certainly wouldn't have meant anything to me."

"Is there anything else you can say about her? I am most interested in what she did with her off-duty time. I'm not asking this question well; are you aware of any risky types of activities Carol may have been part of other than her latest relationship?"

"I'm three years older than she is. Once I left home for college, our lives diverged. We were close in many ways, as I said before, but we didn't tell everything to each other, as you can imagine.

"It was only when we felt down or had a problem that phones would ring one way or the other to offer support other than our usual calls to each other."

"Were your parents available for that kind of advice?"

"Our parents are very social people. They were loving in a way, but not overly affectionate. Many times, they didn't have the right time for us when we were growing up. They were good parents; they did their best; at times, they just couldn't help us when we needed them."

"Thank you, John. I appreciate your frankness about answering my questions. I will call you when I have any news about Carol."

"Thank you, Major. Carol did tell me one time that she felt you and your group were important to her. She felt she was doing vital work and loved her job. Please find her for us."

John seems caring and cooperative, but we really haven't learned much about Carol's private life. Gene Spencer's story does match with her brother's story. Spencer was pushy for sex and probably had gotten her pregnant. Did he panic and kill her? Damn, where are the polygraph results?

"Hi, Kerri, this is Karen. Was the polygraph able to clear Gene Spencer?"

"Not really, he didn't calm down during the test as people usually do. The readings are off the chart for critical questions. I can't say one way or the other. Even the question about his name drove the pens wild. It was hopeless. My recommendation is that he retakes the test."

"Okay, Kerri, thanks we'll let him know. Can you let Susan know your calendar so we can reschedule ASAP?"

"I'll phone her after this call."

* * *

"Thank you for coming in, Mr. Richardson. I have the site interview notes from the two officers who spoke to you. Major Hunter and I would like to talk with you a little more about the body found on Old Macon Road," Susan said.

"I am glad to help if I can."

"This interview is being taped. Do you have any objections to that?"

"No I don't. I have nothing to hide."

"Fine, Aaron, you don't mind if I call you Aaron?"

"Not at all. It's one of the better things people sometimes call me."

"What do you mean by that?"

"I'm just joking around."

"Okay, well, let's get a bit more serious. Do you know Flynn Reynolds and Eugene Spencer?"

"I know Flynn quite well. I am acquainted with Eugene Spencer from classes but I can't say that I really know him.

"Flynn and I are relatively close neighbors. His dad's place and mine are a few minutes away as the crow flies.

"Therefore, I do see him at class and social events. A group of law students from this area formed sort of a club to assist each other in preparation for exams and to test each other before our moot court trials."

"So, Eugene Spencer is not part of the 'club'?"

"No, he has to work, which would often prevent him from meeting with us. I don't mean this the way it sounds, but he isn't really one of us."

I am sure, Mr. Richardson, that your opinion means his family is poor compared to yours and doesn't meet the 'standard.'

"What is your opinion of Flynn?"

"He is a good friend. He and I share war stories."

"What do you mean?"

"He is a hobbyist as I am. We both like gardening, collect stamps, and coins. We tell each other about times we have been hasty in purchasing coins and get ripped off. For instance, he bought a supposedly graded PCGS MS65 1857s $20 double eagle, spiked shield, for a steal price of less than $8000.

"It turned out that what he got was an NGC AU55 1857s $20 double eagle, which was worth about what he paid for it. The spiked shield variety was worth much more. He was livid, but he hadn't been ripped off at all.

"One reason he wanted the 1857 coin was that the SS Central America was a ship that sunk in a hurricane carrying his ancestor Caleb Reynolds. A few years ago, a salvage team recovered most of the gold ingots, coins and even the gold dust. The coin Flynn bought was one brought up from the wreck."

"Does Flynn have a temper?"

"No, he doesn't. He is a calm guy. I guess if that coin purchase had happened to me, I would have been angry also."

"Let's talk about you a bit. What are your interests other than coins and stamps?"

"Right now, I am so involved with finishing up law school that I don't have a lot of time for hobbies. The only one I have indulged this year is deer hunting this fall. That is how I stumbled across the woman."

"What made you choose the area of Old Macon Road?"

"I've been hunting there since I was seventeen. I have gotten a deer every year that I hunted in that area. This year, of course, put a crimp in my wanting to hunt after finding the woman."

"How often have you been to the shed?"

"Just about every time I'm hunting. I use it to get out of the rain when those sudden showers pop up; if I'm near it, I mean.

"My father also hunts near there. When I told him about the woman I found, he said that the place always has had a bad smell. He thinks that animals were slaughtered there. As long as he can remember, the shed has been there. It is all that is left of the old Suggs farm. It had been taken by eminent domain by Middlefield back in 1972."

"Have you ever dated Carol Morgan?"

"I met her at a bar one night. The following Saturday, we went out. We agreed that we weren't suited for each other."

"How do you mean?"

"I'm not a drinker. I go to bars to pick up women. She is a heavy drinker, as far as I could tell, so we didn't hit it off. Maybe it was a bad night for her, but I didn't call her again."

"Do you know if Flynn ever dated her?"

"He never mentioned it, but I strongly doubt that he did. Amy was his one true love. He said he cheated on her now and then, but I truly doubt it, macho talk. Most of his time in college and law school is devoted to studying. He is an 'A' student with an impossibly high cumulative average. He will be a great lawyer like his father."

"To your knowledge then, Flynn rarely dates?"

"He has begun to more recently. As I said before, there are social events, really parties, where girls are definitely invited. Nature takes its course at those times."

"Thank you, Aaron, for talking with us. If we have any further questions, we will call you."

"That is quite alright. Call me anytime."

* * *

"What do you think of him, Karen?"

"He seems like a nice kid. He has normal interests and goals, but his taking credit for discovering the body bothers me. He only found the pile of clothes as far as we know. He told Charley and Brian that he did not go into the shed that day. Maybe it is just bravado. What do you think?"

"I feel the way about him as I do Flynn. They are two

fine kids who make their parents proud. I think they will be great citizens. As far as his statement about finding the woman, I believe it's just bravado, as you said.

"Aaron seems to have a bit more of the money snobbishness, though that I didn't see with Flynn. However, I don't feel that that makes any difference in my overall opinion of them both."

"It does make me wonder, though, Susan. Intelligence and money were the ingredients for the infamous Loeb and Leopold case. We will keep him on our list, at least mentally."

* * *

"Karen, Susan here. Missing Persons just called with a report they received from Hartford, Connecticut. Jim sent it over to us because of the woman in the shed.

"A twenty-year-old woman left her home in the morning ten days ago to go to work and did not return. The baby sitter was concerned when she did not pick up her daughter at the end of the day and notified her husband. Her husband reported that she did not answer their home phone or her cell the evening before. They had a fight on the phone earlier in the day.

"Her husband said that she had been despondent over the death of her mother. The Hartford police have checked out his story. They have had marital troubles, but he has a solid alibi. He was on business in New York at the time.

"They are sending this report out everywhere. It turns out that the missing woman is the daughter of the Senate

President of the Connecticut legislature."

"Obviously, they sent a description and picture."

"Yes, I have it here. Five foot five, blond hair, medium build, slim figure, one hundred fifteen pounds, no tattoos, or other identifying marks. Pretty woman, if I say so.

"They want to know if we can send them dental x-rays of our woman. I am a bit squeamish telling them that our victim has no head."

"Right. That's sad, Susan. I don't know what we should do next. The only way we can help is to provide them with our dead woman's DNA profile.

"I will put money down that Hartford does not have a biological profile of her. Generally, there is no reason to conduct a DNA test on a living, healthy person. On the other hand, check back with them; ask if we should send our information."

"We should tell them about our woman's condition, Karen. There's no sense in toying with them about it."

"Send them the DNA profile anyway. They can decide if they have a use for it."

* * *

Karen scheduled the next MCU meeting to address the strategic tactics that the MCU was using in the effort to solve these murders. The Mayor and City Council were collectively starting to demand results by the MPD. The honeymoon between the press and City leaders after the killing field discoveries was quickly fading.

Because of the audacious letters sent to the *Patriot*, there had been noticeable patience by the citizens of Middlefield to allow the MPD time to solve the ciphers and ultimately arrest the killer, but tempers were rising and threats were coming fast.

"Morning, Folks. We are on the verge of what we experienced a few years ago. Unless we can show results very soon, the more aggressive members of the Council and the Mayor will micromanage our investigations. We can't let that happen again. Chief Tate has said we cannot let that happen. I am saying it again; we cannot let that occur."

"We can all agree to that, Karen, so what are the ideas that Chief has to combat this threat?"

"Richard, you know very well that orders come down from above, not useable ideas to accomplish the orders."

"Yes, it is Chicago again."

"Well, I do have some thoughts about the direction we will need to take. First, I want us to review what has been accomplished to date. Second, we have to critique the accomplishments to find the weakness in our strategy. To shorten the outline, 'S' will equal 'Suspect,' 'NS' will equal 'Not a Suspect,' finally [S] means a strong suspect.

"Let's take the accomplishments and impose a critique identifying those people whom we believe are potentially our killer. We have to put Carol's disappearance aside for now.

"First let's look at the interviews:

- **Abutters of Waters' farm**

- o Jenkins family
  - ▪ Edgar and Mary, NS and NS
  - ▪ Edgar, Jr and James, NS and NS
  - ▪ Alicia and Anne, NS and NS
  - ▪ Greg Moran, [S]
  - ▪ Jack Mullen, [S] Alibi/story shaky
- o Melville family
  - ▪ Laurie and Gene, NS and NS
- o Reynolds family
  - ▪ Lincoln and Mary, NS and NS
  - ▪ Lizbeth, minor child, NS
  - ▪ Flynn, college student, NS
- o Jason Richardson, [S] behavior
- o John Jackson, kooky but NS
- o Richardson family
  - ▪ Craig, NS
  - ▪ Aaron, [S] keep on radar
- • Other people involved
  - o Spencer family
    - ▪ Helen, NS
    - ▪ Harold, NS
    - ▪ Eugene, [S] Social problems
  - o Fifteen law students, NS
  - o Michael Pitts, NS for the moment. Must interview

"We need to rank the suspects from 'most likely' to 'least likely' and state why," Karen directed.

"From our list, I would rank them this way: 1) Arnold, 2) Mullen, then 3) Pitts, 4) Richardson and finally 5) Spencer," Richard volunteered.

"You haven't articulated why, Richard," Karen said.

"Okay: Arnold is first on my list because he is a loner, which gives him plenty of opportunity; he has a terrible way of treating people, which leads me to believe he is callous enough to kill; he has access to the field; his wife mysteriously went missing; I believe that she lies in that field also.

"Mullen is second because of his general behavior; he has an alibi for that night, which was not corroborated by his wife; he has a lifestyle that gives him the opportunity in time and location to kill.

"Pitts is my third choice because his profession and schedule gives him the opportunity to meet women by bar hopping; we don't have a first-hand view of his demeanor or life-style, we only have the information from Waters' niece. We definitely have to interview him ASAP.

"Richardson is my fourth choice because from your interview reports, he has a rich boy's haughtiness, which may translate to killing activities to prove how smart he is. He has the opportunity and access to the field.

"Finally, Spencer because he has had an affair with Carol. You have said to put her aside while we focus on the field murders and the latest victim. Although he may have done something to Carol, he is not, in my mind a serial killer."

"Thank you, Richard, I agree with your assessment. How do others feel?"

Sarah and Susan did not agree that Aaron Richardson should be included on the list, but agreed to accept it.

"I have one last statement about our list," Karen said, "Every one of the people on the list is capable of writing the letters and the ciphers, in my opinion."

"Now what do we do?" Susan asked.

Chapter Fourteen

Nothing great is created suddenly, any more than a bunch of grapes or a fig. If you tell me that you desire a fig, I answer you that there must be time. Let it first blossom, then bear fruit, then ripen. Epictetus

The answer arrived the next day at the MPD.

October 2015
I have decided to communicate directly with you. The newspaper does not seem to get it. I have sent them a hundred-page manifesto of my demands to print. They have not done it, so the killings will continue. You really should do something about that.

I understand by your news story that you have not found your officer. You wonder where she could be. I can tell you, but I won't.

I promised to send you another, harder cipher and here it is. Let me give you a tantalizing offer. Solve this last cipher, if you can, and your troubles with me will be over. I have included my name in this three-line cipher.

I have sent a sprinkler to help you. Have you received it yet? It is a pretty, blue plastic one with all sorts of designs and flowers on it. It will make your life so much easier, if you know what I mean.   Baphomet

2594573038282898002167304736058807777761
7612360436235227277024509462510485391108
124817925448482265755042659299135369562

"Here we go again. Another message from the crazed cryptographer," Tate said as he handed the note to Karen.

"Oh, God. This one is all too familiar. He has resorted to the Vic cipher, I trust. Only time will tell if we can crack it. Don and I had a hell of a time working the ones from the Mendosa case. If he hadn't had his insight, we probably would have never solved them, I am not feeling optimistic about this one; these are devilishly tough to crack."

"Shall I call Marcus to ask that Don be freed up to assist with this one?"

"That would help. My thought is that Richard, Don and I may be able to come up with a solution, but again, I'm not really optimistic about it."

"Well, let me call Marcus; I'll get back to you."

"Thank you, Chief. In the meantime, I have a meeting with Martha Whittingham from GBI. She is a forensic anthropologist there. Gordon sent over the skeletal remains to her for her analysis of each one. Would you care to sit in on the meeting?"

"I'm interested, of course, but I have some other things to attend to. Keep me posted, Karen."

After Tate left, Karen called the MCU together for a one o'clock meeting.

"Folks, you have probably already heard that we have received another letter from 'demento' that includes another code. Richard and I will start to work it. I will have a copy of it for each of you later today.

"I do have some other news. I received a call from GBI this morning requesting a meeting with us to discuss the Waters' field skeleton evidence. An expert wants to come to see us as soon as possible. I told her today would work, so she'll be here at two."

"Who is 'she'?" Richard asked.

"Her name is Martha Whittingham. She says that she can give us some important information about our victims."

"I know Martha," Susan said, "She and I went to college together."

"Well, that's a coincidence; I suppose that she knows that you work here," Karen said.

"Yes, we have stayed in touch over the years."

"Is that her married name?" Richard asked.

"Down, boy; she is happily married with two rugged boys," Susan said.

"Damn, just wanting to expand my horizons," Richard replied.

"Richard, since we last talked, have you been able to make any progress with the first cipher?" Karen asked.

"Sorry to say, Karen, I haven't; every technique that we have discussed only leads to gibberish."

"Too bad, I need to free up some time after our meeting with Martha; Tate is contacting Marcus to see if Don can help us with these ciphers."

"Should I continue with the cipher work instead of this meeting?" Richard asked.

"No, I think we all need to hear what Whittingham has to say."

"We'll break for now. Please be here promptly at two."

* * *

Martha arrived on time and after introductions were completed, she began her presentation to the group. Whittingham appeared to be a college undergrad with her hair in a ponytail and rimless glasses on a sleek nose against a face that could be said to have never basked in the sun at the beach. A thin woman standing five foot eight inches tall with a throaty voice that spoke with years of experience.

"First, I should give you some idea of my educational vitae. I hold Masters and Doctorate degrees in forensic anthropology from the University of Florida. In 1999, I became board certified from the American Board of Forensic Anthropology.

"I spent seven months after 9/11 helping to identify human remains from the World Trade Center. It was exhausting, sad work. The reason I've asked to speak to you today is that Doctor James Gordon, Twiggs County ME, sent me the remains of the nineteen graves. Actually, he also sent to me the few bones found in McCrery Park."

"Doctor Whittingham, the news may not have gotten to you yet, but the McCrery Park remains have been identified from DNA testing as Kaye Billington. That may have been a waste of your time, I'm sorry," Karen explained.

"Thank you, Detective Hunter, I learned about that at the last minute. I didn't have time to change my slides for this meeting, so please overlook that.

"Let me explain briefly what I do when I receive a

199

skeleton in the lab. The bones are laid out as completely as possible; then multiple photos are taken. Generally, the bones received are not clean, so the first step is gentle cleaning. This step is required because dirt and other detritus may mask injuries that may have been inflicted on the bones.

"Sometimes I can determine how the person died; whether death was from suicide, homicide or even from natural causes. In most cases, I am able to determine the approximate age, the sex, and the height of an individual accurately.

"It is possible for me to determine the person's overall health status at the time of death. In addition, I can sometimes determine, with some accuracy, the type of occupation a person may have had in life.

"Let me start with the first partial skeleton found by the surveyors in Waters' field. In this case, the body was not buried deeply enough. Animals intruded the site; destroyed the grave and carried off some of the remains. The few bones from that gravesite showed teeth marks consistent with an animal's stripping of the flesh. The other eighteen field burial sites were more deeply dug. From Doctor Gordon's reports, the graves were several feet deep and the bodies were wrapped in rather sturdy cloth, perhaps bedsheets. None of these remains showed any evidence of animal intrusion.

"I have summarized my results of the twenty, really nineteen, women on the following list: None of the sites had complete skeletons as you know."

"We are now certain that the twentieth woman was murdered also," Karen interrupted.

"That just makes this whole mess worse. When I look at my list, it turns my stomach," Whittingham said.

Site #	Location	Sex	Age	Height	Cause	Site Remains
1	Field	Female	>35	≈ 65"	Homocide	Femur, tibia, pelvis
2	Field	Female	<25	≈ 63"	Homocide	Complete, w/o skull
3	Field	Female	<25	≈ 66"	Homocide	Complete, w/o skull
4	Field	Female	<25	≈ 64"	Homocide	Complete, w/o skull
5	Field	Female	>35	≈ 68"	Homocide	Complete, w/o skull
6	Field	Female	<25	≈ 61"	Homocide	Complete, w/o skull
7	Field	Female	<25	≈ 65"	Homocide	Complete, w/o skull
8	Field	Female	>35	≈ 60"	Homocide	Complete, w/o skull
9	Field	Female	<25	≈ 65"	Homocide	Complete, w/o skull
10	Field	Female	<25	≈ 66"	Homocide	Complete, w/o skull
11	Field	Female	<25	≈ 67"	Homocide	Complete, w/o skull
12	Field	Female	>35	≈ 64"	Homocide	Complete, w/o skull
13	Field	Female	<25	≈65"	Homocide	Complete, w/o skull
14	Field	Female	<25	≈ 68"	Homocide	Complete, w/o skull
15	Field	Female	<25	≈ 63"	Homocide	Complete, w/o skull
16	Field	Female	<25	≈ 67"	Homocide	Complete, w/o skull
17	Field	Female	>35	≈ 61"	Homocide	Complete, w/o skull
18	Field	Female	<25	≈ 63"	Homocide	Complete, w/o skull
19	Field	Female	<25	≈ 66"	Homocide	Complete, w/o skull
20	Park	Female	?	?	Undeter.	Humerus/Pelvis

"Only Sites 1 and 20 displayed evidence showing that animals had ravaged the sites by leaving deep teeth mark striations on the bones.

"Since I've now learned about the Park identification, the following statement about Site 20 on my slide is moot, but I'll tell you what I thought at the time.

"With Site 20, I could not say about the age or height. She may have been a homicide, but not enough was known; she could have had a natural death. For her, the humerus provided enough information to say that she was an adult, but not much more.

"Perhaps what is surprising is the fact that the other skeletons are complete except for their heads. Your killer, I suspect, did this to obscure the identification of the women, but that's my speculation only."

"He has succeeded. We have no idea who they are yet," Susan piped up.

"Yes, it certainly makes the task harder."

"Martha, do you believe that there is a pathological reason for decapitating the victims, I mean other than just to obscure their identities?" Susan inquired.

"Susan, I am not certain that I can answer that, in any meaningful way. Since my expertise is forensic pathology, my focus and abilities are concentrated to the facts of what he has done, not necessarily why it was done. From the viciousness of how he left the remains; it would only be my personal opinion.

"From the table above, I have estimated the average height of the women is 5 foot 4 and a half inches; the average age is 27.6 years using 25 and 35 as the lower and upper age limits. Of course, the women I have labelled younger than 25 are most likely between the ages of 20 and 25; subsequently the average I have given you is skewed, but then exact ages are difficult to determine."

"Doctor Whittingham…," Karen began a question.

"Martha, if you please."

"Martha, what you are stating is very useful information for us. Having a sense of the ages involved, suggests that our killer is someone who easily earns the trust of the younger women."

"I agree, Karen. I believe it is similar for the few older women in the list, but perhaps they are in harm's way for different reasons; the disarming result is the same, however; they are trusting; they are killed.

"Doctor Gordon also sent to me all of the sifted items from each grave site. The item in his report that caught my eye was an unusual remnant, a penny, found in the siftings of each site with two exceptions. Again, disregard the Park data.

"I prepared a table of grave sites Take a look."

Site #	Location	Coin	Date	Site #	Location	Coin	Date
2	Field	Yes	2010	5	Field	Yes	2013
4	Field	Yes	2011	12	Field	Yes	2013
7	Field	Yes	2011	9	Field	Yes	2013
20	Field	Yes	2011	10	Field	Yes	2014
15	Field	Yes	2011	16	Field	Yes	2014
3	Field	Yes	2012	19	Field	Yes	2014
14	Field	Yes	2012	8	Field	Yes	2014
17	Field	Yes	2012	18	Field	Yes	2015
6	Field	Yes	2012	13	Park	?	NA
11	Field	Yes	2013	1	Field	None	NA

"Your table really puts things in perspective, Martha,"

Richard interrupted.

"Thank you, Richard. To make sense of this, I sorted the coin data by increasing date with the corresponding site to yield the result shown in the 'Coin' columns.

"Notice that Site #2 and #18 each had a single penny dated 2010 and 2015, respectively. For Sites #4, 7, 20, and 15, there were coins dated 2011. Looking further at the chart, you will see that there are three sets of four sites exhibiting pennies, which have the same date!"

"Martha, you are saying that this killer has kept track of his murders. How thoughtful of him! An annual track record; four murders, four graves, four coins. We also know that he wanted the coins to be preserved by putting them in waterproof containers, but we don't know why."

"My conclusion is that he is extremely organized; obviously, he is a cold-blooded killer who must be devoid of any feeling for his victims."

"Martha, I have no doubt that he is rational in a way that he is able to plan these murders to the last detail. I suppose his throwing a penny into each grave tells us exactly what he thinks of the women he kills."

"Karen, I could not agree more strongly with your assessment; however, this psychopath operates in a way, which is different from anything in my experience."

"Martha, we had a serial killer a few years ago who killed six women in the City, but he left us with corpses that were in pristine condition, if you remember. It's just the opposite with this killer; he wants them mutilated."

"I do, the papers dubbed them the 'Lost Cipher Murders,' as I recall. However, as ruthless as that killer was, he didn't abuse his victims' bodies after death. This killer seems to take pleasure in the destruction of his victims."

"In the Lost Cipher Case, we eventually realized that our killer was 'Mission Oriented' and very organized. This person also seems to be extremely organized, so I believe that we can make an assumption that he is highly intelligent," Susan said.

"That makes sense, Susan, however, beyond that specific idea; there are very few characteristics, which I believe, we can use to further to distinguish him. The problem is that the attributes normally used to categorize serial killers are established only after the fact of actually identifying them," Martha replied.

"I know that you are right, Martha, because we have no idea if this guy exhibits any of the usual symptoms. We don't understand if he was a bed wetter; sexually or psychologically abused; or loved to torture animals, for instance, so it gets us no closer to any clues to identify him," Susan continued.

"This is interesting dialogue, Folks, and I agree that it doesn't get us any closer to the killer's identity. I suggest that we move on," Karen proposed.

"Okay, Martha, from the penny evidence, we can reason that the killer started his field work in 2010 and tells us the last one he did was in 2015. That now makes good sense because Site #18 has the most complete remains," Richard said.

"Of course, that assumes that his method of operation has never changed. He could have murdered and not thrown pennies in with the bodies; worse he may be killing in other cities or even states," Martha added.

"Do you suppose, Martha, that the Park Site and field Site #1 are enigmas to these cases; that they were done by different killers whose murders just happened to become entangled with our field data?" Karen mused.

"That is entirely possible. I don't envy your task to sort that out," Martha agreed.

"Martha, I'm sure you noted a sick item in Doctor Gordon's reports; that a cola bottle was found wrapped with each body, eh, remains in the graves?" Karen asked.

"I did, Karen. Since only the body in Site # 18 had significant flesh remaining, I am tempted to conclude that this was a sign of the killer's final degradation of his victims; but the bottle lay at her feet, so I do not feel comfortable with that line, although it may be true."

"We thought it might be his final toast after killing each victim," Karen said.

"We can't forget the letters we have been receiving from someone claiming to be the murderer of the woman in the shed and, God forbid, possibly Carol," Susan added.

"I agree, Susan, but that shouldn't necessarily involve Martha at this point," Karen said.

"Karen, I trust that I have given you some information

you need. I do hope it helps you."

"Martha, I have a last question."

"Yes, Susan?"

"I realize that you only have bones to work with; can you speculate how the women were killed?"

"It's only a guess, but I have given considerable thought to that; my belief is that given the size of some of the women, compression of the carotid arteries was the method to immobilize them. If done expertly, it is quick with unconsciousness produced in nearly five seconds and death in approximately twelve seconds. I saw no evidence of knife wounds to any bones; so my belief is that the decapitation occurred post mortem.

"If the person were alive when beheaded, the killer would not have been able to make such a clean cut; it was surgically beautiful, if I may say so with much sorrow."

"That is what we concluded in a discussion with Doctor Gordon," Karen said.

"That does take some of the gore out of these deaths, but not much," Susan added.

"Thank you again for your valuable insight about these murders."

"Karen, you are welcome. If you have any questions, please don't hesitate to call me."

After Whittingham departed, Karen and the team began to bat around ideas for their next steps to identify the killer.

"Susan, do you remember that a skull that was found in a field in Macon in 2006? We were informed of it by the

Macon PD, but we had our hands full with the Mendosa case; we didn't have any reported missing persons at that time. Maybe this was our killers first time."

"I remember it happened, but that is all that I recollect of about it," Susan answered.

"Sarah, please call Macon PD and see if they know what happened to the skull."

"I will, Karen"

"In the meantime, Richard, I want you to track down the full details of the disappearance of Jason Arnold's wife. When, where, and any more information that you can glean. I suggest that after we have your report, we haul Mr. Arnold in here. Once we find the skull, we can try to squeeze him. Even if it isn't his wife's, it will put a shock into him."

* * *

"Karen, after a few phone calls, I reached a Detective Bryant at Macon-Bibb's MCU and established that the skull found buried in Macon in 2006 is housed in the Bibb's ME's lab," Sarah reported.

"Right, Sarah. What about the skull?"

"At my request, several x-rays are being delivered to Doctor Gordon. They will not part with the skull itself unless it is needed for court."

"I appreciate that. Also, send copies of the x-rays to dentists in Macon, Atlanta, and here for any matches."

"That was already done in March 2006. No luck."

"Dead ends are all we seem to find. Sarah, at least

compare the 2006 list with a current one of dentists in Macon, Atlanta, and Middlefield. Check dentists who have purchased a practice or sold their practices since that time. That may help us."

"I understand, I've been told that earlier files of patients are often not updated, so that one more look may be worth it. I'll start right away."

"Good, please keep me informed of any developments. In the meantime, I am going to my office and continue to try to find a decryption for the two unsolved ciphers we have."

Karen sat in her office and decided to re-read significant parts of the three notes the killer had sent. Karen had decided that the first cipher was, most likely, not worth the time to decrypt.

I really feel that he has not included information about himself of any value in the first cipher; it's just his way of mocking us by boasting that we cannot solve that cipher. As I said to Richard, Mr. Cool may be correct in this case. It would be nice to break it, but I'm not optimistic that we will learn anything of value; nevertheless, I am going to try the first three lines of the cipher using a keyword list, which we could try to develop at a group meeting. If I don't have success there, I will move on to the numerical cipher.

Richard thinks we shouldn't give up on it; nevertheless, I have to keep the group re-interviewing our possible suspects, so Richard will not be able to help with the decrypting for a while.

We have to move on with that other work. Am I correct about the first cipher? Chief wants results today, but that is not going to happen. He wants Carol back safe and sound. We have a ruthless killer; I can't believe he has Carol in his clutches. But, where is she?

September 2015

Greetings to the Sleuths of Middlefield. I see that you have finally stumbled upon my handiwork. Here is something for you in your spare time. I will send you a sprinkler to help you along with your work.

Baphomet

October 2015

...See if you can solve them. The next one will come in due time; it will not be easy, but it will give you answers to all your questions. Unfortunately, having the Middlefield Police solve my ciphers is like sending a sprinkler to a 3-alarm fire. *Baphomet*

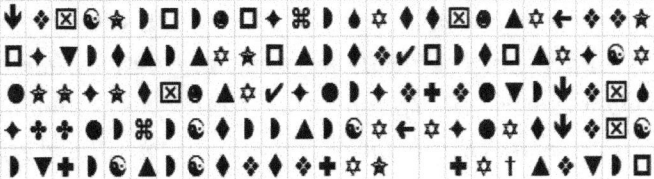

October 2015

...I have sent the sprinkler to help you. Have you received it yet? It is a pretty, blue plastic one with all sorts of designs and flowers on it. It will make your life so much easier, if you know what I mean. **Baphomet**

**2594573038282898002167304736058807777 61
76123604362352272770245094625104853910 8
12481792544848226575504265929913536956 2**

After reading the letters, Karen was bewildered by the wording in each message.

I can't understand what he means by a 'sprinkler.' The third letter explains the watering can reference; but the purpose of sending some kid's sandbox toy to us is inexplicable to me. I have no doubt that he believes he is so intelligent that we cannot possibly figure out what the symbolism is. Unfortunately, at this point, he may be right.

Richard thinks the guy is just playing with us; he believes that the toy watering can has no meaning at all in solving this case. I think Richard is wrong. This killer is handing us a vital clue; I just can't see it yet.

We have not been able to break the first cipher and possibly never will. I know that it must be a Vigenère; however, he has messed with it. I made a long, hard effort at it and came up empty. I now believe he has changed keywords somewhere in the nine lines, so it becomes very difficult to solve.

Richard may be correct in that it may tell us something about how or why he kills. I don't really believe it contains his name and I don't believe it would help solve this case. The three line Vic cipher though is where we need to spend our time. I believe this psychopath when he says it has his name in it. It fits his arrogant profile.

I feel Richard and I need a boost from GBI. I need to call Marcus to give us some of Don's time.

"Hello, Marcus, this is Karen. Has Chief Tate given you a call?"

"He did, Karen."

"I know I am asking a huge personal favor, but can you free up some of Don's time to help with these ciphers?"

"I wish I could Karen. I told Tate that we are working an assassination plot against the Governor. I know that I can trust you two to hold this information. Tell no one. The evidence that we have just gotten our hands on confirms what the informant gave us. I have faith that we will nab the plotters, but until that happens, I can't let Don go."

"I understand, Marcus. Good luck."

I guess it is up to me. I have the entire crew out re-

interviewing the suspects we've identified to this point. Not much to go on, but something may turn up. I'll work these ciphers until I have them.

First, I will have the brainstorming session with the staff over this 'sprinkler' clue.

Chapter Fifteen

By learning, you will teach; by teaching, you will learn.
Latin proverb

Karen set up her brainstorming meeting with the MCU.

"Okay, Folks. We'll start brainstorming with the clue 'sprinkler,' which the killer referenced in all three letters. I don't understand it, but my feeling is that we should develop a list of words relating to it. Then, I think that it will help when we attempt to decrypt the cipher.

"Richard feels strongly that the killer left clues that we can use to identify him from the Vigenère ciphers. I am not as certain, but we should attempt it with the understanding that if our ideas prove futile, we have to abandon that approach in favor of trying to decipher the last one he gave us, the Vic cipher."

"You know my opinion about that, Karen; it's a hoax; he is only trying to play with our minds. I ask you; is the 'sprinkler' word a keyword and if so, how did he apply it?" Susan voiced.

"That is what we have to find out, Susan. Karen and I both feel that this guy's ego is telling us exactly how to solve these ciphers. He thinks we are too dumb to figure it out. I don't know enough about ciphers to say how he may have applied it, but there is a reason he repeated it," Richard countered.

"Thank you, Richard. Susan, I am convinced that what he has said is true. The killer has no respect for us. Maybe it's the Loeb-Leopold disorder again. Killing for the thrill of it, having a masterful mind, which is so intelligent, mere humans cannot grasp the subtleties of his capabilities and clues. We need to move on. Okay, for a start, how many different words related to 'sprinkler' can we come up with today?"

"I have one, 'sprayer,' Richard said.

"Good, I'll write these on the board; keep them coming," Karen volunteered.

At the end of the session, the team had developed a list of possible synonyms, which covered the board.

"I'm tired of writing these, but let's consider the ones we have; we can review them and then weight them. At this point, I don't know if one word or the other has greater importance, but I think it is worth our time," Karen said.

"Karen, can I assume that the word list we've developed here is not useful for solving the first cipher he gave us?" Sarah asked.

"Yes, as far as I'm concerned, Sarah, we should put our effort on the last cipher. Don and I were able to decipher the Vic codes in the *Lost Cipher* case. I do admit that it was serendipitous achieving the final solution, but we did get the answer. Vic codes are extremely hard to solve, but we've proven that it can be done."

"So this list could help for the third cipher?" Sarah asked.

"The first cipher is undoubtedly a Vigenère, to which we could certainly apply this word list, but I don't believe he is telling us anything useful. Again that is only my opinion, but this list may also be useful as keyword source for the Vic cipher," Karen said.

"Sarah, I agree with Karen on this point. The killer says the third cipher contains his name. I'll accept that that is true, so we should work on both ciphers. We deciphered the second one, but as you know, it was rambling on with some story he made up," Richard said.

"Right, her physical description of blond hair, etc. he could have gotten from the *Patriot's* article we had them publish. I think the rest of his message was just tripe," Karen added.

"Okay, but where can Carol be?" Sarah pushed.

"That is the million-dollar question; we have to move on if we have any chance of finding her," Karen answered.

Richard turned to Sarah and mouthed 'alive.'

"Please, Richard, I am distraught about her."

"I'm not being callous, but every day only adds to the probability…"

"I know; let's move on with the task this morning; here's the possible keyword list reordered: fog, vaporizer, moisture, froth, droplets, drizzle, sprayer, atomizer, aerosol, and of course, the word 'sprinkler' itself," Karen added.

"So, what do we do with this list now?" Susan asked.

"At this point, as a team we are not going to do anything with it. I need to have you all carry on with the interviews and hope something breaks there. I will tackle the ciphers. I asked Marcus if he could help me with that, but they are tied up presently, so I will go it alone. If there is any time in your day, Richard, I will ask that you assist me. Is that fair enough?

"Let's break and you get on to the interviewing. If someone refuses your request, Tate is going to the DA for some support. Let him know. Thank you."

After the meeting, Richard approached Karen.

"Are you angry or upset with me?"

"Absolutely not, Richard. I know that we feel immense pressure with Carol missing and no progress to speak of on the ciphers. Let me show you what I have in mind for the matrix."

"Here is what I plan to do. From the decryption of the 'Baphomet' cipher we decrypted, I know that the first row of the Vigenère matrix must look similar to this:

	A	B	C	D	E	F	G	H	I	J	K	L	M	N	O	P	Q	R	S	T	U	V	W	X	Y	Z
A	✿	✛	●	★	☽	✔	←	▲	✦	✳	♥	♣	▼	●	◆	†	☯	☕	♦	□	⊠	✖	♠	✚	▼	↑

"The four undetermined letter and symbol combinations will be figured out as we test the keywords. I don't believe that testing our keyword list will take me more than a day. I would like us to get back together tomorrow morning at nine to discuss the results."

"I wish I could help, Karen," Richard said.

"Finish the interview with Jason Arnold; then help with the ciphering."

"Thank you, Karen. I appreciate that."

* * *

I've been awfully tough on Richard. He is a good man and a good detective. I guess that I will never be able to control him. I suppose there is too much Chicago influence on his behavior. If he chooses to leave, there is nothing I can do about it.

Karen went to her office and began work on the first cipher. Using her proposed Vigenère matrix, she focused on the first cipher line; testing each of the 'sprinkler' word variations that the team had developed. The idea was to examine how the Vigenère keywords may have been used.

The first words I'll use are Fog, then Vaporizer, then Moisture. If I get nothing, I'll have to keep on with the list. Fortunately, I can run through these pretty quickly.

♥	□	★	)	♥	☺	♆	)	♦	✚	♥	✚	♦	✝	✦	←	♦	†	♥	✳	□	✚	★	▼	✦	◉	⌘	†
F	O	G	F	O	G	F	O	G	F	O	G	F	O	G	F	O	G	F	O	G	F	O	G	F	O	G	F
F	F	X	Z	W	K	T	Q	M	G	F	F	R	J	C	B	E	J	F	V	N	G	P	G	D	O	P	K

Nothing there, or here!

♥	□	★	)	♥	☺	♆	)	♦	✚	♥	✚	♦	✝	✦	←	♦	†	♥	✳	□	✚	★	▼	✦	◉	⌘	†
V	A	P	O	R	I	Z	E	R	V	A	P	O	R	I	Z	E	R	V	A	P	O	R	I	Z	E	R	V
P	T	O	Q	T	I	Z	A	B	Q	K	W	I	G	A	H	O	Y	P	J	E	X	M	E	J	Y	E	U

Or, here.

♥	□	★	)	♥	☺	♆	)	♦	✚	♥	✚	♦	✝	✦	←	♦	†	♥	✳	□	✚	★	▼	✦	◉	⌘	†
M	O	I	S	T	U	R	E	M	O	I	S	T	U	R	E	M	O	I	S	T	U	R	E	M	O	I	S
Y	F	V	M	R	W	H	A	G	X	C	T	D	D	R	C	G	B	C	R	A	R	M	I	W	O	N	X

Since her attempts using the next seven possible keywords (Froth, Droplet, Drizzle, Atomizer, Aerosol, and Sprinkler) yielded nothing useable, Karen terminated the work.

♥	□	★	)	♥	☺	♆	)	♦	✚	♥	✚	♦	✝	✦	←	♦	†	♥	✳	□	✚	★	▼	✦	◉	⌘	†
F	R	O	T	H	F	R	O	T	H	F	R	O	T	H	F	R	O	T	H	F	R	O	T	H	F	R	O
F	C	P	L	D	L	H	Q	Z	E	F	U	I	E	B	B	B	B	R	C	O	U	P	T	B	X	E	B

♥	□	★	)	♥	☺	♆	)	♦	✚	♥	✚	♦	✝	✦	←	♦	†	♥	✳	□	✚	★	▼	✦	◉	⌘	†
D	R	O	P	L	E	T	S	D	R	O	P	L	E	T	S	D	R	O	P	L	E	T	S	D	R	O	P
H	C	P	P	Z	M	F	M	P	U	W	W	L	T	P	O	P	Y	W	U	I	H	K	U	P	L	H	A

♥ □ ★ ☽ ♥ ☯ ⬇ ☽ ♦ ✝ ♥ ♣ ♠ ╪ ✦ ← ♦ † ♥ ✳ □ ♣ ★ ▼♦ ● ⌘ †
D R I Z Z L E D R I Z Z L E D R I Z Z L E D R I Z Z L E
H C V F F F U B B D L L L T F P K Q L Y P I M E J D K L

♥ □ ★ ☽ ♥ ☯ ⬇ ☽ ♦ ✝ ♥ ♣ ♠ ╪ ✦ ← ♦ † ♥ ✳ □ ♣ ★ ▼♦ ● ⌘ †
S P R A Y E R S P R A Y E R S P R A Y E R S P R A Y E R
S E M E M M H M D U K N S G Q R B P M F C T O V I E R Y

♥ □ ★ ☽ ♥ ☯ ⬇ ☽ ♦ ✝ ♥ ♣ ♠ ╪ ✦ ← ♦ † ♥ ✳ □ ♣ ★ ▼♦ ● ⌘ †
A T O M I Z E R A T O M I Z E R A T O M I Z E R A T O M
K A P S C R U N S S W Z O Y E P S W W X L M Z V I J H D

♥ □ ★ ☽ ♥ ☯ ⬇ ☽ ♦ ✝ ♥ ♣ ♠ ╪ ✦ ← ♦ † ♥ ✳ □ ♣ ★ ▼♦ ● ⌘ †
A E R O S O L A E R O S O L A E R O S O L A E R O S O L
K P M Q S C N E O U W T I M I C B B S V I L Z V U K H E

♥ □ ★ ☽ ♥ ☯ ⬇ ☽ ♦ ✝ ♥ ♣ ♠ ╪ ✦ ← ♦ † ♥ ✳ □ ♣ ★ ▼♦ ● ⌘ †
S P R I N K L E R S P R I N K L E R S P R I N K L E R S
S E M W X G N A B T V U O K Y V O Y S U C D Q C X Y E X

* * *

Karen re-assembled the team to give them results of her effort.

"Good morning. I have made copies of the deciphering attempts using the key words we developed yesterday. I still feel certain that the symbol-letter assignments are valid, but as you can see, absolutely no luck with the list we generated! They didn't work. We may be just chasing ghosts about the 'sprinkler' keyword association; I'm beginning to think that the keyword he used has nothing to do with the idiotic watering can."

"Karen, what do we do now? I am very worried about

Carol. This guy's terrible message about her is scaring me," Susan confessed.

"I think we are all distraught about Carol, but…"

"If I may interrupt, Karen, I think the focus of our efforts has to be the Vic cipher. I agree that the first cipher may help us to identify him in some way; I'll accept the idea that he <u>did</u> give us his name in the Vic cipher. It fits his psyche if I may say so. <u>That</u> is where you and I should spend our time to decrypt," Richard said with passion in his voice.

"I believe that you are right, Richard. I need to give up the idea that anything useful will come out of all the manpower we put into the first cipher. How do the rest feel about this?"

With consensus of the group, interviewing of possible suspects was to continue; Richard and Karen would attack the Vic cipher, which is the type the killer had sent with his name.

Chapter Sixteen

Everything passes; everything wears out; everything breaks. [Tout passé; tout lasse; tout casse.) French proverb

Chief Tate came to Karen's office. As soon as she saw his face, she knew why he was there.

"Karen, I…"

"Don't say it, Chief."

"I'm sorry. They just found Carol's body in a ditch along Old Macon Road. She's been there for a day."

Karen felt agony that drove her emotions back to earlier times in her life.

"Chief, she was the sweetest kid. It never should have happened to her. That son-of-a-bitch! Was she mutilated?"

"No, at first glance she simply looked as though she was asleep. She was almost fully clothed. Gordon will autopsy her this afternoon."

"Almost, huh? I will be there. I don't know how I will handle it, but I will be there."

"You can send someone else."

"No, I have to do it. I owe it to her. She went to the hospital on my orders and into oblivion. I can't forgive myself. I thought that I had protected her with the uniformed officer, but…," said Karen completely breaking down with long painful sobs.

"You can't blame yourself, Karen. You're a good cop. These things will happen. I don't need to say it, but we have to nail this guy."

"I rushed to tell her parents that the body found last week wasn't Carol; now I have to call them with this news. I'm telling you; Chief, sometimes I hate this job."

"I do know how you feel, Karen. My uncle was a detective in LA and he was gunned down that time when the bad guys had all the firepower and the police had none. He was shot twenty times by some clown with a fully automatic AR15. A lot of good cops died that day."

"You never told me that. I'm sorry."

"I don't like to talk about it. I have a request into the Council to approve automatics for us. It has been sitting on someone's desk for two years. The wimps will probably never approve it; much less bring it up for discussion. The mayor doesn't believe in guns."

"You never know, Chief, they may surprise you yet."

"They may, but I'm not optimistic."

"I need some time alone, Chief, I don't handle things like this very well. Carol is, was dedicated to us; I can't help but feel responsible for her death. I don't know how I'll handle telling her parents after the…"

"It isn't your fault. He's gotten one of us; don't allow him to damage us further. Let me take care of notifying her parents. I will call them as soon as I leave here."

"I should be the one to tell them," Karen sobbed.

"You're in no shape to do that. They have to be told right away. It would be criminal to wait."

"I know that you're right, Chief, I just can't…," Karen said sobbing.

"Leave it to me, Karen."

"Thank you for doing that, but I will attend her autopsy. That is the least I can do for her. I will ask Susan to attend with me."

"As soon as you and Burnham are up to it, Karen, get back to the cipher work. I agree with you that it may be our only hope to catch this creep."

"We will, Chief," said Karen still shedding tears.

* * *

Later that day, Karen attended Carol's autopsy with as much courage and control as she could gather up.

"Karen, if this is too much, please don't hesitate to leave," Gordon said. "I know what Carol meant to you and the team. I have to tell you that she made an impact on me. Very professional and caring."

"Thank you, James. Let's get this over with."

At the completion of the autopsy, Gordon assembled, bagged, and labeled all the physical evidence for analysis at the GBI labs.

After Karen and Susan left, Gordon completed his report; death was caused by strangulation and evidence of rape was noted. Additionally, Gordon had noted tumors on Carol's ovaries, which could have misled Carol into believing that she was pregnant.

* * *

Karen went home to her apartment and called David.

"I'm sorry to bother you at work, Love, but today we found Carol. I've just gotten back from the autopsy…"

"Tate had you go to the post-mortem?"

"No, Love, but I felt I had to go. I want to catch this guy who has been killing women in Ely. Now he's killed Carol. I hate him and I want to be part of every facet of this investigation, so that I can put him on death row."

"Honey, is there anything that I can do?"

"No, Sweet, just provide that shoulder for me to lean on. Right now I am a wreck; I've been crying all day since Tate told me."

"I've got ER duty this evening, so I won't be able to come over."

"That's fine, David, I need time alone, actually. I'm going to spend tomorrow at home thinking about the cipher that Richard and I have to master. It's our only hope of catching this bastard."

"Okay, Darling, call if you need anything."

"I will. See you soon."

Karen made a light dinner for herself and went to bed. Drained from the emotional day, she quickly fell into a deep sleep. Dreams flooded her mind; those brain waves that her subconscious tried to parse and make sense of.

One of the vignettes was so vivid and revealing that she awoke. She hurriedly turned on the lamp sitting by her nightstand; writing down what she had envisioned, since she knew that such imaginings are fleeting and momentary, but sometimes very important. In fact, it had been a dream such as this that had allowed Don Martinelli to break the encryption in the Lost Cipher Case.

In the morning, Karen immediately read her scribbled notes from the night. As she looked at them, it became clear that the dream had not been as revealing as she had hoped.

Realizing that she needed to free her foggy thoughts; she showered and breakfasted. With her morning cup of warm coffee, she sat in her comfortable chair; then read and re-considered her notes.

This looks as though I was silly last night. What do these words mean? 'sprinkler', 'rose', 'field', 'bush,' 'bloom', 'shed' and 'bud'. Now I have no idea what my mind was trying to tell me.

Finishing her coffee, Karen's eyes slowly closed and she began to doze. Suddenly, she awoke.

I know what my brain was trying to say. Put some of those words together and see what you get. He sent us a kid's sprinkler can. What does a sprinkler can have on it? It has a handle so you can pour water, naturally, but what else? It has a 'rose' on it to disperse the water. That's it, but what in hell does that mean? A rose is a rose is a rose, but wait, a rose is a flower! Was that the hint 'Baphomet' was giving us? So what, what does that have to do with Carol, the other dead woman, and the graves in Ely? Tomorrow, Richard and I will work on this. His opinion may help.

* * *

"Good morning, Richard. How are you today?"

"I'm fine, Karen, but like you I am bumming about Carol. She was vulnerable and I was no help."

226

"I know. I think we all have a bit of responsibility in that we didn't pull her closer to us. She had such a strong 'I can take care of myself' posture that we didn't spot the weakness of her character or her needs. For whatever reason, she was dependent on men to make her feel fulfilled; that's so sad."

"Well, Carol was young, but you must admit that we all are dependent upon others. Their opinions affect us; they can make or break the strongest psyche. You remember what happened to Charlene Smith, and I hear tell what happened to you in a messy case a couple of years ago, which left you in a terrible state."

"Yes, it's true. Because of Carol, I'm going to talk with the Chief about putting in place a mentoring program so that any new person to the Unit or the Force will have an advisor assigned to them for a while. It would make sense that the older, seasoned folks take on that responsibility. Hopefully, it will bring us closer together throughout the entire MPD."

"I like that idea. You said that you have some ideas about how we can get to decrypt the last cipher sent."

"My subconscious has been working overtime. Last night I had a series of dreams that woke me up. I was only able to record one of the dreams. But that dream I consider worthwhile to talk about."

Well, Karen, dreams can be very telling about a person.

"I'm all ears; what happened?"

"I'll give you the simple version: the dream forced me to look at the words of this killer. We've been puzzled by the references to the sprinkler and the fact that he sent us a kid's toy. What was different about the kid's toy?"

"Well, for one thing, the size wouldn't be useful for a gardener, also the thing at the end of the spout is molded on so it wouldn't get lost," Richard suggested.

"Bingo. What's that 'thing' usually called?"

"I don't recall its name; I'm not a gardener. I have someone hired to take care of watering my plants."

Oh, right. You're rich.

"Well, apparently my subconscious made me think about the 'thing' at the end of the spout. It is called a 'rose' and its purpose you know. A rose is also a plant."

"Okay, Karen, I'm not quite following your logic yet. How does that get us closer to a possible decryption of the last cipher?"

"I hope my idea is not too far-fetched, but I'm thinking that this may be one of the important clues that this guy left us. We know that he is filled with his own self-worth. He <u>knows</u> that our abilities are too feeble to parse out what his genius has given us."

"What is your idea?"

"It's this in a nut shell: we believe that the numerical three-line cipher is a Vic cipher, and that he is smart enough to have played with a straddling keyboard."

"That opens up an immense number of permutations, which the keyboard could have. We don't have enough firepower here, or long enough lifetimes to try each possibility," Richard responded.

"I know that you are right about that, but think about this: in my dream, words other than 'sprinkler' came to my mind. The word, rose, was a logical jump from the sprinkler as we've noted, but there were also other words that somehow made me aware of them; I wrote them down: field, bush, bloom, shed and bud."

"Karen, some of those words you just listed are so common that they don't seem relevant to this case. How do you think they are significant to the cipher?"

"I spoke with David about them. He has a good mind like yours, but he asked the same questions, I wish I had a better rationale for what I'm telling you. I need to spend more time just thinking about them; perhaps that will open up more ideas that we can work with."

"Well, I will try to spend time on the words also."

"Good, in the meantime, can you re-interview Jim Parsons over in Traffic? He was the one who found Carol. Susan did a preliminary interview, but I want every bit of information we can get from him. In particular, we need to know if he was ever intimate with her."

"Are you saying that you have some doubts about him?"

"No, but take a look at Susan's report. Something is bothering me. I can't put my finger on it. Susan also had some reservations, but remember that he is new to the Force, and this is his first dead person, so maybe…"

"I understand, my first many years ago freaked me out

also."

"Okay, let's get along then. I need to spend time thinking."

* * *

Karen sat at her office desk when her phone rang.

"Karen, I just got back from talking to Jim Parsons. He was very reluctant to share what was bothering him, but I finally got it out of him."

"And that was what, Richard?"

"It seems that Carol and he were a sometime on and sometime off item. In fact, they had planned to go on a date the night that she disappeared, but you detailed her to the hospital, so that was out. He did speak to her that evening; she told him they would go out the following night. He seems pretty broken up about it; I don't believe it is an act."

"Why didn't he tell Susan about it?"

"I asked him; he said he heard that Susan never took the man's side in these kinds of things."

"That's ridiculous, Richard, Susan is as fair a person as I've ever met. Feminism isn't her main interest in life."

"Well, she has a reputation over in Traffic."

"Forget it. Let's keep an eye on him. I'll talk to his supervisor. Did he say that he had relations with Carol?"

"He finally admitted that they did on a couple of occasions. He was very embarrassed. It took a while to get it out of him. He heard about Robert and Caroline; he swears he didn't know there was a policy about fraternization with Force members."

"Right; that adds fuel to my thoughts for a mentoring program. For now, I'm headed to HR for a talk. Thanks."

"Any more thoughts about the 'words'?"

"No, nothing to report. I'll keep at it."

"Okay, Karen, talk to you later."

At the end of the day, Karen went home powerless to shake her thoughts about the words that she thought were important to this case, but was unable to find a reasonable track for her to pursue them to the killer.

David is coming over for dinner. Perhaps we can play word games and see what falls out. He may be good at that.

* * *

After Karen and David had finished dinner, they reviewed the word list looking for nuances.

David opened the game with his thoughts.

"I think that the word 'field' is important because of the place where the nineteen bodies were found in Ely. The word 'shed' could be important since it may relate to Carol and the other two women's deaths. I wonder if a shed also comes into play in the Ely murders."

"Perhaps, but Billington's, Carol's, and the last victim's murders are different in some ways from the Ely murders. The shed on Old Macon Road may be coincidental to those three murders. The differences are frustrating."

"Do you have any ideas why the killer changed his, what do you call it, MO?"

"No, at this point, we are treating all the deaths as our

serial killer's handiwork."

"Do you think my thoughts about the 'field' and 'shed' words are valid?"

"I don't know. I've thought that about them myself, David, so they may not have the meaning that I had hoped for. What do you think about the other three words?"

"I think without any other knowledge of the cases, that 'bush,' 'bloom', and 'bud' are all related to the 'rose' as a plant, not as a sprinkler head."

"Yeah, that's been my nagging thought exactly, but it still isn't very helpful. Maybe my mind is just playing tricks on me."

"What are your next steps?"

"Quite frankly, David, I don't know. Maybe the killer will slip up somehow and give us something really good to work with, but I'm not optimistic there."

"This guy is evil, Darling, I hope you get him soon."

"I'll do the best I can, Love."

"I've got to roll, Love. Thank you for dinner; I'll talk to you tomorrow."

Chapter Seventeen

To the good listener, half a word is enough. Spanish Proverb.

"Good morning, Karen; James Gordon here; I just received the toxicology lab results from GBI. Carol had an elevated level of blood alcohol at the time of her death. There were no signs of the usual tested drugs."

"That's good to know she wasn't using. It confirms my belief that Carol was a good cop, but I am very concerned that she was drunk. Your initial autopsy report indicated that she had been raped. Has the semen profiling come back yet?"

"No, the lab said that I should have it in a couple of days; I'll send it to you, but they are going to enter it into CODIS for a match."

"I hope Lady Luck is with us on this. I want to nail this guy."

"I agree, Karen; let's hope She is."

"Is there anything else I should know, James?"

"Yes, there were growths on Carol's ovaries. They have been biopsied and confirm my initial thought that they were cancerous. I wanted to be sure before I told you. Other than that, I have nothing else right now. I will send over copies of the lab tests for your case records."

"Do you consider that these growths would have misled Carol into thinking that she might be pregnant?"

"There is a very strong possibility that may be true, but she was not pregnant."

"Knowing that might make a difference for us since she did tell a beau that she was pregnant."

"That is sad, Karen. I'll let you know as soon as I receive the other results."

"Thanks, James."

* * *

Later in the day, Karen and Richard devoted time trying to unravel the last cipher sent.

"Richard, last evening David and I spent some time trying to make sense of the dream words I told you about yesterday. The best we could do was to parse all the words into two categories; the first one involved the belief that the two words, shed and field, are important because they are somehow associated with the grave sites in Ely. We weren't as certain about shed having the same meaning for the Old Macon Road murders.

"The other words, we felt, were related to roses, the plants. We thought that the killer was toying with us by sending the silly kid's sprinkler can. David wondered if what the word roses really meant, if anything."

"So, Karen, perhaps we were wrong; what's the next step?"

"Frankly, I'm not sure. We've interviewed everyone who had any possibility of involvement with the women killed in the field. Did I say 'killed in the field?' I meant who were killed; we don't know where they were killed."

"I know, Karen; I've had the same thought. I can't get it out of my mind that these deaths have been going on under our noses. Families must be reporting the women missing, but our systems do not have the ability to link reports to bodies found. How can that be?"

"Exactly, think of the anguish family members have when a loved one simply walks off the face of the earth! However, it is partially our fault, I think, Richard; missing person reports from the States are available. How many times do we detail someone from the Unit to scan them? Even when we do, we are more concerned about the missing from Georgia, not elsewhere. Some of the bodies in the field were recent enough to obtain some biological samples for profiling, but it will be a cost and time issue to get results."

"Sad. Does James have any idea when the semen test from Carol will be available?"

"He thought in a couple of days. He did put a priority on it because of who our Carol is, sadly was. Otherwise we have to wait and hope that this killer is in CODIS."

"Do you mind if I bug him about it?"

"Be my guest, but please be understanding that he has a great deal of pressure on him with this whole mess. Hansen isn't too happy with us, either. Lots of bodies and no suspects that we can reasonably build a case around."

"Well, I'm off. I think I will go to James's office instead of calling. I might learn more that way."

"Okay, Richard. Let me know if anything interesting pops up."

"You know I will. Catch you later."

"In the meantime, Richard, I am going to try some ideas with a straddling keyboard. I need to go over the killer's letters again to see if he gave away some information we've missed that might help."

* * *

An hour later, Karen's phone rang.

"Hi, Karen, as I was leaving the morgue, Carol's results arrived. You are not going to believe this; the guy who had sex with Carol is in the CODIS system. His name is Daniel Russell. I will come to your office and explain more."

* * *

"Okay, Richard, who is this Russell guy?"

"His name is Daniel Aaron Russell; white; age thirty-seven; six-foot two inches tall; gray hair; blue eyes software engineer; home state is Massachusetts; Stoneham in particular; Stoneham is a suburb of Boston."

"I know; I lived in Boston for a while. He is in CODIS obviously because he has served time, or was arrested. What was the crime?"

"He spent eight years at MCU-Walpole State prison for raping and killing a woman. I've heard that that is one tough prison. He stood trial for that; hence Walpole. He served eight years and was released, a model prisoner, I guess. He also had two years of probation, which he completed satisfactorily without any problems."

"When did he complete his probation?"

"It was December 15th, 2009. He told his parole officer that he was planning to start fresh and move South."

"Any idea where he moved to?"

"Yes, Russell was moving to Jacksonville where he has relatives and his parole officer notified the Jacksonville PD. I have their names."

"Well, clearly, he has been in Middlefield. Okay, you know what to do. I will let the Chief know you will be in Jacksonville for a while. I want you to stay in touch with us with any information, which we can begin to work here. I want him found and interrogated, and I do mean seriously interrogated."

"Got it. I'll pack and be on my way."

"Before you leave, something in his description rings a bell; does it with you?"

"No. Maybe we should check with Susan."

"I will. Get on with you."

Karen called Susan to her office.

"Susan, we have identified the guy who had sex with Carol and may have killed her. His name is Daniel Russell. I will give you the details of his past. Does that name mean anything to you?"

"Not off hand. Should there be?"

"Not necessarily, but something nags at me. This Russell is a software engineer. Didn't we interview someone about the Ely murders who was an engineer?"

"The only thing that I can remember about that was the person that Caroline Fielding told us about. Let me get my notes."

"While you are doing that, I need to talk with Chief

about how we represent us at Carol's funeral."

* * *

"Okay, Karen, from my notes, the guy's name is Michael Pitts, but we never interviewed him. He rents a house on the Waters' farm; he was out of town when Richard went there."

"I want you and a uniformed officer to go out to Ely and get Pitts on record. See if he will give us a swab. We have a DNA profile of Russell. I doubt if there is anything there, but since we never interviewed him; I think it's about time. If anything it is a hole in our investigation. Richard is going to talk to Russell's relatives in Jacksonville."

"You know, Karen, this is probably a dead-end. There are thousands of software engineers."

"Well, since we have never talked to him, it is a weakness in our investigation."

"Got it, I will get out there this afternoon."

"Thanks, Susan. Update me when you get there."

* * *

* * *

Karen, we just got here. Michael Pitts is home. He is willing to talk to us. Will update you later.
* * *

Great. Can't wait to hear from you.
* * *

* * *

"Mister Pitts, thank you for talking to us. We have been interviewing all the residents of the Ely area who are

238

somehow connected to the Waters' property. You were out of town when we were here earlier."

"It's quite alright. I have been hearing about the terrible situation in the nearby field. It is hard to believe that something like that can happen here. Those things always happen somewhere else."

"That is certainly the perception; it is always wrong. How long have you rented from the Waters' family?"

"I moved here about five years ago. It was in May or June, if I remember correctly."

"What do you do for employment?"

"I am a software engineer. I subcontract with large software firms. I travel a great deal both stateside and internationally, and to some spots not so safe, politically."

"Can you document your travel schedules over the past several years?"

"It would take me some time to do that. Each year I archive my files, so I would have to retrieve them. To meet IRS requirements, I keep them for seven years."

"How long will it take to retrieve them?"

"It will take at least a week. I can retrieve them fairly quickly, but I have to redact the items that I feel are proprietary to my business."

"I understand, as long as the redaction process is not excessive. We do need to know when you were in Middlefield and where you were when traveling."

"I can give you the locations, but not the contracted company names. My contracts require that I hold that information confidential."

"We have an agreement. If we can have the past five years that will be sufficient. Will you bring the information to the station, or do you want us to return for it?"

"I will drop the sheets at the station."

"Thank you, Mr. Pitts. There is one last thing I have to ask. Would you be willing to give us a cheek swab today before we leave?"

"Why is that necessary? Am I a suspect?"

"We have taken samples from everyone who has been living in this area near the burial sites. Since you live on the Waters' property, we will be able to eliminate you as we have with the others."

"Well, I'm not sure of that. I don't want to be stubborn about this, but I don't like the idea of submitting to a test if you believe that I am not a suspect. It's the old 'Live Free or Die' kind of thinking."

"It's all right for now, Mr. Pitts, but I may have to insist on it at some point. We definitely want to exclude you. We can get a court order, but we would rather not do that, if possible."

"I promise you that I will think about it. I'll give you my answer next week when I bring in the schedules."

"Thank you. One last question, Mr. Pitts. Did you know a Carol Morgan or a Kaye Billington?"

"I can't say that I do. Because of my schedules, I don't have a chance very often to sample the local femme fatales of the area."

"I understand. We look forward to seeing you next week. Please ask for me at the front desk. Here is my card."

* * *

Susan returned to the station and settled in; then she went directly to Karen's office.

"I know it's late in the day, Karen, but I wanted to tell you about Michael Pitts."

"I have time. How did the interview work out?"

"He is quite personable and was willing to answer some questions. He was not willing to give us a swab today, but he promised to think about it."

"Were you able to determine his schedule for the past year?"

"He told us that his yearly records are archived and that he would have to remove any of his contract references."

"I am surprised that the current year is archived. He should have been able to give you that, at least," Karen said.

"I thought that it was a little strange also, but I decided not to press him about it. He said that it would take him a week to gather the information. He would deliver the information to us and give us his answer about the swab."

"Okay, Susan, we will give him four days to deliver the schedules. After that, I want to get an order to search his place. Something bothers me about this. What does he look like?"

"He's a bit over six feet tall; he has black hair; blue eyes; he has a large build, not fat though. He appears to be in

241

good physical shape. He speaks very well with a slight Boston accent. I thought that was interesting because he told me he was from Valhalla, New York. Carlos and I visited there one year on vacation. I remember remarking to him that some people there had a pronounced southern accent. Carlos told me that I was imagining it, but I think he was wrong."

"That's interesting, Susan. However, you said that Pitts has a Boston accent?"

"To me he does, but what is a bit weirder for me is the reason he gave for not wanting to agree to the swab."

"What was that?"

"He said that it was important not to be coerced into things. He used the phrase 'Live Free or Die.' That's the motto on New Hampshire tags."

"That may not mean anything, Susan, if he does travel all over."

"I know, but I still find it interesting," Susan answered.

"Do you have anything else?"

"Yes, I asked him if he knew Carol or Kaye Billington and he denied that. He said that he didn't have time for the local femme fatales."

"Do you believe him?"

"I'm not the best judge of character, but, yes, I think he was honest and will deliver the goods. I'm not as certain about the swab."

"That's a strange way to refer to Middlefield's bevy of available young women."

"Yeah, I thought so at the time."

"Anything else about him that I should know?"

"No, he seems very pleasant to talk to. For some reason, I don't believe that he is connected to the Ely murders."

"Did you get a cell phone number from him?"

"He gave me his business card, which has it and the Ely address on it. It's quite plain, and does not have an email address."

"Okay, we give him four days from today to deliver the goods. Off you go. Have a good evening."

"See you tomorrow, Karen."

* * *

On the second day after Susan's interview with Michael Pitts, Susan's phone rang.

"Ms. Ramos, this is Michael Pitts calling. I was planning to see you on Thursday, but I will be unable to come to the station this week. I have an emergency situation with one of my contracts that requires me to be out of town."

"When do you think that you will return to Ely?"

"It's difficult to say. The contract involves banking, so it may take a while."

"That's disappointing, Mr. Pitts. We want to get this cleared up as soon as possible. Can you mail them to us?"

"They will need some explanations so it's best if I don't."

"Can you tell me where you are you going?"

"I can't tell you exactly because I will probably wind up going to several sites. I can tell you that I will be in the southwest area of the U.S."

"Please stay in touch. Give me a call two days from now. The original time that you agreed to come to the station. Is that acceptable?"

"I will call you Thursday morning at ten o'clock."

"Thank you, Mr. Pitts. I will be waiting for your call."

* * *

Later in the day, Richard returned from Jacksonville and went directly to Karen's office.

"Karen, just got back and wanted to brief you on Russell."

"What did you find out?"

"First of all, Russell has no relatives in Jacksonville. I couldn't find any records of where they may have gone, if they were ever there. Supposedly he had a brother and a sister, but nada."

"Well, that's interesting. Another dead end."

Chapter Eighteen

We are never deceived; we deceive ourselves. Goethe

Ten o'clock on Thursday came and went. Susan phoned the cell phone number on the card several times. The call answered directly to voice mail. At two o'clock, Susan phoned Karen with the news.

"Karen, I believe Michael Pitts has bailed on us. He didn't call me at ten as he promised."

"Somehow I suspected that would be the case. Let's get a search warrant signed, and get out there."

* * *

When the search team went to the house Michael Pitts rented in Ely, it was apparent that Pitts had moved out.

"Rip this place apart," Karen ordered.

* * *

"I think that we have enough from the search to identify Michael Pitts," Karen said at the MCU meeting.

"His fingerprints have been sent to GBI for CODIS. Also, we gathered biological samples from a cup and utensils sitting in the sink. Fortunately for us, they had not been rinsed. That sample is also at the GBI lab," Susan said.

"Any news about the disk drive found in the closet?" Karen asked.

"Julius has assigned Marcus and Don to do a forensic search of the available data. I expect to hear from them as soon as they have something to report," Richard replied.

"Good, let us know as soon as you hear from them. I am

very interested to know if that disk has any information about the letters we have received from this 'Baphomet' creep," Karen said.

"I will, Karen, I am planning to go to Atlanta and help out, if that is okay," Richard replied.

"Be my guest. Keep us informed of the progress."

* * *

One week later, the DNA results came back. Karen assembled the MCU to plan the next steps.

"I have good news and I have bad news. I will give you the good news first. Michael Pitts' DNA profile matches the profile found in Carol, so we know he lied to us about his association with Carol. Unfortunately, the fact they had sex does not mean he killed her," Karen cautioned.

"If that's the good news, Karen, what's the bad news?" Richard asked.

"The bad news is that Michael Pitts is Daniel Russell, the felon who served time in Massachusetts. Pitts' DNA profile matches Russell's."

"What did he serve time for?" asked Sarah.

"He raped and murdered a woman in Boston in 1996. He went to trial in 1997 and was convicted. He was sentenced to thirty years."

"What's he doing on the street?" Sarah asked.

"What is he doing in Middlefield?" Susan asked.

"He was released in 2007 and finished two years of parole in 2009. He then left for Jacksonville according to his parole officer."

"Ten years for murdering a woman? Is that all a woman's life is worth?" Susan asked indignantly.

"We are no better in Georgia. Sometimes a brutal killer is sentenced to several lifetime jail terms, but the sentence includes eligibility for parole. The Pardons' Board has to consider parole for that person. There have been times when a person has been granted parole, the parolee has gone on to murder and rape again. Who do you blame: the DA, the Judge, the Parole Board? No, we can't judge how other states work their systems," Karen added.

"Julius told me that the GBI has put out an APB for him," Richard said.

"Pitts, well, Russell told me that he was going to the southwest part of the country for business. I'm willing to bet that he went in the opposite direction, the northeast," Susan said.

"There is nothing that we can do directly about that now. The GBI and FBI need to track him down. Once he's nabbed, we will go get him," Karen instructed.

"I want to let the group know that the forensic people at the lab were not able to find anything incriminating on the disk drive," Richard said.

"Are you saying that the drive was cleaned by Russell?" Karen asked.

"Files had been deleted, but the forensic gurus restored enough to read them. As you know, deleting a file simply removes the pointer to that file; the actual file data is generally undisturbed if it has not been overwritten and can be recovered with software available today. We were lucky that he hadn't defragged the disk; it may have made their efforts futile," Richard explained.

"If that's the case, Richard, what did you mean by 'they had not found anything incriminating'?" Sarah asked.

"You remember the message that we decrypted from the 'Baphomet' letter? It said that Carol, but did not mention her name, was his victim and he had a good time with her. What was interesting about his statement was that he knew that she was a detective and he knew her hair color, etc., but, of course, he could have picked that up from the description, which we had put in the *Patriot*."

"I'm not following you, Richard," Sarah pushed.

"My point is that the forensics folks did not find any files containing the taunting letters, which this 'Baphomet' had sent to us. They did find many business and personal letters. He apparently really is a software engineer. The personal letters were to it seems, young women. They were suggestive, not porn, but clearly the content was in that direction. As far as we can tell, he wrote five letters to Carol. I assume that she answered him."

"There is something I don't understand about this, Richard. Carol knew that we were looking at Pitts as well as others as possible suspects in the serial murders. Why on earth would she get involved with him?" Sarah probed.

"My guess is that she knew him as Russell, not Pitts, so she had no idea that she was dealing with a possible suspect," Susan volunteered.

"We didn't have a clue about his background, either. We knew that we had to talk to him, but we weren't suspicious of him until he bailed on Susan. That's when we did a background check on him," Richard interjected.

"Oh my God, this is such a mess. Carol, we didn't protect you," Karen sadly acknowledged.

"But Carol worked in the Boston PD. Wouldn't she have known about Russell?" Sarah questioned.

"Not necessarily, Sarah. His crime happened long before she was on the force, and even if she did, it's quite possible that she didn't suspect that he was the same individual," Karen answered.

"What is our next step, Karen?" Susan asked.

"We will continue to examine the remaining items that we removed from Russell's house to beef up our evidence against him. Richard and I will continue our work on the ciphers."

* * *

Two days later, Karen received a call from Julius at GBI.

"Karen, I have good news. We arrested Daniel Russell this morning on the DA's warrant for suspicion of murdering Carol."

"That is great news. How did you spot him?"

"You are not going to believe this, but he was holed up in Milledgeville."

"That was finally a break for us, Julius."

"Yes, we never expected to find him in Georgia, but since his picture was smeared across the State; a store owner called us after he came in to buy cigarettes."

"Where is he now?"

"We have him in Atlanta, but we are transferring him to the Twiggs County lockup."

"Has he been read his rights?"

"He has."

"Is he willing to talk to us?"

"No, he asked for a lawyer."

"Right, he knows the system well enough."

"When he was arrested, he had a laptop computer, which I have sent over to the forensics lab. Maybe we'll find something there."

"That's good news. Okay, Julius, thanks. Once he's in Twiggs, we'll get over there."

The following day, Karen received a phone call from Attorney Kenneth Sharpe.

"Good morning to you, Attorney Sharpe. What can I do for you?"

"I'm representing Daniel Russell who is in the Twiggs County Detention Center."

"Not even a 'good morning,' Mr. Sharpe? I am surprised."

"Let's cut the fake niceties, Major. I do not want you talking to my client."

"That's his right, Attorney, but it might be better if we could spend a few minutes with him. Otherwise, this might expand into a larger case that you want."

"You are not referring to the murders in Ely, are you? I

understand that you are holding Pitts in connection with the murder of your detective. Is that true?"

"Yes, for the moment, that is the reason, but there are two other deaths that we have to consider, Kaye Billington and Jane Swanson. Those two women are on missing persons' lists from Massachusetts and New Hampshire."

"But you have no proof of any involvement by my client for those deaths. In fact, you don't even know if the bones that were found are Jane Swanson's. For that matter, you have no evidence implicating my client to your detective's death. I demand that you charge him or release him."

"Attorney Sharpe, we know the bones are those of Kaye Billington. The body found in the shed we now know is Jane Swanson. Your client may be involved with those deaths."

"You need to prove it."

"DA Hansen is calling the Grand Jury together as we speak. Any evidence that we have will be presented to them. We will hold him for a hearing later today, but you know that already. He is a flight risk; I wouldn't hold my breath that the Judge will release him."

"I will not let my client become a railroad case as it was with Doctor Carlson."

"Perhaps, it would be best for your client if you let us talk to him. You can be there and then it will be videotaped. Obviously, you will be given a copy. What do you say?"

"I am knee deep in an Atlanta case. I will have an associate at the meeting, but you cannot talk to him until after the hearing today. I will talk to my client to see if he agrees to speak to you; my advice to him is to keep his mouth shut. But if he does agree, you'd better toe the mark, Major, you only have one hour to interview him."

"I believe that is very wise, Mr. Sharpe. I don't want to waste our time or Mr. Russell's."

"If Mr. Russell agrees, I will have my associate at the station by ten o'clock tomorrow morning, but remember this, if the interview turns ugly, my associate, Attorney Mary Sutherland will stop it immediately. Do you understand?"

"It's a deal; I honestly believe it is in the best interest of Mr. Russell."

* * *

The interview began at ten-thirty the following morning with Susan and Karen.

"Mr. Russell, why did you identify yourself as Michael Pitts when Detective Ramos spoke to you recently?"

"Because I am Michael Pitts. I served my time in Mass. and didn't want to have to explain to nosy people about my past. I had it legally changed here in Georgia."

"I understand, Mr. Russell."

"His name has been changed. Please address him as Michael Pitts," Sutherland insisted.

"All right, Mr. Pitts. Did you know Carol Morgan?"

"I did have a couple of dates with her."

"Were you ever intimate with her?"

"Don't answer that, Michael," Sutherland interrupted.

"Did you know Kaye Billington?"

"I went out with her once. She was a nut case."

"Were you intimate with her?"

"Don't answer that, Michael," Sutherland advised.

"Did you know Jane Swanson?"

"I never knew a Jane Swanson, and no, I was never intimate with her."

"Mr. Pitts, are you familiar with the area of the Waters' field where several bodies were found buried?"

"When I first moved to the house on Waters' farm, I had a dog, a black Lab, and we took walks on several hay fields. So yes, I probably walked that field."

"Did you ever notice anything unusual about the field?"

"No, not when Spike and I walked there. You know how dogs are; they poke their noses at any smells. He never acted as though he found any bodies or anything. Spike was killed by a car four years ago, and I haven't done any field walking since."

"So, you've never seen any unusual cars or activity around your house leading to the field?"

"Not that I can ever recall."

"Mr. Pitts, if I ask you to tell me what words come to mind when I say the word 'Evil' or 'Satan,' would you be willing to do that?"

"Major Hunter, what is the purpose of this little game?" Sutherland asked.

"Well, it is not a game as you call it. It helps us to understand some information that we have received. We are asking anyone we interview the same question."

"Michael, you do not have to play the game. In fact, I am about to close this interview," Sutherland cautioned Pitts.

"I'll play her silly game, Mary," Pitts answered.

"I demand that you not answer, Michael."

"You are my lawyer, not my mother; I am going to answer."

"Mr. Pitts, when I say the word 'Evil,' what words come to mind?"

"Malevolent, wicked, vicious, and hideous."

"Thank you. What about 'Satan?'

"Antichrist, Devil, Beelzebub, Demon, and let's see, Lucifer, Baphomet, and Mephistopheles."

"Thank you, Mr. Pitts, you seem well versed in present day common and old names used for Satan."

"I have read many books on the subject. I enjoy reading about mythology. My time in prison was well spent. I used the library extensively. Did I tell you that I finished a Master's degree in engineering from the Northeastern? I did it on line. You must have found my sheepskin in your search."

"Yes, it is still at the house."

"Major, did this wasted exercise help Michael at all?" Sutherland asked.

"As I said earlier, Ms. Sutherland, we are asking all of our interviewees the same questions. It hasn't helped or hurt any of them," Karen answered.

"Well, our allotted hour is nearly up; do you have anything else, Major?"

"Just one question. Mr. Pitt, do you consider yourself rehabilitated?"

"That's it, Major. This interview is at an end. Michael, do not answer any more questions by the police."

"Thank you, Mr. Pitts. Thank you, Ms. Sutherland. We appreciate your time and cooperation. I will have a copy of this interview tape sent to your office."

* * *

"Well, how did it go?" Richard asked.

"It went as we suspected it might. He lied about Carol, so he may also be lying about Billington and Swanson."

"Of course, we know that the bones found in McCrery's Park are Billington's. If Sue Miller's DNA profile that we sent to Hartford is confirmed to be their missing person, that ends speculation about the body in the shed. We should know that very soon," Richard stated.

"Yes, but the identities of those buried up in Waters' field are still a mystery," Susan said.

"We know Russell had opportunity and means to kill these women, but what is the motive?" Richard asked.

"He's a psychopath, Richard. He's done it once, perhaps, many times. Who knows what drives a mind like his?" Karen offered.

"I'm still surprised that we found nothing on his disk drive about Baphomet," Susan said.

"I am also, Susan. He failed the 'Satan' test. Not one of

the other people interviewed ever used the synonym Baphomet for Satan. I hope my eyes didn't light up when he said it."

"No, but Sutherland's eyes narrowed when he said it," Susan answered.

"Have we given them any information about the killer's use of that word?" Karen asked.

"No, Karen," Susan said.

"Well, she must know something that we don't know about Pitts."

"More than ever, I am sure the forensics folks must have missed something on that disk," Susan said.

"Well, I'm not. He probably has a couple of computers. I suspect that he has laptops, which we don't know about. He travels frequently and what better way to have your work with you, sinister or not," Richard pushed.

"Speaking of laptops, Julius just left a message that Russell's laptop has nothing but his travel schedules on it. No sinister letters as he hoped," Susan disclosed.

"I still have a feeling that Russell is our serial killer, but proving it will be a nearly impossible challenge. Right now we have nothing to tie him to the Baphomet letters or Waters' field. We do know that he had sex with Carol and killed her, well, only that he had sex with her," Karen backtracked.

"I hate to state the obvious, but we don't have much of a case. If it weren't for his prison record, we wouldn't have looked at him twice," Richard said.

"So, the only thing that we have is a semen profile. Richard, we have to crack those codes," Karen said.

Chapter Nineteen

The Devil's boots don't creak. Scottish Proverb

"Richard, I want to try something different with these ciphers."

"What do you mean by different, Karen?"

"Let's look at the last cipher he sent to us. We are quite certain that it is the Vic type. The question we now have is what type of straddling keyboard he devised."

"I understand that, but what's the difference you spoke about?"

"Look, he sent us that stupid sprinkler. We tried a series of word games to try to understand what the jerk was talking about. He thinks we are as dumb as rocks. What if he used some of those words we fooled around with to make up his straddling keyboard?"

"What do you mean?"

"What I mean is this: what if he changed the usual Vic format of the straddling keyboard. We know in the 'Cipher' case, the killer kept the third and fourth rows of the keyboard the same as the original Vic keyboard. With the first letter row, he used the letters to make up words that made sense to him. Why couldn't Russell have used letters from the second and third rows in the first row?"

"Karen, do you realize what you are saying? What tools can we possibly use to discover that?"

"I don't know, but I have been racking my brain for weeks about this. I would love to say that Sloan might be able to help us, but really I don't believe that is possible and I'm not going to call her."

"The straddling keyboard configuration problem is a nearly impossible task; the keyword itself would not be possible to find. No, Karen, I think this is a futile effort."

"Well, do you have a better idea?"

"Frankly, Karen, I don't. I have no great inspiration to offer."

"I feel that this guy is definitely telling us what is on his mind. We just can't see it yet. I have faith we can crack his code. In the meantime, I want you and Susan to contact the State Police in Massachusetts and New Hampshire to get any further information on their missing persons."

"We have set up a notification system with them, so we get weekly briefings. I've asked them to particularly note women whose families reported that their missing person was headed for Georgia."

"Good thinking, Richard. Can I assume that we've covered all the neighboring States?"

"All but Florida. It seems that they have a problem working with us; they only want to contact Julius at GBI."

"Well, okay. Get us fresh updates from the others. Talk to Julius. We have to gumshoe our way to find out who the Ely bodies are. Okay, then off with you. I want to spend time with my code cracking ideas. Thank you for all your support, Richard."

After Richard left, Karen wrote down the list of words the MCU had considered several weeks ago. Then began to place the words in a way that formed short phrases. She remembered that the group had finally decided that the words bush, bloom, and bud were all related to the word <u>rose</u>, but not the <u>rose</u> on the watering can. Baphomet had used the watering can to give a serious clue, which he mistakenly believed the police would not be able to discover. Karen thought that she might have an answer to the straddling keyboard.

I think I am beginning to understand how this guy's mind is working. If I arrange the words like this: A Rose Bush, or A Rose Bloom, or A Rose Bud, we might have something. Let's see, a straddling keyboard can be set up like this, so common vowels and consonants are in the first letter row.

	0	1	2	3	4	5	6	7	8	9
	E	T		A	O	N		R	I	S
2	B	C	D	F	G	H	J	K	L	M
6	P	Q	#	U	V	W	X	Y	Z	&

I can use this keyboard to encipher a message by converting an alphabetical letter to a number. So, E is 0, T is 1, etc., and B is 20 in the third row, P is 60 in the fourth row, and so on for each letter.

Karen then began to experiment with the word phrases for the first row of her straddling keyboard.

	0	1	2	3	4	5	6	7	8	9
	A	R	O	S	E		B	U	S	H
5	B	C	D	F	G	H	J	K	L	M
	P	Q	#	U	V	W	X	Y	Z	&

No, that one can't be it. The S is repeated making any message that I make ambiguous. The other problem with this configuration is that it has only one space at 5 in the first column. There is no way that I can rearrange the third and fourth rows to replace the letters used in the second row. What would I do with the double S problem? No, Karen, don't waste any more time with this keyboard.

Let's see how A Rose Bloom looks.

	0	1	2	3	4	5	6	7	8	9
	A	R	O	S	E	B	L	O	O	M
	B	C	D	F	G	H	J	K	L	M
	P	Q	#	U	V	W	X	Y	Z	&

That is even more ridiculous, if Baphomet is really using the Victor cipher. There is no way to differentiate the letters A, B, and P, or any other letters from each other. Let's see how the last one might look. The blank spaces in row two allow me to assign 1 to the third row and 6 to the fourth row.

261

	0	1	2	3	4	5	6	7	8	9
	A		R	O	S	E		B	U	D
1	B	C	D	F	G	H	J	K	L	M
6	P	Q	#	U	V	W	X	Y	Z	&

This appears much more useable. I can put the numbers 1 and 5 at the start of the second and third rows to define the other letters, but it still isn't right. I am missing the letter T and the letter U appears in the fourth row. Okay, I'll rearrange the keyboard to this:

	0	1	2	3	4	5	6	7	8	9
	A		R	O	S	E		B	U	D
1	T	C	I	F	G	H	J	K	L	M
6	P	Q	#	N	V	W	&	X	Y	Z

No, it still isn't right. I should arrange the third and fourth rows to have the letters match their sequence in the alphabet. I'll put the ampersand and hash tag under the two blank spaces in the second row. I don't know if that is how Baphomet did it, but it is logical, and he appears to be a logical, if not a diabolical thinker.

	0	1	2	3	4	5	6	7	8	9
	A		R	O	S	E		B	U	D
1	C	F	G	H	I	J	K	L	M	N
6	P	Q	#	T	V	W	&	X	Y	Z

Voilà!! I think this is it! You're not as clever as you think you are crazy man. We may get you yet. Now on to the keyword. That is going to be a tough nut to crack. I need to get the team together.

* * *

Karen's euphoria was interrupted by the ringing of her phone.

"Karen, this is Tom Hansen. We have a "True Bill" for the death of Carol Morgan by Michael Pitts. We were not successful for Kaye Billington or, of course, Jane Swanson, but I still feel good that we can go to trial for Carol's murder."

"That is great news about Carol. I am very worried that Kaye's and Jane's murders will go into deep freeze and never be solved. What do we need to do further to assist you with Pitts trial?"

"I will be calling you, Susan, and Richard to testify when I can get this thing to trial. I need to be certain that all our records, reports, and interview notes are without flaws. I will have to turn over copies of much of that to Sharpe for discovery. This case is on thin ice as it is; I don't want a typo here and there to give him any ammunition to destroy the case."

"We will pore over all the paperwork, Tom. Keep us up to date."

"I will. If anything, and I mean anything pops up, let me know immediately, Karen."

"You know that I will. Take care, Tom."

The next morning Karen called the MCU together to deliver her good news about the straddling keyboard, and to advise them that all the records pertaining to Carol's murder case would have to be scoured to ensure that there were no embarrassing or contradictory contents.

"You know we'll do this for Carol, Karen, but what a waste of time. We have all been on top of this and have been very careful not to botch anything up," Richard said.

"I know that all of you have been very conscientious in working this case, but we have to do it for her and for Tom," Karen said.

"And for ourselves. We must do a superb job in any case, but this one is special," Sarah voiced.

"Sarah is right. Let's get to it. I will hold off on the ciphering until we all can complete this work. In the meantime, ..."

Karen's phone rang interrupting her.

"Karen, this is Sue Miller from GBI. We have a DNA profile of the humerus marrow. We sent that to New Hampshire for their comparison with a profile they had for Jane Swanson. It's a match! Karen, you must have had bones from Billington and Swanson and not realized it."

"That is good news, Sue, but it's sad that they came to Middlefield to meet their killer. Thank you. I will spread the word."

* * *

Two days later, Tom Hansen called Karen.

"We've gotten a lucky break! Sharpe called to say that

264

Pitts wants to cut a plea."

"What are they proposing, Tom?"

"If we will not pursue the death penalty, he will plead guilty to Carol's murder."

"Why the change of heart, Tom?"

"Massachusetts does have the death penalty, so he has gotten scared in Georgia, and wants to avoid that. I've told Sharpe that I will only agree to the plea if they agree to a sentence of life without the possibility of parole. The guy is a repeat killer and I don't ever want him back on the streets. I need to get in touch with Carol's family, and tell them this is probably the best route at this point."

"What about Billington and Swanson?"

"He denies anything to do with their deaths. From your interview information, I did ask him about the Waters' field. He denies anything to do with that, but I sincerely doubt that."

"Well, Tom, that is good news and bad. Good for Carol's family, but it means we have to break the ciphers to prove it was him that killed those people we found in the field. That will be a tough job, but at least Pitts will be confined until we can finish them."

"We all want to solve the Ely murders. Let me know if there is anything that we can do to help you, Karen."

"Thank you, Tom, but Richard and I will have to struggle through the ciphers. We'll keep you posted."

* * *

"Okay, Richard, let's get back to this last cipher. I feel

265

certain that we have the correct straddling keyboard. Our next step has to be unravelling the keyword."

"Before we get started, Karen, I have some very good news. Aretha and I are going to get hitched."

"That is great news, Richard. Have you planned the wedding date?"

"We know your wedding will be in June, so we are planning ours for July fifteenth. That way we don't step on your toes in June."

"Don't be silly, Richard, if she wants a June wedding, plan for it then. It won't bother David or me."

"I'll tell her, but she is happy with July."

"I'm very happy for you both. I wish the best for you."

"Thank you, Karen. Let's get back to our work. I really want us to nail him."

"Good idea. As I was saying about the keyword, finding it won't be easy. Do you have any suggestions?"

"Let's set up a program on your computer to try some common keywords. I suggest that we first try some prime numbers, Karen."

"That works for me as a first trial. Can I suggest that we take the first half of the first line cipher and work with that? If we get something legible then we can do the same for the second half."

"Karen, the way we've set this up, the 'Letter Cipher' row is the cipher that he gave us in his letter, and the 'His Cipher' row is the cipher that we think he converted the plaintext to."

"Also notice, Richard, that the prime numbers that we are using with our program must be broken up to allow one number per position. By that I mean, 11 becomes 1, 1, 31 is 3, 1 in the program."

"Is that a valid way to use the numbers?"

"It is how we did it the last time we dealt with the Vic cipher. It may not be the only way, but it worked then; we got the killer. It is worth a try now."

Letter Cipher	2	5	9	4	5	7	3	0	3	8	2	8	2	8	9	8	0	0	2	1
Key (Primes)	2	3	5	7	1	1	1	3	1	7	1	9	2	3	2	9	3	1	3	7
C–K	0	2	4	-3	4	6	2	-3	2	1	1	-1	0	5	7	-1	-3	-1	-1	-6
Mod 10	10	10	10	10	10	10	10	10	10	10	10	10	10	10	10	10	10	10	10	10
His Cipher	0	2	4	7	4	6	2	7	2	1	1	9	0	5	7	9	7	9	9	4

"Richard, now if we use our straddling keyboard to convert the 'His Cipher' row back to letters we get this garbage string: ARSBS QBR FDAEBDBDDS in the decipher."

	0	1	2	3	4	5	6	7	8	9
	A		R	O	S	E		B	U	D
1	C	F	G	H	I	J	K	L	M	N
6	P	#	Q	T	V	W	&	X	Y	Z

Letter Cipher	2	5	9	4	5	7	3	0	3	8	2	8	2	8	9	8	0	0	2	1
Key (Primes)	2	3	5	7	1	1	1	3	1	7	1	9	2	3	2	9	3	1	3	7
C–K	0	2	4	-3	4	6	2	-3	2	1	1	-1	0	5	7	-1	-3	-1	-1	-6
Mod 10	10	10	10	10	10	10	10	10	10	10	10	10	10	10	10	10	10	10	10	10
His Cipher	0	2	4	7	4	6	2	7	2	1	1	9	0	5	7	9	7	9	9	4
Plaintext	A	R	S	B	S		Q	B	R		F	D	A	E	B	D	B	D	D	S

"Well, Karen, one or the other is wrong: the key or the keyboard. There's no sense in trying the second half of the cipher."

"I still feel that the keyboard is logical and right. It's my feeling that Pitts with his engineering degrees wants to be logical. I think it fits with his persona."

"Okay, Karen, let's try either some dates or the Fibonacci series. I must admit that I don't have much faith with this process."

"Don't lose confidence, Richard. We have to succeed."

"Okay, let's try the first numbers of the Fibonacci series."

Letter Cipher	2	5	9	4	5	7	3	0	3	8	2	8	2	8	9	8	0	0	2	1
Key Fibonacci	0	1	1	2	3	5	8	1	3	2	1	3	4	5	5	8	9	1	4	4
C–K	2	4	8	2	2	2	-5	-1	0	6	1	5	-2	3	4	0	-9	-1	-2	-3
Mod 10	10	10	10	10	10	10	10	10	10	10	10	10	10	10	10	10	10	10	10	10
His Cipher	2	4	8	2	2	2	5	9	0	6	1	5	8	3	4	0	1	9	8	7
Plaintext	R	S	U	R	R	R	E	D	A		#	E	U	O	S	A		N	U	B

"Nothing but junk again, Karen."

"Right, let's try the date that Carol was found. Better yet, she was killed the day before she was found so, June 13, 2015, so we use 06132015."

Letter Cipher	2	5	9	4	5	7	3	0	3	8	2	8	2	8	9	8	0	0	2	1
Key Date	0	6	1	3	2	0	1	5	0	6	1	3	2	0	1	5	0	6	1	3
C–K	2	-1	8	1	3	7	2	-5	3	2	1	5	0	8	8	3	0	-6	1	-2
Mod 10	10	10	10	10	10	10	10	10	10	10	10	10	10	10	10	10	10	10	10	10
His Cipher	2	9	8	1	3	7	2	5	3	2	1	5	0	8	8	3	0	4	1	8
Plaintext	R	D	U		H	B	R	E	O	R		J	A	U	U	O	A	S		M

"This is no good, Karen. We aren't getting anywhere. I can see nothing but a waste of time."

"I know how it feels, but are you willing to grind through other dates and possible number keys? We know more about Pitts than we did before the interview. Maybe there are some other ideas we can try."

"What do you mean by that?"

"Numbers have always grabbed peoples' attention. 666, for example, is supposed to be the epitome of evil. You know, from the book of Revelation."

"Karen, that number also means the creation and perfection of world to Kabbalistic Judaism, and for Jehovah's Witnesses it represents the world's unified governments in opposition to God, so it is universally recognized. How does that apply to Pitts?"

"It may not, Richard, I'm grabbing at straws, but it may yield something. Try many number combinations; now that we are set up, it doesn't take much time to run through them."

"I hate to say it, Karen, but it's a fool's errand."

"I'll ask you again; are you willing to keep working these number keys to catch this guy?"

"I will do as you ask, Karen. I don't know if this guy is

into magic numbers but I can also try magic numbers."

"What are those?"

"Since you asked; I will explain. Atomic nuclei have stabilities, which seem to follow certain numbers. For instance, it is the number of neutrons or protons in an atomic nucleus that determines the stability of the nucleus. The numbers for neutrons are 2, 8, 20, 28, 50, 82, 126 and 184. For protons, the numbers are 2, 8, 20, 28, 50, 82, and 114. Atoms with these numbers result in strongly bound and extremely stable nuclei."

"So you could try those numbers after we've done others."

"I will, but honestly, I think this exercise is futile. I've said it before. Unless our killer has a background in physics or chemistry, he wouldn't think of those numbers."

"Well, Richard, you did suggest them."

"I know. I am very discouraged."

"Okay, Richard, you have convinced me. Why don't you please spend your time getting ready for Pitts' trial. That is coming up in a couple of weeks and we need to be ready. Susan is preparing now. I will handle the rest of the cipher solution work myself. Off you go."

"Okay, Karen, I am sorry to disappoint you, but I just don't have it for the grind."

"I understand. Catch you later, Richard."

As Karen returned to work the ciphers, the DA called.

"Hello, Karen, we have reached a plea deal with Pitts and Attorney Sharpe. I will inform the sitting judge and see if he agrees to hear it."

"I know you have to work this case to keep him behind bars, but we have the Billington and Swanson's deaths. How do we handle those?"

"There is simply no evidence you have been able to find to link him to those murders. I would rather let those cases sit until something more becomes available. The worst case would be to have a jury find him not guilty of those. He would have gotten away with murder, Karen."

"I know that you are right, Tom, but it galls me that we haven't been able to pin them on him."

"Keep your fingers crossed that the judge will accept his plea."

"Let me know what happens, Tom."

Chapter Twenty

When its time has come, the prey goes to the hunter.
Persian proverb

Karen continued with the drudgery of the cipher key search. Don, Marcus, and Julius had all given her ideas for approaching the solution of a key. Several algorithms had been tried with no success.

I'm beginning to lose my faith that we can ever find the key. I have one idea to try. What if Baphomet used the same phrase, A Rose Bud, for the key? What if he used the straddling keyboard to convert the phrase to the key? Let's try it.

	0	1	2	3	4	5	6	7	8	9
	A		R	O	S	E		B	U	D
1	C	F	G	H	I	J	K	L	M	N
6	P	#	Q	T	V	W	&	X	Y	Z

Using the keyboard, then the phrase numerically becomes this: 02345789.

A	R	O	S	E	B	U	D
0	2	3	4	5	7	8	9

Letter Cipher	2	5	9	4	5	7	3	0	3	8	2	8	2	8	9	8	0	0	2	1
Key (New)	0	2	3	4	5	7	8	9	0	2	3	4	5	7	8	9	0	2	3	4
C–K	2	3	6	0	0	0	-5	-9	3	6	-1	4	-3	1	1	-1	0	-2	-1	-3
Mod 10	10	10	10	10	10	10	10	10	10	10	10	10	10	10	10	10	10	10	10	10
His Cipher	2	3	6	0	0	0	5	1	3	6	9	4	7	1	1	9	0	8	9	7
Plaintext	R	O		P	A	A	E		H		Z	S	B		C	D	A	U	B	B

Nope, that doesn't work for a keyword either. Wait a minute! What if he used the position of the letters in the alphabet, not the straddling keyboard to make the conversion? This is how the letters are sequenced in the alphabet.

1	A		8	H		15	O		22	V
2	B		9	I		16	P		23	W
3	C		10	J		17	Q		24	X
4	D		11	K		18	R		25	Y
5	E		12	L		19	S		26	Z
6	F		13	M		20	T			
7	G		14	N		21	U			

So, the phrase, <u>A Rose Bud,</u> becomes this: A = 1, B = 2, R = 18, etc. This could really be it!

A		R		O		S	E	B		U	D
1	1	8	1	5	1	9	5	2	2	1	4

Now, to plop this keyword into my program…

Letter Cipher	2	5	9	4	5	7	3	0	3	8	2	8	2	8	9	8	0	0	2	1
Key (New Rev)	1	1	8	1	5	1	9	5	2	2	1	4	1	1	8	1	5	1	9	5
C–K	1	4	1	3	0	6	-6	-5	1	6	1	4	1	7	1	7	-5	-1	-7	-4
Mod 10	10	10	10	10	10	10	10	10	10	10	10	10	10	10	10	10	10	10	10	10
His Cipher	1	4	1	3	0	6	4	5	1	6	1	4	1	7	1	7	5	9	3	6
Plaintext		I		H	A		V	E		K		I		L		L	E	D	O	

This is working!!!!!! I get something readable!!

273

"I have killed o"

What's the rest? I need to format the second half. Let's see what that looks like.

Letter Cipher	6	7	3	0	4	7	3	6	6	0	5	8	8	0	7	7	7	6	1
Key (New Rev)	2	2	1	4	1	1	8	1	5	1	9	5	2	2	1	4	1	1	8
C–K	4	5	2	-4	3	6	-5	5	1	-1	-4	3	6	-2	6	3	6	5	-7
Mod 10	10	10	10	10	10	10	10	10	10	10	10	10	10	10	10	10	10	10	10
His Cipher	4	5	2	6	3	6	5	5	1	9	6	3	6	8	6	3	6	5	3
Plaintext	V	E	R		T		W	E		N		T		Y		T		W	O

Here it is: "I have killed over twenty-two"
Yes, I've got you now. Here it is in two steps again.

Letter Cipher	7	6	1	2	3	6	0	4	3	6	2	3	5	2	2	7	2	7	7	0
Key (New Rev)	1	1	8	1	5	1	9	5	2	2	1	4	1	1	8	1	5	1	9	5
C–K	6	5	-7	1	-2	5	-9	-1	1	4	1	-1	4	1	-6	6	-3	6	-2	-5
Mod 10	10	10	10	10	10	10	10	10	10	10	10	10	10	10	10	10	10	10	10	10
His Cipher	6	5	3	1	8	5	1	9	1	4	1	9	4	1	4	6	7	6	8	5
Plaintext		W	O		M	E		N		I		N	S		I		X		Y	E

Letter Cipher	2	4	5	0	9	4	6	2	5	1	0	4	8	5	3	9	1	0	8
Key (New Rev)	2	2	1	4	1	1	8	1	5	1	9	5	2	2	1	4	1	1	8
C–K	0	2	4	-4	8	3	-2	1	0	0	-9	-1	6	3	2	5	0	-1	0
Mod 10	10	10	10	10	10	10	10	10	10	10	10	10	10	10	10	10	10	10	10
His Cipher	0	2	4	6	8	3	8	1	0	0	1	9	6	3	2	5	0	9	0
Plaintext	A	R	S		Y	O	U		C	A		N		T	R	E	A	D	A

"I have killed over twenty-two women in six years. You can't read a"

Well, buddy boy, I am reading your stupid cipher. Now

for the last line. I've got you!

Karen prepared the final cipher line to decrypt using the same keyword.

Letter Cipher	1	2	4	8	1	7	9	2	5	4	4	8	4	8	2	2	6	6	4	5
Key (New Rev)	1	1	8	1	5	1	9	5	2	2	1	4	1	1	8	1	5	1	9	5
C–K	0	1	-4	7	-4	6	0	-3	3	2	3	4	3	7	-6	1	1	5	-5	0
Mod 10	10	10	10	10	10	10	10	10	10	10	10	10	10	10	10	10	10	10	10	10
His Cipher	0	1	6	7	6	6	0	7	3	2	3	4	3	7	4	1	1	5	5	0
Plaintext	A		K	B		&	A	B	O	R	O	S	O	B	S		F	E	E	A

Letter Cipher	6	4	4	7	1	1	4	3	9	9	1	3	5	3	6	9	5	6	2
Key (New Rev)	2	2	1	4	1	1	8	1	5	1	9	5	2	2	1	4	1	1	8
C–K	4	2	3	3	0	0	-4	2	4	8	-8	-2	3	1	5	5	4	5	-6
Mod 10	10	10	10	10	10	10	10	10	10	10	10	10	10	10	10	10	10	10	10
His Cipher	4	2	3	3	0	0	6	2	4	8	2	8	3	1	5	5	4	5	4
Plaintext	S	R	O	O	A	A		Q	S	U	R	U	O		J	E	S	E	S

The bastard changed the key for the last cipher line! Nothing but junk again for both halves. He hinted that it would have his name. I guess he wasn't as positive as he bragged that we wouldn't solve his codes.

* * *

At the MCU meeting the next morning, Karen updated them with her success decrypting the first two lines of the Vic cipher.

"The problem we have now is that Pitts has changed the keyword for the last line. I think he realized that we haven't just fallen off the turnip truck; we have more on the ball than he gave us credit for."

"Well, Karen, where do you go from here?" Richard

asked.

"I'm not certain; I have a couple of ideas that I may try. We have got to find some evidence that Pitts is responsible for the Ely murders."

"Karen, every bit of sifted soil from each burial site has been exhaustively examined. We've found nothing that remotely links Pitts to the murders," Susan cautioned.

"And further, the articles of women's clothing found during the search at Pitts' house have been examined. In some cases, we have enough biological samples to test, but we haven't done it. We will need more money in the budget to fund those tests," Sarah warned.

"Tate said that he would get the funding. Let's get the samples out to the GBI lab ASAP," Karen ordered.

"Julius told me the other day that he doesn't know how much longer he can hold off the FBI. They want in on the Ely cases because of the number of bodies," Richard said.

"Yeah, I know; he called me the other day also. It would be a feather in their caps and a black eye for the GBI," Karen responded.

"How is the plea bargain coming along for Pitts' confession?" Susan asked.

"Tom is calling me today, but he is very positive that Judge Redding will accept it. He has to be sure that Pitts understands that by this deal, he will spend the rest of his natural life in a high security slammer."

"If Redding doesn't accept the plea and sends it to trial, we could wind up with nothing. Juries have become very unpredictable in these cases," Susan said.

"I know, I know," Karen answered.

"Let's hope that the Judge realizes that he may let off a serial murderer," Richard said.

"I will let you all know as soon as Tom calls me. In the meantime, get the samples out for testing."

"We don't have any cash left in the usual account that we use for these tests. What account am I going to use?" Sarah asked.

"Use the same account number. I will take responsibility for that," Karen ordered.

Later that afternoon, Tom called with the good news. Pitts would be going to jail for the rest of his life. Karen emailed the news to the MCU staff, and then got on with her decrypting work.

I've tried some weird combinations of keywords, which did not work. I wonder what I would get if I try the first idea I had; use the straddling keyboard letter number to generate the keyword. It didn't work with the first two lines but what happens now?

A	R	O	S	E	B	U	D
0	2	3	4	5	7	8	9

Letter Cipher	1	2	4	8	1	7	9	2	5	4	4	8	4	8	2	2	6	5	7	5
Key (New)	0	2	3	4	5	7	8	9	0	2	3	4	5	7	8	9	0	2	3	4
C–K	1	0	1	4	-4	0	1	-7	5	2	1	4	-1	1	-6	-7	6	3	4	1
Mod 10	10	10	10	10	10	10	10	10	10	10	10	10	10	10	10	10	10	10	10	10
His Cipher	1	0	1	4	6	0	1	3	5	2	1	4	9	1	4	3	6	3	4	1
Plaintext		C		I		P		H	E	R		I	D		I	O		T	S	

My God, it looks like it works! The first half says "cipher idiots." What does that mean? How about the second half? "cotty's rose heads?"

Letter Cipher	5	0	4	2	6	5	9	2	9	9	1	3	5	3	6	9	5	6	2
Key (New)	5	7	8	9	0	2	3	4	5	7	8	9	0	2	3	4	5	7	8
C–K	0	-7	-4	-7	6	3	6	-2	4	2	-7	-6	5	1	3	5	0	-1	-6
Mod 10	10	10	10	10	10	10	10	10	10	10	10	10	10	10	10	10	10	10	10
His Cipher	0	3	6	3	6	3	6	8	4	2	3	4	5	1	3	5	0	9	4
Plaintext	C	O		T		T		Y	S	R	O	S	E		H	E	A	D	S

Okay, the two halves read: "cipher idiots, cotty's rose heads." No, that's wrong. It actually reads: "cipher idiot. Scotty's rose heads."

The complete message now could be read.

Exultant, Karen immediately called the MCU together.

"It looks like we may be on the right path; I've finished the decryption; here it is," Karen said rather smugly.

"I have killed over twenty-two women in six years. You can't read a cipher idiot. Scotty's rose heads."

"Who's Scotty?" Susan asked.

"I have no idea and worse, I can't understand what he means by <u>Scotty's rose heads</u>," Karen replied.

"Karen, I need to congratulate you," Richard said.

"There is no need, Richard, it was blind luck that we made any progress."

"I didn't help at all; I gave up."

"If we are correct in thinking that Michael Pitts is our Ely killer, how does the name Scotty fit that scenario?"

Susan asked.

"That's right, Susan, Pitts is an old English surname," Richard said.

"Who knows. It could be another one of Pitts' little jokes on us," Karen said.

"Can I say something here?"

"What is it, Sarah?"

"Because of my disability, Karen, I have had much time over the years to study things that really interest me. Genealogy has fascinated me for years."

"Go on."

"Well, English families moved into Scotland, Wales, and Ireland over the eighteenth and nineteenth centuries. I am not saying that family migrations didn't happen before that, but you do have to remember the fierce pride of the Irish and Scottish peoples before English domination. Therefore, there may be family connections of a given English family surname to Scotland or Ireland."

"What are you saying, Sarah?" Karen asked.

"I am saying that the Pitts' family may have migrated to Scotland or Ireland, and that parts of that family may have or had kin in Ireland or Scotland. Michael Pitts' family may very well have had roots in Scotland."

"Let me be certain that I understand what you are saying, Sarah."

"I'll paint a scenario for us. Michael Pitts many-great grandfather and grandmother moved at some point from London to Scotland with their two sons. Let's suppose that one son decided to move from Scotland to Ireland. The family is divided simply because of distance. Over time and generations, the two factions of the family no longer regard each other as direct family, giving credence to our idea that one could have an English surname, but Scottish or Irish roots," Sarah explained.

"Thank you, Sarah. That's something to think about. Richard, would you please contact Attorney Sharpe and Michael Pitts for another interview? It may be futile. but Pitts may be willing to talk about family history," Karen said.

"It could be that Michael Pitts was called by a nickname growing up, maybe Scotty," Sarah added coyly.

"Richard, test that idea if you get to speak with Pitts," Karen ordered.

"I'll set it up in the morning," Richard said.

"Well, Folks, it's late in the day. See you in the morning. Thank you."

* * *

Several days later, Richard reported back to the MCU.

"I finally received permission to visit Michael Pitts at Reidsville. I can tell you that Sharpe was not happy, but Pitts gave permission, so I made the trip."

"I know that you'll tell us, but was it worthwhile?"

"I can't be certain. He told me that his family immigrated to the States in 1915. His great-grandfather, Alpin, and great-grandmother, Arabella, came from the village of Paisley in the Central Lowlands of Scotland, and settled in the Central Massachusetts town of Lancaster where he bought a small farm. Michael's father, Graham, was born in 1945 and married his mother, Nancy, in 1970. Michael was born ten years later in Boston where his parents had moved after their marriage. He said that beyond his great-grandparents, he did not know much of the family history. They both died in 1985 when he was only five years old."

"Was he ever called Scotty by his parents?" Susan asked.

"In fact, he was. It is a nickname that acquaintances still use. I checked his high school in Boston and sure enough, his year book has him listed as Scotty."

"Now we are getting somewhere," Susan said.

"Perhaps, Susan, but isn't it strange that he would readily admit to that nickname since we know that he wrote the cipher we decrypted?" Karen cautioned.

"Well, he's not a dumb-bell by any means, but…"

"It is a public record, so denying it wouldn't have helped him," Richard added.

"Are we focusing too much on the nickname?" Sarah asked.

"Frankly, we don't have much else."

"Karen, can I suggest that we brainstorm the ideas we have about Pitts?" Susan inquired.

"I think that that is something we could try, Susan," Karen replied.

"Let's start with the very basic. I will scribe on the

board," Susan volunteered.

"Okay, Folks, let's get started," Karen ordered.

1. **Michael Aaron Pitts**
   a. **Birth name: Daniel Michael Russell**
   b. **D.O.B: 7/15/1976**
   c. **Place: Stoneham, MA**
   d. **Scottish descent: does that matter?**
   e. **Only one of all suspects who is a convicted murderer**
   f. **Has confessed to killing Carol Morgan**
   g. **May have killed Kaye Billington and or Jane Swanson in Middlefield**
   h. **Educated at State Universities**
      i. **Bachelor's degree: Software Engineering**
      ii. **Master's degree: Software engineering**
   i. **Inmate #: MA12372**
   j. **First Degree Murder**
   k. **Served 10 years/2 years' parole**
   l. **Russell name legally changed to Pitts**
      i. **May 15th 2009**
      ii. **Moved to Ely: June 2009**
2. **Ely murders**
   a. **Estimated murder dates from coins**
      i. **2010 through**
      ii. **2015**
   b. **Number of murders: >twenty?**
   c. **Pattern:**
      i. **one each 2010 & 2015**

        ii. 4 in 2011
       iii. 4 in 2012
       iv. 4 in 2013
       v. 4 in 2014
    d. Cause of deaths
       i. Unknown
       ii. Decapitated remains
       iii. Skulls not at burial sites

3. Possible known suspects with possible MOM
    a. Jack Mullen
    b. Greg Moran
    c. Aaron Richardson
    d. Eugene Spencer
    e. Michael Pitts

4. Murderer or murderers must reside in Ely or Middlefield (Opportunity)
    a) Killings require opportunity
    b) All 5 suspects have opportunity
    c) Greg Moran and Jack Mullen work until midnight

5. Physical ability to kill
    a. All 5 are physically strong men
    b. Greg Moran is not considered as likely to be the killer because of demeanor, but cannot be ruled out
    c. Moran is strongly influenced by Jack Mullen

6. Motive
    a. Other than Pitts, motive to kill the women is unknown.
    b. Moran and Mullen are married
    c. Richardson, Spencer and Pitts are single

d. No conclusion can be drawn for motives of the other 4

"Thank you all for going back through this. I am afraid we are no closer to the killer in spite of this exercise," Karen said dejectedly.

"Let me ask my question again," Sarah said.

"What is that?"

"I asked a while ago if we were putting too much focus on the name Scotty."

"Where are you going with this?" Karen asked.

"The cipher you decrypted ended with <u>Scotty's rose heads.</u> My thought is that <u>rose heads</u> may be the more important clue, not necessarily the name. Once we understand what <u>rose heads</u> means, then the name may be as important."

"You may be onto something, Sarah. The whole sprinkler thing has been a sticking point for all of us. For a long time, we had no idea that it referred to the sprinkler head on a watering can," Karen said.

"Let me voice one more opinion, if I may," Sarah added.

"Of course, what is it?"

"I think that 'rose heads' means exactly what it says. Rose is the flowering plant. Heads are the decapitated skulls of the poor women he killed."

"What the hell do we do with that?" Richard asked.

"I just raise the questions; I don't have answers for them, unfortunately."

"That's okay, Sarah; you are helping us to consider

something that we have possibly overlooked," Karen said.

"Well, with that in mind, what do we do now?" Richard asked.

"I recommend that we consider Sarah's idea that <u>rose heads</u> have a real meaning. By that, I suggest that we take a hard look at the Reynolds clan again. Of all the Ely people, they are the only ones who have publicly said their hobby is growing roses. Exactly what <u>heads</u> means, I don't dare say, but it feels sinister, given the body finds," Susan said.

"But aren't they English?" Richard asked.

"What if, in fact, they claim Scottish heritage?" Sarah pushed.

"Good point again, Sarah," Karen agreed.

"Are you suggesting that someone from the Reynolds' clan is called Scotty and wrote the ciphers?" Susan asked.

"Susan, the Scottish thing coupled with growing roses could be a clue from the decrypted ciphers. So we should look at that. Do you have a better idea?" Karen asked.

"When do you want to re-interview the family?" Richard asked.

"Today, Richard, make the set-up calls and plan to get our butts up there tomorrow. I'll call Tom Hansen to work with us to get a search warrant for their home and gardens," Karen commanded.

"You know, Karen, that it will take a strong judge to sign off on a warrant; Lincoln is, after all, a powerful lawyer. It's not going to be easy," Susan warned.

"That may be true, Susan, but we are going for it. You, Sarah, and I will spend the day working up the details of the warrant. I will see if Tom can join us," Karen said.

* * *

"Tom, thank you for helping us. I want to have these items included in the search warrant:"

1. **Papers related to the heritage of the family**
2. **Documents written by the family or written for the family related to Scottish background**
3. **Family Bibles because they may contain papers noted in Items 1 & 2**
4. **Permission to dig in gardens on the property for evidence of human body parts**
5. **Permission to search any out buildings for evidence of human body parts or blood**
6. **Permission to dig at other locations on the property deemed important by the searchers**
7. **Home computers including thumb drives or any other data storage devices**

"Karen, that is an ambitious list. I have a feeling that Judge Redding will not approve all of it. In fact, he may balk at the whole thing due to stature of the person and whose effects we are requesting. You understand that any data on any device or paperwork relating to legal cases Lincoln Reynolds may have or had is strictly off-limits," Tom cautioned.

"You have to convince him, Tom; over twenty women have been brutally killed. He can't say no; it would be a travesty," Karen pushed back.

"Hey, I'm on your side; I just giving you fair warning that Judge Redding may not want to fight politics," Tom warned again.

"Well, maybe he should develop a pair of gonads."

"Karen, please be fair; Judge Redding is a well-respected Magistrate; he has handled many sensitive cases in his time on the Bench, and he generally does not fear political issues, but there are times one must choose the battles."

"Okay, Tom, please do your best. Would you like me to accompany you?"

"I think it's best if I handle this one alone. I know the details of your concerns."

"Thank you, Tom. Oops, I need to stop Richard from calling the Reynold's until we have our warrants."

* * *

Three days later, Karen and the MCU had their warrants in hand with the exception of digging up the rose beds. Judge Redding had delayed the digging up of the rose gardens until a better case could be made for their disruption. Karen was incensed at the stop order, but dutifully obeyed it. Tom Hansen and Karen's staff began work on a rebuttal to the delay, but that would take a while to complete.

"Good morning, Mrs. Reynolds. I have a copy of a warrant for you allowing us to search your home and outbuildings," Karen announced.

"What is this all about?"

"You may read the warrant. Are any other family members at home today?"

"My daughter is here. My son is at law school and my husband is in his Boston office. He is there most weekdays and commutes home on weekends. I will have to call him before I let you in."

"That's wrong, Mrs. Reynolds. You and your daughter may remain outside, but not in the house nor in any of the outbuildings while we conduct the search. We are beginning our search now."

"This is an outrage! We have done nothing wrong! I am calling my husband."

"Do what you need to do, Mrs. Reynolds. Please step aside."

"You will be hearing from my husband and I mean right away," said Mrs. Reynolds as she called her husband.

"Put her on the phone," Lincoln Reynolds shouted at his wife.

"He wants to talk to you," Mrs. Reynolds said while handing the phone to Karen.

"What do you think you are doing?" he shouted.

"We are conducting a search of your home, gardens, and out buildings by order of Judge Redding. You may call DA Thomas Hansen for any further information," Karen replied and hung up the phone.

Mrs. Reynolds answered the phone, which rang again immediately.

"My husband says that you are not to begin your search until an attorney from Middlefield arrives," Mrs. Reynolds said.

"Tell your husband that we will search now and will listen to his attorney, but we will finish this search," Karen responded forcefully.

Chapter Twenty-One

Some people handle the truth carelessly; others never touch it at all. Anonymous

The search of the house and outbuildings had taken a day to complete. Karen had arranged support from GBI to minimize the disruption to the Reynolds family, but cooperation from Lincoln Reynolds and the rest of the family was non-existent, as most searchers expected.

Back at the station in Middlefield, the MCU, the DA's office and GBI members met to discuss the search results. Anything deemed to be of evidential nature had been properly handled by the criminologists called to support the investigation.

The chain of custody for all evidence was strictly followed, especially in a case such as this. The team knew that any slip-up in procedure could result in the destruction of their case, if one existed at all.

Because of the explicit nature of the search warrant, all suspected evidence not included in the warrant directives had to be ignored. However, one major piece of family background evidence was found in the one of the family Bibles and was covered under the original warrant. The document had been written by Caleb Reynolds' wife after Caleb had been killed on the return trip home.

Karen read the document to the assembly.

The account that I have to tell comes down from the traditions passed from family member to family member of

the Reynolds' clan. My Dear Husband, Caleb, told me much of this, which I recorded while he was alive.

The Reynolds' family line in America began when Flynn Reynolds emigrated from Ireland in early 1739. His Gaelic name meant 'son of the red-haired man.' Standing nearly six-foot-tall, Flynn was a hulk of a man whose massive biceps were a testament to the hard labor the twenty-five-year-old had faced working the hardscrabble potato farm of his father Séamas. His mother, Bernadette held fast to the old rules of the Gaelic clan tradition teaching her nine children the ways of old. Flynn was the oldest of the siblings driven by an inner desire to escape the life that he knew could never change. The rising and setting of the sun year after year would only break his spirit and soul as it had his father's. Without any formal education, life for him would be nothing more than a grinding spiral into old age and death.

Séamas was adamant that Flynn stay on the farm, as he was already too ill from age and the backbreaking work; it was up to Flynn to carry on the farm to support the family. It was only by his mother's pleading with Séamas that his father finally relented. Flynn knew that his leaving would place additional burdens on his only brother, Darren, to help his father, but Flynn would not stay.

Had Flynn been able to foresee the future, he might have remained, but the drive for adventure was too strong; he would leave his birthplace traveling to Belfast with only two silver pence in his pocket given to him by his tearful mother. Flynn hugged his family and said goodbye with promises to return to see them some day. That day would never come.

In Belfast, he signed on as an indentured servant to a Lord Riggby traveling to Pennsylvania on a ship destined for Philadelphia. On February 9, the two hundred and twenty foot, three-masted William and Mary weighed anchor; setting sail for the new world. The fourth week out, the ship was struck by a north Atlantic storm wrenching the ship by violent pitching and rolling waves.

Lord Riggby, feeling the pangs of seasickness, had foolishly gone topside of the passenger berths to the primary deck where he was thrown against one of the main masts, knocking him unconscious. A wave violently washed upon the deck and receded pulling Riggby against the railing and over the side.

Flynn, who had seen what was happening, dove into the water to save the patron of his voyage. Grabbing Riggby by his jacket, Flynn watched in horror as the ship began moving away from the pair.

"Throw me a line," Flynn yelled over the roar of the seething sea.

A crewmember threw a life ring, which Flynn missed at first, but then by some miracle threw an arm into the life preserver while still holding onto the seemingly lifeless man.

Two crewmembers pulled the ring line to the rolling ship and hauled them aboard. Once aboard, Flynn and two of the crew dragged Riggby below deck where he subsequently slowly recovered from his experience.

The next day, the Lord sent for his servant.

"Reynolds, crewmembers have told me that I was washed overboard. Your heroic deed saved me from death. Because you are Irish, I did not want to take you on as a servant, but the ague took away my servant in Belfast. I needed someone. My thought was that a filthy Irishman would do for a while."

The insult slapped Flynn's pride with such force that he nearly started to trounce this ungrateful Englishman, but for once in his life, he let the anger cool and stood there. Flynn stood defiantly and thought:

You are lucky, English pig for I could kill you with my bare hands. Perhaps tonight I will throw you overboard and let the sea eat you alive.

The English system had abused him and his family all their lives; calling them filthy, dirty papists looking down their noses with their sniffing, nasal voices. His father Séamas, at least owned his farm; many Irish farmers were merely tenants working the land for far away English landowners who kept them at subservient states of survival. Flynn made a promise to himself:

No, you will not defeat me, Sire. Your heirs will bow before me someday. I am already a better man than you, Sire, but I will learn and take from you all that I can to use and defeat you.

"Flynn, I apologize for calling you a filthy Irishman.

You are a man of honor. You have contracted with me for seven years. Because of the service you have done for me, I will reduce the time of the contract. In the meantime, you will follow me and learn. I will teach you the ways of the English and you will learn to read and write. I have need for a strong right-hand-man in this boiling colony to help me run my plantations. After four years, you will be set free; a better man."

"My Lord, I thank you for your wisdom and kindness. I will not let you down."

Three days later, the William and Mary docked in Philadelphia where Flynn continued his servitude to the Lord he had saved.

Lord Riggby was better than his word. In Philadelphia, Flynn threw off his tattered farmer's garb. Lord Riggby outfitted him with the newest and stylish clothing worn by professionals of the city. It was then that Flynn began to understand his role with Lord Riggby, not a servant, but a respected aid to the Englishman.

In 1740, word was reached in the colony that a great famine had decimated Ireland. Flynn asked Lord Riggby if he would make an inquiry about his family. In early 1741, the devastating news reached Flynn. His entire family except for his brother, Darren, had fallen ill, starved, and died. To his immense relief, he found that that Darren had moved his family to Scotland when the famine started and settled in the Central Lowlands where he continued farming.

Three years later, Flynn was released from his contract and moved to Boston. Several years later, he sent for Darren and his family to join him. Darren had a son, Scotty, who died on the trip to America. He was buried at sea, and as you can imagine, to the great distress of the boy's mother.

By 1840 in America, the Reynolds' clan had split into two strong branches from the loins of Flynn and Darren and become Boston Brahmins owning large tracts of Massachusetts and New Hampshire as well as major real estate in the city. Their sumptuous houses on Brattle Street spoke of their success, but in the climate of the time, they had become English Reynolds; giving up their heritage. At the time, to be Irish or Scottish was not an asset.

It was the California gold rush of 1849, which lured my dear husband, Caleb, great grandson of Flynn, to Sutter's Mill. Before the area had played out, he had amassed a small fortune in gold nuggets, which he shipped to me. When the Sutter's Mill area went bust, my Dear Caleb moved to the open Arizona territory to try his hand again at prospecting.

In a few letters to me, he told of finding a claim, which he believed would make us rich beyond anything we could imagine.

In July of 1857, he staked a claim, and traveled to San Francisco to begin his voyage home. In those days, the fastest travel time from the west coast to the east coast was to take a ship from San Francisco to Columbia; then travel on land over the isthmus; then take another ship from the port of Colón to New York City.

On September 3, my Dear Caleb boarded the side paddle wheel ship, SS Central America, loaded with over six hundred passengers, crew, and untold ounces of California gold. Six days later, the ship foundered in a hurricane off North Carolina and sank, taking with it Caleb and tons of gold and silver.

Before Caleb left San Francisco, he sent me several letters to be carried overland, one of which he had written in a language, a puzzle, that he said I would not be able to read. On September 23, I received a letter from the shipping company telling me that my Loving Dear Caleb had perished on the SS Central America. It had sunk during a hurricane and with it, my Dear Caleb and the puzzle keyword. Three weeks after news of the ship's sinking, his letters to me arrived.

Looking at the unreadable letter, I placed it in the back of the family Bible as Caleb had requested. All my hopes and dreams have died with my Dear Husband.

I believe this to be a true testament from oral and written documents of the Reynolds' family.

Lisbeth Reynolds   *May 25th 1858*

"Well, Karen, it looks as though the Reynolds' family line holds both Irish and Scottish backgrounds. What do you do with that?" Tom Hansen asked.

"We know that both the Irish and Scottish pride is still

evident in the Reynolds families. It is clear that the two brothers, Flynn and Darrell, were very close. It is not impossible to think that the nickname, Scotty, may have been given to male descendent children over the years. We need to interview them to confirm it."

"Good luck there," Hansen said.

"Maybe not," Richard said, "I've been re-reading the interview notes with Mary Reynolds. We overlooked something that she said as an aside. She told us that her husband had been called Scotty growing up, but his friends had stopped calling him that years ago as Lincoln's law stature grew."

"Why didn't you bring this up at our brainstorming meeting a few days ago?" Susan asked incredulously.

"As I said, I've just started re-reading the notes."

"Okay, let's let that go for now. I believe that we have enough to ask the Judge to allow us to dig up a few plants at least. We can be careful with them. In fact, why don't we recommend that a specialist in roses be called to do the digging so that their precious rose plants aren't injured," Karen suggested.

"Okay, I will suggest that one plant from each of the three rose beds be dug up and replanted. That should be acceptable to Judge Redding," Tom said.

"Tom, can you get on this right away?" Chief Tate asked.

"I'm on my way to him now."

* * *

An hour later, the team had their approval in hand. A local horticulturist was called.

Lincoln Reynolds met the searchers at his front walk.

"Get off of my property, now," Reynolds shouted.

"Sorry, Mr. Reynolds, we are here to dig up one plant from each of the three rose beds. Here is the warrant."

"This is an outrage, I will have your jobs," Reynolds yelled.

"In the meantime, we are digging. Jason Wagner here will do the digging up. He is a certified specialist in roses. Our goal is to dig up the rose bush and then replant it," Karen said.

At the first bed, Karen said, "Who has been digging here?"

"We are always digging around these beds to aerate and move plants as we need to improve them. We don't dig; we use a pitchfork to loosen the soil around the rosebush," Reynolds said disgustedly.

"I understand, Jason dig up this plant," Karen directed.

"Not that one, please; it is an award winning "Teasing Georgia" variety developed by hybridizer, David Austin of England. It is truly a wonderful rose," Reynolds pleaded.

"All right, Mr. Reynolds; Jason dig up this one located next to it."

"No, no, not that one!"

"Look, Mr. Reynolds, I am not playing this game with you. Dig it up, Jason."

Nothing was found of any evidential value and Jason

replanted the bush. The same scenario followed with the second rose bed.

In the third bed, Karen noticed that much of the rose bed soil had been disturbed compared to the first two beds.

"Mr. Reynolds, why does this patch look more worked on than the others?" Karen asked.

"Oh, this is our newest bed. We started planting here about five years ago. We have been planting bushes here for later removal to the other two beds. That way we can control any diseased plants and keep them from our special award winners," Reynolds said.

I wonder if more disruption in this bed means something else.

"Okay, Jason dig up this plant here," Karen ordered.

By this time, Reynolds had given up protesting.

As Jason finished loosening the plant; he gingerly pulled it out of the ground.

What is that at the bottom of the hole?

"Jason, set the plant down and dig a little deeper, but be careful," Karen ordered.

As careful and gently as an archeologist excavates, Jason slowly exposed a human skull.

"Well, Mr. Reynolds, is this your idea of fertilizer for your precious rose bushes?" Karen asked with a sneer.

"What the hell! I don't know how that got there."

"Mr. Reynolds, I am arresting you on suspicion of murder."

"I don't know anything about this!"

"You can't arrest my husband; he is a very famous man," Mary Reynolds shouted as she began to move toward Karen.

"You had better calm down, Mrs. Reynolds, or I will arrest you also," Karen shouted back.

"Shut up, Mary; get into the house and call Mervin; he will know what to do; also call Flynn," Lincoln Reynolds yelled at his wife.

"Are you willing to talk to us about this?"

"Of course not," Reynolds shouted.

"Fine. It is time to call your lawyer, Mr. Reynolds. Richard, take him back to the station," Karen said with immense satisfaction.

Lincoln Reynolds was taken to the Middlefield lockup; read his rights; and booked on suspicion of murder.

"What do you want done next, Karen?" Susan asked.

"Phone Tom with the details of what we've found. Then have him get to Judge Redding for permission to uproot all three beds. I'll call Chief Tate; I want three of the best criminologists and forensic photographers available to get up here ASAP."

"Are you done with me, then?" Jason asked.

"No, Jason, you are our digger for the next few hours, maybe days. I want only one person digging up the plants; are you able to do it?"

"I can, but my boss, Mr. Collins, at the Institute needs to know."

"I will let him know that you are needed here. Thank

you, Jason."

* * *

Two hours later, Tom called Karen.

"Judge Redding has signed a change to the warrant; you are allowed to dig up all plants."

"Great, Tom; the criminologists are arriving now; we'll get started."

Six hours later, the last rose bush had been uprooted, and the holes inspected.

"Susan, this has been an exhausting day. I cannot believe what we have found. It is interesting that only the third bed held any evidence; I don't know what to make of that fact, yet," Karen said.

"Every plant except for three, had a skull beneath it, it's horrible. What kind of monster did this?"

"We've known for a long time that we had a monster on our hands; now we know who he is," Karen replied.

"Tom is going to have his hands full prosecuting this case, Karen," said Richard who had returned to Ely.

"I know, Richard; let's get this work wrapped up; I told Tate that we needed to have two officers stationed here, 24/7, for the next week. We have to ensure that no one is able to tamper with this site. No family member or anyone else is allowed out here. We cannot afford any slip-up that Reynolds' lawyers can pounce on. Chief is setting that guard up now."

"Karen, I need to get back home. Carlos has late duty tonight and Aretha cannot sit the kids."

301

"Yes, Susan, you need to leave. I want to meet tomorrow to go over the sticky parts of our evidence. Tom has requested that we consider having another brainstorming session. I think it is a good idea; we have some serious evidence ambiguities to clear up."

Chapter Twenty-Two

He who excuses himself, accuses himself. Anonymous

In the morning, Julius and Marcus from GBI, Tom Hansen and his staff from the DA's office, and the MCU gathered in the large conference room to discuss the Ely murders.

"Thank you all for coming here this morning. We have arranged coffee, tea and Danish to get you wound up for the work we have this morning. At lunch time, we will have sandwiches and cold drinks catered in," Karen announced.

"You are too kind to us," Julius said, "But thank you, it's well appreciated."

"I hear that you have a new detective coming on board soon," Tom said.

"Good news travels fast," Karen admitted, "Yes, Chief Tate gave the final okay to hire a detective from the Los Angeles PD, Charles Sanderson, who applied for our position. He is one of their best detectives; they didn't want to let him go."

After the ice-breaking chatter slowed, Karen moved the group to the business of the day.

"I suggest that we complete a brief review of the evidence and information that has been collected to date for the Ely murders. I'll play scribe today and give Susan a break from that duty. I'm going to use the easel pads and tape the pages to the white board so that we can refer to them. We will start with the evidence collected at the Ely grave sites."

1. Waters' field with the gravesites
   a. Nineteen dismembered skeletons, all women
   b. Most are shallow gravesites with no evidence of animal intrusion
   c. No grave site had skulls present
   d. A coin was found at each site
   e. Speculation is that the coins indicate the year each death occurred
   f. Coins had been placed in plastic sealed bags
   g. Coin dates span from 2010 to 2015
   h. One grave found with a 2010 and one with a 2015 coin
   i. Four graves each with 2011, 2012, 2013, 2014 coins
   j. An empty cola bottle was found at each gravesite
   k. Speculation is that the killer had a "farewell" drink after each killing
   l. There is no basis for this assumption, but it is worth noting for its potential psychological meaning
   m. No clothing of victims was present at the gravesites
   n. No fingerprints were found on coins or cola bottles in the graves
   o. No other useable evidence was found in the field area
   p. Evidence shows that the killer had ample time to kill and bury bodies

2. Search of Lincoln Reynolds' home
   a. Old Lisbeth Reynolds' record of family history found
   b. Various papers found in three family Bibles had no evidential value and were not taken
   c. One Bible inscribed to "Scotty" found and taken
   d. Search of Lincoln's computers revealed no reference to 'Baphomet' or 'Scotty'
   e. Mary Reynolds' computers also revealed no reference to 'Baphomet' or to 'Scotty'
   f. Lizbeth Reynolds' computer contained no evidential value
   g. No ciphers or codes were found on any of the computers
   h. Flynn Reynolds' laptop computer was not present; said to be with him or at his law school
3. Search of the Reynolds' property
   a. Two outbuildings were searched
   b. A garden shed, 8 ft. x 16 ft., was located within twenty feet of the rose gardens
   c. It contained the usual garden tools, shovels, hoes, rakes, etc.
   d. The tools, shed walls and floor were tested with Luminol, no suspicious stains were noted
   e. Another garden shed, 20 ft. x 40 ft., was located 500 feet from the rose

   gardens set in a wooded area of the
   property
 f. It also contained the usual garden
   tools, shovels, hoes, rakes, etc.
 g. Suspiciously, several butcher knives
   were also found
 h. History reveals that this shed was
   originally an abattoir
 i. Therefore, many dark stains on the
   walls and floor were noted
 j. All tools, knives, walls and the floor
   were tested with Luminol
    i. Lit up like a Christmas Tree
    ii. GBI has some samples, which
     were taken before testing with
     Luminol
    iii. No test method to determine if
     blood is human or animal
 k. Awaiting test results of samples

"Marcus, when do you expect that we will have any word on the tests?" Karen asked, breaking the pace.

"I expect within the week, Karen."

"Great. The time is approaching noon, so I suggest that we break for lunch; we'll continue this afternoon with a quick review of the cipher content and messages," Karen suggested.

During the lunch break, Tom left the room to take a call from his office. He returned twenty minutes later with some news to share.

"I've just spoken to Attorney Sharpe, Pitts' lawyer, he is now insisting that Pitts case be reviewed. This discovery in Ely has given him ammunition to demand a hearing on Pitts' 'coerced' confession, his words, not mine. I'm just letting you know; I don't intend to do anything until he files paperwork. Sharpe knows that we have been looking at his client as the suspect in the Ely killings. It does pressure us to get a confession out of Reynolds."

"You know that won't be easy, Tom," Julius said.

"I agree, but we have to find a wedge to get Reynolds to talk. No offence, Tom, but trying to get this lawyer to 'fess up' won't be easy. He's spent his professional life in court," Karen said.

After lunch, the group continued with the task. Karen was afraid that most would fall into a post-prandial dip and nod off, but that didn't happen.

 4. Reynolds' family history, 1800s
  a. Flynn Reynolds immigrates to Boston from Ireland
   i. Flynn's descendants stay in Boston to the present day
   ii. Lincoln, son Flynn, and daughter Lizbeth are the latest off-spring in that side of the family line
  b. Darren Reynolds immigrates to Boston from Scotland several years after Flynn
   i. Darren's descendants move from Boston to San Francisco, Calif. in 1909
   ii. Three sons, Darren, Jake, and James, and two daughters, Rachel and Charity, are the latest

off-spring in that side of the
family line

iii. All presently reside in California

5. Family traditions that we know of
   a. Strong linkages between old Darren's
      and old Flynn's descendants
   b. It has been family tradition to call the
      oldest son by the nickname 'Scotty' in
      the Darren Line
   c. Lincoln refuses to say if the Scotty
      naming tradition follows in the Flynn
      line

6. Reasons for pursuing the Scotty issue
   a. Ciphers are signed Baphomet
   b. Decryption of the cipher, which gave the
      line 'Scotty's rose heads,' led us to the
      Reynolds' home site
   c. We believe that whoever this Baphomet
      is; he is or has been known as Scotty at
      one time or another
   d. As already noted, we have not found a
      computer, which has any reference to
      the messages, or the names Baphomet or
      Scotty

7. Suggestions for the next steps
   a. Complete the computer search by
      obtaining young Flynn's computer(s)
   b. Send Rep. to Boston to obtain Reynolds'
      background information from friends
      and foes
   c. Work with DA Tom Hansen to sew up
      any issues with interviews we have
      completed

d. Reconvene this group when any major developments of the case occur

"That is all we have at this point," Karen said.

"I'd like to suggest, Karen, that whoever we send to Boston be instructed to press the Scotty nickname item on the list during interviews of Lincoln's friends and associates in Boston. Push the question if Lincoln ever went by that nickname," Marcus said.

* * *

Richard was detailed to Boston after the Boston PD Chief agreed to provide a detective to accompany him for the interviews. The detectives began their interview work with a list of Lincoln's law associates. As expected, some would not talk to Richard and those that did were very cautious with their comments.

The most interesting item that Richard learned from the brief discussions was that most people respected Lincoln as a lawyer and power broker, but did not care from the man on a personal level. The detectives were able to compile a short list of Lincoln's friends, actually acquaintances, who were willing to share more information than the associates.

One such acquaintance was a crusty old man, Amos Henderson, whose early life had been spent on the sea out of Provincetown fishing for cod in the Georges Banks. Lincoln had been a God-send to Amos by helping him retrieve his large boat and livelihood from Amos' partner who had illegally mortgaged it, unbeknownst to Amos.

From that day forward, the freshest sea delicacies from Amos' boat were hand delivered to Lincoln's family, at no cost, in a gesture of friendship for several years. Suddenly, one year, Lincoln presented Amos with a legal invoice for over fifty thousand dollars for representation in Amos' boat case. Stunned, Amos severed the gift-giving and spent the next three years paying off the debt.

Standing barely five foot six inches, with a weather beaten face that showed years of sun exposure, Amos represented the tough, honorable fishermen of the New England coast. In the tradition of the salt that he symbolized; Amos could turn the air blue with his language; never meaning to insult or offend, nevertheless, what little he had to say about Lincoln was eye-opening for Richard.

"Yes," Amos admitted, "years ago at a clam bake held at Lincoln's beach house, Lincoln shared early stories of his life. He told me some things that he shouldn't have. He had had way too much to drink. Maybe that's why later, he turned on me."

"What vignettes did he share?"

"Vignettes, hah, that's a great word. Some of the stories he told were pure sea stories, and others I do believe. He said that there are bodies buried along the Charles and Neponset Rivers; you know, they are tidal, so twice a day water sits awash the dearly departed."

"Did they involve the Mafia?"

"You know they did."

"Did Lincoln admit that he was involved with the Mafia or know about these burials?"

"He did, but there is no way I can or will remember them. I'm good as dead even in these days of the government's bragging that the crime families have been stopped. You know it ain't true, Mister."

"Is there anything else you can tell me?"

"Well, you know that the Italians and the Irish both have their piece of what you call the Mafia. I just call them gangs, but make no mistake, if they are after you; you are as good as dead. Somehow his relatives seem to be pretty active. Slimy is how I think of him and his lot now."

"How about any family traditions about naming sons?"

"It was true," Amos said, "that in Lincoln's family, it was a tradition to give a moniker to the oldest son in memory of old Darren Reynolds, Flynn's brother who had immigrated from Scotland back in the 1800s."

"And what was the nickname given?" Richard asked.

"Well, of course it was Scotty," Amos replied.

"Did Lincoln admit that he was ever called Scotty?"

"He told me that he was called that as far back as he could remember, but in college he insisted that his family start calling him Lincoln. He was going to be a famous lawyer, he had boasted, and he was embarrassed by the name," Amos replied.

"I take it that he wouldn't name his son Scotty, since he hated it," Richard queried.

"You'd have to ask him that," Amos replied.

With that interview completed, Richard packed his bags and returned to Middlefield.

* * *

"What's been happening since I went to Beantown?" Richard asked Karen.

"Plenty. Reynolds was booked as you know. Tom convened the grand jury with the obvious results for this case. He was arraigned on Tuesday and the trial date is set for sometime in May. I expect that the date will get postponed; you know how that goes."

"What happened with the search warrant for the son Flynn's computer? Richard asked.

"Oh that. We took two laptops of his and had Julius scour them; no low level messages were found. He may have reformatted the disks or replaced them. In any event, they were clean," Karen responded.

"That's too bad, I had really hoped that would break the case."

"What have you found out?" Karen asked.

"No was no surprise there. An old fisherman I met told me that Reynolds was called Scotty in his younger days, but Reynolds blew it off when he was in college. Apparently he hated the sobriquet."

"Sobriquet, such a big word! Well, that is interesting, but it doesn't do us any good. Unless we can find the computer that Reynolds used to write the cipher letters, we are stuck. We need that evidence on it; however, there is no chance of getting that that I can see. Most of the stuff on his computers relates to legal cases and, of course, that is all off limits. We couldn't read any of the contents, so we don't know if we missed anything. For all we know, he could have buried the messages within the legal briefs. Go on please."

"The other thing that the old fisherman told me was that the Reynolds' family has always been involved with the underworld; Lincoln Reynolds isn't as clean as he wants us to believe."

"There again, that is an interesting story, but it does us no good. Now that you have confirmed that Reynolds may have used the nickname, Scotty, I am wondering if his son Flynn was ever called that. Do remember if any of Flynn's friends mentioned or called him by that name?" Karen asked.

"It would have stood out if they did. I don't think anyone called him that. We should re-check the interview notes. I know that we wouldn't have asked any of them that question because we hadn't decrypted the messages at the time. Remember that we focused on the Baphomet thing."

"Keep nosing around, Richard, we have to find something to nail this guy."

* * *

That afternoon Karen received a telephone call. The caller ID was blocked when she answered.

"I have some information for you."

"What is it?"

"I know where the computer is that you are looking for."

"What computer is that?"

"Don't get cute with me. The Reynolds' computer."

"Well, where is it?"

"Can I get a reward for the information?"

"It depends how good the information you have is," Karen answered.

"When do I get the reward?" the caller asked.

"I'm beginning to believe that this is a prank call," Karen pushed.

At that, the caller hung up. Karen immediately dialed *57 to trace the number; then she called Susan to notify the phone carrier and get a warrant to search the home of the caller.

* * *

"Karen, the phone number you had traced was Craig Richardson's. I have written up the probable cause information for him to take to Judge Redding. Redding has signed it and Tom is sending it over as we speak."

"Excellent, Susan; Richard and I will head out for Ely with the warrant. Please organize a stand-by team to conduct the search. I will call you from Ely when we need to execute the search."

"Suppose it was not Craig who called you, but his son Aaron," Susan cautioned.

"You could be right; I have never spoken to Aaron, especially on the phone."

"The reason I've mentioned this is that Flynn and Aaron are classmates at the law school. If anyone would know about a computer having information we need, it would be Aaron, not Craig."

"First we will talk to Craig, and if he is not cooperative, we will tear his house apart. We are going to find that computer!"

* * *

"Good morning, Mr. Richardson, I am Detective Hunter from Middlefield; this is Detective Burnham."

"Good morning, Officers. What is this about?"

"We are here because I received a phone call from this residence. The caller was asking about a reward for supplying critical information to us."

"Well, I made no such call, and I can't believe that my son would have any information like that."

"Is there anyone else living here?"

"Yes, my son, Aaron, and my housekeeper, Alice."

"Can we speak with Aaron?"

"I think he is getting ready for class. Let me check. Please make yourselves comfortable."

Moments later, Craig Richardson re-entered the room.

"As I thought, he just stepped out of the shower. He will get dressed and be down shortly. Can I get you some coffee or tea?"

"That would be fine, thank you," Karen and Richard answered.

As they sat drinking their coffee, idle weather talk turned more serious.

"Mr. Richardson, do you remember a call from the

Middlefield Police some time ago?" Karen asked.

"I remember that a woman called me to ask if a detective had come to my home for an interview."

"That caller was me and the detective I was asking about was Carol Morgan."

"Oh, yes, I read about her in the paper. Terrible thing to happen to a young woman; well, anyone for that matter."

"At the time, we had received several letters claiming responsibility. We have been looking for some items related to that."

"I'm sure that I don't know what you are talking about," Richardson said.

"I feel confident that you are being truthful, but Aaron may have some information that we would like to have," Karen answered.

"Are you saying that Aaron may have had something to do with that officer's death?"

"Not necessarily, we have a confession from the person we believe killed her, but the Ely murders are still unsolved."

"Detective Hunter, haven't you arrested my friend and neighbor, Lincoln Reynolds, for that?"

"We have; yesterday's phone call to me has presented some ideas that we need to check out."

"I can't believe that Lincoln or Mary had anything to do with those murders. An upstanding person like that couldn't possibly murder nineteen women!"

"A person's outward image to a community sometimes

hides an evil heart. Stranger things have happened," Karen answered.

"But you are not saying that Aaron has anything to do with that mess, are you?"

"Not necessarily, but I now believe that it was Aaron who called me."

"I think I need to call my lawyer."

"That is your right, Mr. Richardson, but may I suggest that you let Aaron confirm or deny the call first? It may save a lot of time and heartache."

Shortly after, Aaron came down the stairs and entered the room.

"Aaron, these detectives believe that you made a phone call to them yesterday."

"It couldn't have been me, Dad, I was in class all day yesterday."

"Aaron, we traced the call to this phone line. We also checked your school schedule; you were not in class when the call was made from this house. Please don't lie to us, Aaron," Karen warned.

"All right, that's enough. I am calling my lawyer," Richardson exclaimed.

"No, Dad, don't. I did make the call yesterday. I do have information that may help them solve the case," Aaron interrupted.

"Aaron, shut up. Don't say another word. I am calling my lawyer."

"Mr. Richardson, I am going out on a limb here with this

317

statement. We do not believe that Aaron is involved with murder, but we do believe that he has some information that may help us. Are you willing to listen to that?"

"Dad, you may want to hear what I have to say," Aaron pleaded.

"Detective Hunter, if I do listen and you change your mind about Aaron, I will ruin your career."

"Let's not pre-judge what Aaron has to say," Karen said.

"Dad, I don't know anything about any murders. The other day, someone told me that there exists a computer, a laptop, which has some interesting information on it related to all these murders. I have never seen what is on the computer."

"Who told you about the laptop?" Karen asked.

"I can't tell you that; I promised that I wouldn't. Please don't ask me to break that promise."

"I'll let it pass for now; does this person own the computer?"

"No, but she, uh, he only knows what the person told him about where it might be."

"Where is it now?"

"The person told my friend that the laptop owner said he stashed it in the house on Waters' property after you had finished searching it, you know, the Pitts' place."

"Did your friend tell you who told her, uh him, about the computer?"

"No."

"Aaron, this chain of someone who knows someone, et

cetera, doesn't really help us. Would you be willing to ask your friend if she would also give us a statement?"

"I will ask if you can promise that she will not be charged with anything."

"I can't promise that, Aaron, but if what you are saying is the absolute truth, she need not worry. Do the right thing to help us bring this fiend to justice."

"I will ask her."

"Thank you, Aaron, we will need to have you come to the station to sign a statement of our conversation today."

"I will come to the station with my son, Detective."

"Thank you both. Please come to the station this afternoon," Karen said.

Chapter Twenty-three

Jupiter is slow looking into his notebook, but he always looks. Zenobius

After Karen and Richard left the Richardson's home, Karen called Susan.

"Susan, get the team back to the Pitts' house. The laptop is there someplace."

Later that afternoon, the Richardsons arrived at the station. In tow, was Aaron's friend.

"Detective Hunter, this is my friend Ellen Rhodes," Aaron introduced.

"It is nice to meet you, Ellen. Where are you from?"

"I live in Atlanta; I'm a law student; that's how I met Aaron."

"Aaron tells us that you know who owns a laptop, which we are interested in," Karen said.

"Actually, I don't. Someone sent a letter to my family's home about a week ago. Obviously, the envelope was addressed to me but the letter was not. The letter stated where the laptop had been hidden. I told Aaron and my father about it."

"Do you still have the letter and envelope?"

"Here is the letter. The envelope was mistakenly thrown out," Ellen answered.

Karen asked, "That's too bad. Are you the only one who has handled this letter?"

"No, I showed it to Aaron and my father, and they both read it. At first, Aaron and I weren't sure if it was a hoax or not. My father said that I should take it to the police, but you can see the warning for yourself."

Karen took the typewritten letter and read:

Pamela,

I am sending this note to you because I know that you can be trusted. A person who shall remain nameless was told by her friend, Anne, that Anne's boyfriend had hidden a special computer in a shed near the house Pitts' rented in Ely. Anne told me that her boyfriend threatened to kill her if she told anyone about it.

I am very scared thinking that her boyfriend may come after me if he finds out that Anne told me. He has bragged about killing women, but Anne said that she didn't believe him at first. After he gave her gory details; she knew she was dating a killer, but there is no way she can break it off. She knows that he will kill her if she tries.

She said that he told her about killing a detective. He bragged that the cops would never find out he did it. She is petrified with fear, and doesn't know what to do.

If she breaks down and tells him that she has told me about the computer, he will come after me. I want someone to know about this if anything happens to me. Take this letter to the police.

Helen

"Who are these people, Anne, Pamela, and Helen?" Karen asked.

"I am acquainted with a Pamela Smith; I met her at one of our law school ice-breakers, and we chatted for a while, but I don't know who the others are," Ellen replied.

"How long ago was this ice-breaker?"

"Aaron, wasn't it about three weeks ago?" Ellen asked as she turned toward Aaron.

"Yes, it was on Saturday evening, the fourteenth," Aaron said.

"When you spoke to Pamela, was there anything that seemed out of the ordinary?" Karen asked.

"As I say, I had just met her, but she did seem antsy. I recall thinking at the time that she was expecting to see someone there. She kept looking over her shoulder, so I moved on. I didn't see her the rest of the evening."

"Do you have any idea why she would send the letter to you?" Richard asked.

"I have no idea why she would pick me. She said that she would like to speak with me sometime, and asked for my phone number, so we exchanged numbers."

"Can you call Pamela Smith while you are here to ask if she sent the letter to you?" Karen asked.

While Ellen dialed Pamela's phone number, Karen asked Aaron if he knew Anna or Helen. He did not.

Pamela did not answer her phone. The Richardsons and Ellen were excused and left the station.

* * *

* * *

We found it!! There is no shed near the house. We

322

searched the house, nothing. We went back to the large shed at the Reynolds place. We asked and Mary Reynolds gave us permission to search the shed again. The laptop was found stuffed behind a box under the bench.

* * *

That's great, Susan. When are you back in Middlefield?

* * *

We'll be back by six. I've called Marcus at GBI. He will be here in the morning to look at the computer.

* * *

Okay, plan on a group meeting at ten. Tag, bag, seal, and lock the computer in the evidence room. I will have Tate assign officers to guard the room. NO mistakes. See you then.

* * *

The MCU convened at ten with DA Tom Hansen and Marcus Strong from GBI.

"Marcus, have you found anything on the laptop to report?" Karen asked.

"I have; fortunately, it wasn't password protected, so that made it easy."

"Well, don't keep us in suspense," Karen chided.

"Right; all the letters and ciphers were on it. There were other ciphers and letters, which you do not have. Maybe they were never sent."

"Is there any indication who owns the computer?" Tom asked.

"There is nothing on it that says "Here I am.""

"Susan, did you ask Mary Reynolds or her daughter if

they knew anything about the computer?" Karen asked.

"We did, they both denied any responsibility for it."

"Both Pitts and Lincoln Reynolds are in jail; it can't be either of them who put it there. My guess is the son, Flynn. We have to pull him in for questioning," Karen said.

Early in the afternoon, Flynn Reynolds was escorted into an interview room at the station.

"Flynn, I have no doubt that you know why we want to talk to you," Richard said.

"Actually, I have no idea why you want talk to me. You've harassed and arrested my father for a crime he didn't commit."

"How do you know that, Flynn?"

"I just know that my father would never hurt anyone; much less torture and kill those young women."

"How do you know they were tortured, Flynn?"

"I don't; it's just a guess on my part, but I know my father."

"Well, evil may be in many hearts; just because we don't think it can happen, doesn't mean it isn't so," Karen pushed back.

Suddenly, Flynn's face hardened into a sneer.

"You don't know what you are talking about, bitch. The dufus you've been talking to knows nothing."

"What do you mean?"

"The jerk who loves his father so much is an idiot. He didn't have the guts to strangle them. I had to take over."

"Who am I talking to?" Karen asked.

"I'm not answering you, bitch, I'll talk to that jerk next to you."

"All right, who am I talking to?" Richard asked.

"I'm Scotty. The dufus doesn't know I exist. He is weak; I am strong. When I kill, I make sure that they suffer. They are so stupid; they believe my lies until I have my hands around their throats."

"How many have you killed, Scotty?"

"Many, many, I love to use them and take their heads. Do you know that they make good fertilizer for roses?"

"Richard, this interview is at an end. Place Scotty here under arrest."

The sneering and belligerent personality disappeared and the meek Flynn returned.

"Scotty, we have to detain you for a while."

"Why are you calling me Scotty?" Flynn asked.

"Do you remember the conversation we just had?"

"Yes, we were talking about my father."

"We are going to ask you to talk to someone to help you. Are you willing to do that?"

"You mean a doctor? I'm fine; I just don't remember things sometimes. Law school is hard."

"It's not fine, Flynn, we need you to speak with a doctor."

* * *

Five weeks later, the MCU and supporting groups met to discuss the investigation.

"Thank you all for coming here today. I have put

together some facts and feelings about the Ely murders. Please feel free to add or give a critical opinion of what I present," Karen said.

1. Judge Redding ordered Flynn to undergo psychiatric evaluation
   a. The State cannot proceed with charges against Flynn Reynolds until the evaluation is complete
   b. He is to remain in custody at the Central State Hospital at Milledgeville
   c. When the evaluation is complete, Judge Redding will rule on the future legal action by the State
2. Flynn Reynolds has a preliminary diagnosis of dissociative identity disorder by Doctor Henry Adams
   a. Doctor Adams has asserted that the disorder is real. He sees no level of malingering
   b. Time spent with Flynn has opened up repressed pain, which Flynn has discussed with Adams
   c. Flynn has said that his grandfather abused him when they lived in Boston
   d. He was very young when it started and lasted until he was eight
   e. He told his mother, but she did not believe him
   f. His mind split into pieces to block out the pain and shame
   g. Scotty, the alter ego, became his

protector and avenger against women
   h. We are not able to interrogate Mary
      Reynolds' father as he passed away last
      year
   i. Doctor Adams' medical opinion is that
      he is not able to stand trial
3. Lincoln Reynolds has been released
   a. All charges against him have been
      dropped
   b. He is threatening to sue us for the
      damage
   c. His lawyer is advising him to drop the
      threat of a suit
4. Identification of the murdered women
   a. Neither Flynn or Scotty can or will
      name the women killed
   b. Our best guess is that they were run-
      aways, not kidnapped
   c. We will have to check Missing Person
      lists State by State and try to correlate
      when they were reported missing to our
      data
   d. We may never know their identities
5. The Carol Morgan Case
   a. Michael Pitts had sex with Carol, but
      that does not prove he killed her
   b. He has confessed to her murder, but I
      have doubts
   c. Scotty claims to have killed her, no
      proof either way
   d. Judge Redding is unwilling to
      reconsider Pitts' confession
   e. Attorney Sharpe is filing an appeal

  f. **More to come on that, I'm sure**
 6. The Jane Swanson and Kaye Billington Cases
   a. **We've had no new information on those two murders**
   b. **They will remain open, but are considered cold**
   c. **We may not ever solve them**

After several hours of deliberation within the group, Karen arose and went to the easel pads, markers in hand.

"After listening to all of your input, concerns and speculations, I would like to give you my conclusions about this situation.

"Starting with the fifth item on our list, The Carol Morgan Case, I believe that Carol recognized Michael as Daniel Russell. Remember that she worked in their MCU and could easily have come across his picture, etc. She may have tried to do some investigating on her own, although why she would do that without the MCU, I cannot explain.

"Pitts figured out who she was and what she was up to. His solution was to kill her because he knew it would not be long before he would be connected to the murders on Jane and Kaye.

"As far as the Ely murders are concerned, I do not believe that Flynn Reynolds is the murderer. I think he developed a dual personality out of fear of his father. He knew what his father was doing and it terrified him.

Flynn developed the code and letters to send to us to throw us off the trail. Flynn may truly believe that he killed the women, but he didn't. His father is the Ely murderer.

"We need to turn this whole matter over to the FBI as distasteful as it may be; we don't have the resources or skills to bring Lincoln Reynolds to trial.

"With regards to item four, ID of the Murdered Women, I would like to start an initiative to place a monument in the Ely Cemetery, which would represent the many women who have gone missing in Ely and elsewhere. I want this monument tall enough to be seen from all directions when approaching the Cemetery as a reminder that unspeakable Death came to Ely.

As Martha Whittingham is now able to identify some of the women who now rest in Ely, their names will be inscribed to show that we care and that their deaths have not been in vain. It will serve to educate young women about the dangers to this life."

Epilogue

What we look for does not come to pass. God finds a way for what none foresaw. Euripides

Several weeks later, Judge Redding ruled that Flynn Reynolds would be held at the Milledgeville State Hospital until such time the medical staff has deemed him cured enough for his return to society.

Law enforcement strongly opposed the open-ended order.

No one was ever or would be tried for the heinous crimes committed on women in Ely, GA.

Afterword

Karen and Richard may have given up solution of the first cipher too early. Their assumption that the killer most likely did not include information in the cipher that would identify him was definitely wrong.

Had they not made the erroneous assumption, the case may have been solved much more quickly possibly preventing more murders.

After learning clues of the killer, from the Vic cypher, Karen decided to try a decryption of the first cipher again. Since the killer would not directly identify the keyword(s) he used for the Vigenère cipher, Karen and Richard developed a list of possible keywords that might work to solve the cipher. The only clue he gave them was that it was a name from his family. The killer refused to reveal the matrix he used. The possible keywords they developed were **Lincoln, Flynn, Caleb, Lisbeth, Darren, Seamus, Mary, and Bernadette**.

Karen and Richard were then forced to devise a matrix with the most logical placement of the wingding symbols. The Vigenère matrix that Karen had in mind is shown here: The **Plaintext** is comprised by the **columns** and the **Keyword** uses the rows as usual.

Enjoy the challenge. Good luck!

About the Author

Jon A Sanborn, writing as J A Sanborn, has written six mystery novels: *The Lost Cipher, The Orion Factor, Death Comes to Ely, The Stillwater Incident, Of Friends and Others, and Recollections – An Olio of Short Stories.*

The author holds a BS degree in chemistry and a Ph.D. in computational chemistry from the University of Massachusetts Amherst.

He is a U.S. Navy veteran who served in an antisubmarine squadron, VS-34, aboard the antisubmarine aircraft carrier, USS Essex, CVS-9, at the peak of the Cold War during the Cuban Missile Crisis in 1962.

He has had a career spanning thirty years in various management positions in high technology corporations as well as fifteen years in academic settings teaching chemistry.

After retirement, he formed Swift River Publishing to provide publishing services for his own novels, and for people who have written manuscripts and wish to have them published at modest cost.

He has had a lifetime interest in physics, chemistry, ciphers, codes, and mystery stories: fact and fiction.

He and his wife live in Savannah, Georgia with a spoiled tuxedo cat.

www.ingramcontent.com/pod-product-compliance
Lightning Source LLC
Chambersburg PA
CBHW062017170626
46813CB00001B/200